CLAIRE COUGHLAN

AMONG THE RUINS

**SIMON &
SCHUSTER**

London · New York · Amsterdam/Antwerp · Sydney/Melbourne · Toronto · New Delhi

First published in Great Britain by Simon & Schuster UK Ltd, 2026

Copyright © Claire Coughlan, 2026

The right of Claire Coughlan to be identified as author of this work has been asserted in accordance with the Copyright, Designs and Patents Act, 1988.

1 3 5 7 9 10 8 6 4 2

Simon & Schuster UK Ltd, 1st Floor
222 Gray's Inn Road, London WC1X 8HB

For more than 100 years, Simon & Schuster has championed authors and the stories they create. By respecting the copyright of an author's intellectual property, you enable Simon & Schuster and the author to continue publishing exceptional books for years to come. We thank you for supporting the author's copyright by purchasing an authorised edition of this book.

No amount of this book may be reproduced or stored in any format, nor may it be uploaded to any website, database, language-learning model, or other repository, retrieval, or artificial intelligence system without express permission. All rights reserved. Enquiries may be directed to Simon & Schuster, 222 Gray's Inn Road, London WC1X 8HB or RightsMailbox@simonandschuster.co.uk

Simon & Schuster Australia, Sydney
Simon & Schuster India, New Delhi

www.simonandschuster.co.uk
www.simonandschuster.com.au
www.simonandschuster.co.in

The authorised representative in the EEA is Simon & Schuster Netherlands BV, Herculesplein 96, 3584 AA Utrecht, Netherlands. info@simonandschuster.nl

Simon & Schuster strongly believes in freedom of expression and stands against censorship in all its forms. For more information, visit BooksBelong.com

A CIP catalogue record for this book is available from the British Library

Hardback ISBN: 978-1-3985-2179-7
Trade Paperback ISBN: 978-1-3985-2180-3
eBook ISBN: 978-1-3985-2181-0
Audio ISBN: 978-1-3985-2184-1

This book is a work of fiction. Names, characters, places and incidents are either a product of the author's imagination or are used fictitiously. Any resemblance to actual people living or dead, events or locales is entirely coincidental.

Typeset in Sabon by M Rules
Printed and Bound in the UK using 100% Renewable Electricity at CPI Group (UK) Ltd

For my mother, with lots of love

Chapter One

The truth is something people think they want. Until they have it. They kid themselves they want facts, that they value honesty and integrity, and they'd prefer to know what's *really* going on. *Bullshit.* Nicoletta follows the sound of a baby crying, up the stairs and into the bedroom. Of course, what they actually want is something very different. Rosa is properly bawling, her mouth a tiny pink maw. Cara, Rosa's twin, blinks, discombobulated by the noise, and half-heartedly joins in the chorus. Nicoletta knows at this exact moment that she has to acknowledge the unvarnished truth: she's made a terrible mistake. Wracked with guilt, she scoops up both precious babies and cradles them against her neck, before offering them the bottles Barney's mother had warmed in the kitchen downstairs. The crying stops as they latch on and begin to guzzle the proffered formula. Nicoletta sinks back against the pillows, her arms aching. She doesn't regret the babies for a second. But she has already admitted to herself that the fairy tale of moving in with Barney had only ever been exactly that. The image she'd had, of them in a new-build on one of the modern estates, playing house, is so far away from the current reality. The truth might be uncomfortable, but Nicoletta knows she much prefers its imperfect edges to the finesse of falsehood.

When she'd found out she was pregnant again, a few months after Barney had proposed, and after she had miscarried his baby, Nicoletta was initially shocked, and more than a little apprehensive. Delighted, too, of course, after everything they'd been through with the Julia Bridges story and the devastation it had caused her. Her own mother is no longer on speaking terms with her after the series of articles she wrote in relation to the case and the personal bombshells exploding in its wake. Which is how she's ended up living with Barney, his mother Joan, and Barney's son Liam from his marriage to the oft-talked-about, but seldom seen, Marie.

She looks up as the door opens with such force that the handle hits the wardrobe. Surprise registers on Joan's face as she sees Nicoletta with the twins. Surprise, coupled with something else, something Nicoletta can't quite put her finger on. She wonders if it's pity, and she can't help but feel a sudden surge of resentment.

'Oh,' Joan says. 'I heard crying.'

'Yeah, they're hungry,' Nicoletta replies. 'As always.'

'Give Rosa to me here,' Joan says, holding her arms out. 'They're a handful together.'

Joan lies in beside Nicoletta, her back against the pillows, a baby each in their arms.

'They're hard work,' Joan says, breaking the tense silence. Nicoletta doesn't answer. 'But they're here now,'

Joan adds with a false cheery note in her voice. 'Can't send them back.'

'I don't want to send them back,' Nicoletta says, her tone defensive.

'I know that, pet,' Joan says quietly. 'But they're hard work all the same.'

'I just can't wait to go back to work. To my actual job,' Nicoletta blurts out. It's as well they're both looking straight ahead and she can't see Joan's expression.

Joan sighs. 'The days are long, but the years are short. You'd regret it, sure, if you went back. Take it from me.'

When I go back, Nicoletta doesn't say aloud.

They lapse into another awkward silence, until Barney appears in the doorway, a fleck of shaving foam on his chin. He clocks them both on the bed with the babies.

'Mam, what are you doing here?'

'Giving Nicoletta a hand,' his mother says.

He tucks his shirt in at the waist, the lapels sparkling white. Nicoletta could never get them as white as Joan can.

'You'll be all right here?' He kisses Nicoletta on the forehead, shrugging on a jacket, pocketing his wallet and keys.

'Where are you going?' she asks, deflecting the question.

'Work, of course.' He takes a smart fawn trench coat out of the wardrobe, though the day holds promise of being dry, the heat already rising.

'I can see that,' Nicoletta says, sharper than she fully intends. 'I meant, what's the story?' Joan doesn't say anything at all.

He turns around, looking at her as though seeing her for the first time. 'The verdict on Danny Hall's trial is likely to be this morning. I want to get a reaction from his brother Ray beforehand.'

'The Hall brothers?' Nicoletta shifts slightly, bumping Joan's elbow, as Cara drains the bottle. Rosa slurps away beside her at a more ladylike pace. 'I thought they were acquitted of murdering that Garda?'

'They were,' Barney says, with a terse nod. He chucks Rosa under the chin with an extended forefinger. She opens her eyes wide with astonishment, then bursts into tears. 'Garda Larry Grehan. This is a separate trial. For the burglary of Fairfax House.'

'I see,' Nicoletta says, as Cara finishes the bottle. Joan soothes Rosa, propping her up as she winds her, then resettles her in the crook of her elbow.

Barney stands in the doorway and blows them each a kiss. Nicoletta feels the now familiar wrench of bitterness twist her guts. If she doesn't say something, it'll never get said.

'What if I came along too?'

He shakes his head. 'You're on maternity leave, Nic. You're not due to start back until next week. And who'd mind this pair?' He indicates his daughters with a terse nod.

Nicoletta swallows and turns Cara over to wind her. The silence threatens to swallow them.

'I could mind them,' Joan says. 'It'd do you good to get out for an hour.' She pats Nicoletta's arm.

'Really?' The deliberate softness in Nicoletta's voice belies the brittle desperation underneath.

'All right,' Barney says with a shrug. 'Why not?'

Barney taps his foot while Nicoletta gets dressed. She grabs her bag, and they flee downstairs before Joan can change her mind.

Chapter Two

Barney's car is the same rusted shit heap it always was, with detritus from chocolate wrappers and snacks eaten on the move all over the seats. As he pulls off, Nicoletta rubs her hands, turning to face him.

'This is just like old times.'

He looks back at her and winks, and for a moment, nothing has changed.

'Tell me about the Hall brothers,' she says.

'Where've you been, Nic? They're all over the papers.'

She blows a strand of straggly fringe out of her eyes. 'I've been having your babies, remember?'

'The Hall brothers are part of a gang that targets big houses. You know the kind. Stately piles.'

'Does this gang have political affiliations?' Nicoletta glances at him. A muscle is going in his jaw.

He shakes his head. 'What they're interested in is the business of good, old-fashioned anarchy. Or, rather, they were.'

'What do you mean, "were"?'

Barney gives her a long look, and the car almost swerves off the road.

'Ray Hall. He's come up in the world. Owns a lovely old red-brick house in Rathmines, where he keeps pigeons, of all things.' He laughs. 'You can take the boy out of the flats ...' He gives her a sly glance. 'And he's rumoured to be in a ménage à trois with two sisters.'

She keeps her eyes focused straight ahead. The roads are quiet at this time, and he zips along, his small car's engine revving like a hairdryer.

'How do you know that?' she snaps.

'I couldn't possibly reveal my sources,' he says with a dry laugh. 'But you'll soon see for yourself about Ray Hall. He fancies himself as a bit of a gentleman now. He'll say anything for his name in a headline.'

'Why's that?' She peers out the window, at the canal trailing past in a smudged cluster of muddy foliage. They pass a bread delivery van, its engine chugging dispiritedly on the other side of the road, before it cuts out. But other than that, there's a sense that they are the only two people driving across the city.

Barney raises a hand to his cheek before replacing it on the wheel. 'Some people just love the attention, is all.'

'And some people don't,' she answers lightly. She thinks of the scores of letters she'd received from readers in response to her articles on the Julia Bridges story before she'd gone off on maternity leave. Many were angry, some curious, a few admiring. Most were simply incredulous at her hubris. Her own mother among them, refusing to speak to her. She remembers their last conversation a year before, when her mother told her that Nicoletta had broken her heart. Her father had stayed silent. She clenches her hands into fists. Her nails make half-moon-shaped indents in her palms.

'Barney, I was thinking of calling my mother. Asking her to meet Rosa and Cara.'

A frown line deepens between his eyes as he turns to look at her. The car swerves.

'Keep your eyes on the road,' she mutters.

'Are you sure that's a good idea?' Barney taps the brake. They're on residential streets now, in Ranelagh, passing by dozens of red-brick Edwardian terraces, glowing in the morning sun. 'She told you she never wants to see you again. Remember? Unless you're going to apologise for "airing all that dirty laundry in public".'

He slams the brakes suddenly as a slight girl on a bicycle scoots out across the road ahead of them without looking. The car shrieks in protest. He turns to look at her again.

'You're not thinking of apologising, are you? Nic, you were doing your job. She didn't understand it then, she won't now.'

'Keep your eyes on the road!' she shouts with unnecessary force as his hub caps meet the pavement with a sickening scrape. 'I was only thinking about it,' she says with finality. 'Besides, that's not my job anymore. I'm women's pages editor from next week.'

His nostrils flare as he rounds the corner on to Rathmines main street much too fast and overshoots the turn. 'True,' he says. 'You hated writing about yourself, didn't you?'

She didn't think he'd noticed. Maybe he notices more

than she gives him credit for. 'Ah, it wasn't too bad. Just not something I want to do on a permanent basis.'

He takes a hand off the wheel and clasps her fingers with it. 'I know you can't stand being stuck at home all the time.'

She didn't think he'd noticed that either. She clamps her lips together as they pull into a free parking space outside Rathmines library, a distinctive turn-of-the-century building with some young trees and shrubs grouped in ceramic pots outside. 'I love my children,' she says with a defensive jut to her chin. 'I mean, *our* children.' Her voice is in danger of cracking if she continues. She digs into her handbag and applies a stub of frosted pink lipstick, her bare face raw and uncooked-looking in the passenger mirror.

He takes his hand away and pulls up the hand brake, cutting the engine. He bites his lip, as though he's choosing his words carefully.

'You're a good mother, Nic,' he says, opening the door a couple of inches. A squat little lorry trundles by, dangerously close. He pauses, as he plants one foot after the other on the road. 'But you're also a damn good reporter, whether you like it or not.'

She waves away the compliment and they wordlessly start walking at a brisk pace, past the library, shops, houses, blocks of local authority flats, and a green space with an empty children's playground.

The main Rathmines thoroughfare gives way to a wide, residential street of spacious, rosy-bricked Victorian two-story villas which are set back from the road and shaded by mature plane trees. They stride purposefully along, until Nicoletta stumbles over a rise in the footpath where the roots of a tree have disturbed the paving.

'What's this road called?' A sharp pain pierces her left ankle, but she doesn't want to show it in her face.

'Grosvenor Avenue,' Barney says, shading his eyes and looking ahead to the last house on the left, outside which a knot of people has gathered, before the road forks in two like a serpent's tongue of Biblical proportions. 'All very exclusive and well-to-do.'

'I wonder what the neighbours make of Ray Hall living here. The Rook.' Nicoletta can't help but giggle, trying out the nickname the press has given the most prominent Hall brother. Barney has raced ahead, pacing two strides for every one of hers, and she finds herself struggling to keep up.

'They've had a lot of problems with him, because of all the press attention,' Barney says, coming to a stop outside the gate. Nicoletta steels herself. They're not the only ones with the same idea. Several men similarly dressed to Barney, in slacks, shirts and ties, with raincoats over them are leaning against the gate, which appears to be locked. As a collective, they are a round mass of varying shades of fawn, taupe and beige.

'Who else lives in the house?' Nicoletta stands back politely as Barney nods at several acquaintances. A man with heavy-looking equipment balanced on his shoulder has a camera lens angled and pointed in the direction of the front door, like a cocked gun.

'No one really knows,' Barney admits, motioning for her

to stand to one side out of earshot. 'There's Ray Hall, his wife Sandra and possibly her younger sister of late. I think her name's Majella.' He winks meaningfully.

'Any children?' Nicoletta asks, eyeing the heaving scrum. They're getting restless, and she wonders if something's about to happen. The camera angle doesn't waver.

'We don't know,' Barney says. 'The Rook would tell you everything, and nothing. He's a spoofer, a teller of tall tales. They had a son, Tadhg, who died in the early sixties, when his old fellow was inside doing a stretch for armed robbery. I don't know if they had any subsequent children. There are people in and out of the house, at all hours, between his brothers and their assorted wives and offspring.'

'Don't the Guards know?' Nicoletta asks. 'I thought he was meant to be under twenty-four-hour surveillance.'

'Do they fuck,' Barney scoffs. 'He's got millions of brothers and relatives coming out of the woodwork; it's impossible to keep track of them all.'

The hum among the group of pressmen is reaching fever pitch. Nicoletta breaks off from Barney and stands to attention, looking over an untidy laurel hedge in the direction they're pointing at. She can see a shadow behind the stained-glass panes surrounding the front door.

'He's about to come out and do a press conference,' says Barney. 'You'd swear we're about to be granted an audience with the bleeding Pope.'

An engine hums from behind them. Nicoletta turns around as a Garda car pulls up a couple of houses away on the opposite side of the road. A uniformed Guard gets out of the driver's side, and pats the door closed. He shields his eyes against the sun. It's Garda Peter O'Connor. He starts walking towards her, then stops and leans against one of the lopsided pillars to the gate. He gives her a wave, and Nicoletta nods politely. Her eyes travel upwards, to the stone-carved griffin at the top of the column. Barney continues looking straight ahead, pretending not to have noticed her acknowledgement of O'Connor. He's always been odd about their – she wouldn't call it a friendship, exactly – affinity. And there have been so many unspoken moments between them, which have all slid away like rain down a windshield. She turns around and focuses back on the house, looking for something resembling a shed. She's curious to see where The Rook would keep the pigeons Barney had mentioned. Her eyes pass over a small circular-shaped window above the front door, clear and round: a porthole. A face is momentarily pressed against it, like a moth against glass, long dark hair pooling around bare shoulders, before twisting back and moving away.

At that moment, a small rotund man in a sweater vest opens the front door and stands on the step, his chest puffed out, which doesn't quite hide a sizeable paunch. He's holding steadfast onto a piece of paper. The effect is that of tightly packed sausage meat, Nicoletta can't help but think, as he grips the sheet with pinkly swollen fingers.

'Barney King,' he barks to the audience of men in front of him.

'It's showtime,' Barney says with a jubilant air punch, stepping forward, on to the porch. The man has stepped back, as the knot of reporters shuffle together as one, straining against the chain-link fence to hear what is being said.

The man with the camera nearly topples Nicoletta over the fence, such is his eagerness to take shot after shot of the back of Barney's head and the exterior of this beautiful, if crumbling, Victorian house. O'Connor stays in position at the pillar, and when Barney makes his way back, there's a scrum to see what was said to him. By the time they get past the gate, and are halfway along the road, Nicoletta looks back, and O'Connor has gone.

Barney doesn't say a word on the walk back to the car. Nicoletta can tell that he resents having to drop her home before he goes into the office to file copy. Nicoletta wonders if they ever really had anything to say to each other. She rolls down a window, drinking in the damp fresh air.

'What'd you think of all that?' he asks eventually, when they're almost at Joan's road in Ringsend, where Barney had grown up with just his mother and sister. Now they are all piled on top of each other. Surely it would not end well. Nicoletta shakes her head, hoping to banish the morose thoughts.

'Thanks for bringing me,' she says finally, turning to look at him. He doesn't meet her eye, dragging his gaze back onto the road. A rainbow has appeared on the horizon in front of them. Nicoletta wonders if she should make a wish. 'Why did he want to talk to you?'

Barney flicks on his indicators, almost as an afterthought, before taking the corner at a swerve. 'He seems to like me. I don't know. I've spent months trying to get him to talk to me. I think he mostly does it to piss off the other reporters.'

'Why do you think he likes you?' Nicoletta asks the question in all seriousness.

'What's not to like?' Barney answers with a laugh, pulling up outside Joan's pebble-dashed two-up, two-down, and letting the engine run for a bit.

Nicoletta twists her hands in her lap. 'Seriously, why do you think he likes talking to you?'

Barney lays his palms flat on the steering wheel. 'You'd be surprised at the amount of people who are used to not being listened to. He likes being asked questions, taken seriously. I think it makes him feel important.'

Nicoletta hesitates. 'Does he confide in you?'

He cuts the engine, before giving her a sharp look. 'Why do you ask?'

She bites her lip. 'You mentioned that his son died when he was in prison ten years ago. Did he tell you that?'

'Yep.' Barney looks at her, impatient. 'So what?'

Nicoletta shrugs. 'And did he tell you about being in a ménage à trois with two sisters, or did someone else tell you that?'

'Ah, Nic. I'm not telling you. I couldn't possibly reveal my sources.' He starts the engine and revs it. 'Are you getting out or what? I've to get back to Burgh Quay and file copy.'

'I'm just saying, is all.' Nicoletta clears her throat. 'Do you think that he's one hundred per cent truthful with you? He could well be one of these arch manipulators. Telling you what he wants for thrills, or to elicit your sympathy.'

'Either you're getting out of the car, Nic, or you're coming into the *Sentinel* office with me.' His tone is flat, but Nicoletta takes it as a warning that she's gone too far, questioning his professional knowledge. Yet she can't help herself.

'If someone like that thrives on the oxygen of attention, wouldn't the best thing be, really, to deprive them of it? As in, not listen to all their tall tales and bullshit?'

She doesn't need to swivel around to know that his face is like thunder. He revs the engine again with gusto.

'Speaking as someone who's been in this business a lot longer than you, I think I'll manage to get by somehow.'

She exhales. 'I know you know what you're doing. But someone like him could be dangerous. And you've your family to think of. Two small babies, don't forget. I hope you don't tell him your business . . .' She trails off.

'Thanks for the tip, Nic,' he says with heavy sarcasm. 'What would I do without you?'

She loops her handbag through her wrist and gets out of the car, closing the door with a slam, without bothering to say goodbye. She watches him drive off, envious of the time he has to himself, how he won't think of her, or the babies, or anyone else, until he returns home later, whenever he feels like it. She walks to the end of the road and back, trying to get her rage under control before she has to face Joan, who doesn't deserve Nicoletta's wrath;

it's hardly her fault her son is trying on the nerves. She plasters her face with a smile as she pushes open the front door. Joan never locks it.

Joan is sitting at the kitchen table with Liam, both nursing steaming off-white mugs. Joan stops talking when Nicoletta enters the room.

'Hi, Nicoletta,' Liam says. 'The girls are asleep.'

Liam is Barney's twelve-year-old son, who'd already been here when they'd moved in with Joan in the lead-up to the twins' birth. He's an absolute sweetheart to Nicoletta; so helpful and kind. She feels sick with guilt every time she looks at him.

'Thanks, you're a pet,' Nicoletta says, sitting down opposite them, her guts twisting. Joan eyes her warily. Nicoletta blinks first.

'Thanks for earlier,' she says to Joan.

'Isn't it as well I'm here?' Joan replies, lifting her mug with both hands. 'Otherwise, what would you do?'

Nicoletta is at a loss; fortunately, the question is rhetorical. When the phone peals from the hall, she jams the kitchen door on her big toe in her haste to answer it. Her ankle is already swelling from earlier. She limps into the hallway and seats herself on the narrow, flowery fabric-backed telephone chair.

'Can I speak to Nicoletta please?' A familiar, deep, gruff voice mutters. It's Duffy, her editor at the *Sentinel*.

'This is Nicoletta,' she says as calmly as she can muster. 'Hello, Mr Duffy.'

'Good girl yourself,' he says with a cheery bark. 'Would you be around this afternoon to come in and open your post? We've sacks of letters taking up space for you to go through.'

She coughs. She's about to reply, when she realises that he's already rung off and she's busy clearing her throat into dead air.

Chapter Three

When Barney dashes off to the Four Courts for the verdict of the Hall trial, Nicoletta returns to the *Irish Sentinel* offices, somewhere she hasn't set foot in over five months. Her presence goes unremarked when she enters the newsroom and grabs her post from her brand-new desk. Elation washes over her as she fans the piles of letters across the high telephone table of the newsroom: an assortment of envelopes, big and small, all addressed to Nicoletta Sarto, women's pages editor. No one can possibly tarnish this moment.

She picks up an envelope and rips it open with her thumb. A shaky scrawl fills a single page, with jagged blue letters gouged into the paper, the edges frilled where they've been torn out of a shorthand notebook.

The letter hasn't been signed. It simply says, 'I HAVE IMPORTANT INFORMATION ABOUT AN ALIEN INVASION. PLEASE MEET ME AT THE GPO AT ONE O'CLOCK ON 19TH MAY TO FIND OUT MORE.'

19th May was almost two weeks ago. She crumples the sheet and throws it into the wastepaper basket, where it misses, and lands beside Ann's desk. Ann looks up.

'Didn't expect you back so soon,' she says coolly. 'You're not due in until next week.'

Nicoletta can hear Dermot laughing with someone from the row of typewriters. She turns, wistful. She has missed something as everyday as sharing a joke with a colleague.

She bites her lip. 'Duffy asked me to pop in to open some post. Fancy some lunch soon?'

Ann sighs and picks up her bag. 'I've a big file of recipes to look through. You can help me if you like.' She glances up at Nicoletta's pile of letters.

'Any more fan mail?'

Nicoletta gives a sharp laugh. 'No, thank God.' She picks up the alien invasion letter from the floor and smooths it out, placing it in the miscellaneous pile, which is growing higher by the minute. She'll sort through the rest later. Ann clicks her nails against the laminate desk, observing Nicoletta, who sidles over to the typewriters and taps Dermot's shoulder. His frown of concentration relaxes as his eyebrows shoot into his hairline. 'Jesus, you're back!'

'Just for a few hours,' she says with a laugh.

'Here, give me a minute to finish this and I'll be over to you,' he says, resuming his assault on the keyboard.

The racing edition of the paper is distributed and there's a flurry of interest in the diminishing pile. Nicoletta picks up a copy and places it face-up on her old desk. She relishes this oasis of quiet in the newsroom during lunchtime, knowing it'll be short-lived. There's no one else apart from her on the features desk. Ann has disappeared.

Barney has the front-page splash. Nicoletta feels a jolt

of some unwelcome emotion when she sees his byline. She should feel proud of him, she knows that, but it's complicated. She thinks of all the months she's been cooped up with the twins at home, waiting for a respite which never came. An amateur mother, playing house with Barney in his childhood home, his own mother breathing down their necks and finding her wanting. Counting down the days until she could go back to work. And now she's missed so much by being off, but Barney has sailed on ahead without her. She gives the paper a shake and holds it up to her face.

THE WREN JAILED FOR FAIRFAX
HOUSE BURGLARY
By Barney King
1st June 1970
The criminal widely known as 'The Wren', Daniel Hall (39), was today jailed for three months for his part in the burglary of Fairfax House at Blessington, Co Wicklow on January 1st of this year. Hall, along with his brothers Ray 'The Rook' Hall and Ronan 'The Magpie' Hall, was tried and acquitted last month of the murder of Garda Larry Grehan at Fairfax House on the same date. The evidence against Mr Hall for the burglary conviction was 'overwhelming' according to the judgment of Justice Frank Doyle. Three works of art belonging to Sir Ken and Lady Pat Dennehy of Fairfax House were found in the boot of Mr Hall's car on a date in January of this year after Gardaí obtained a search warrant. A fourth painting, *Among the Ruins*, remains missing. It is part one of a diptych by 19th-century Austrian artist Edvard

Dunst. The whereabouts of the other half in the pair is also unknown. Together, both paintings are said to be worth in the realm of £5 million.

The Hall brothers are said to be part of an organised criminal gang known as 'The Birds', which targets big houses around Ireland, formerly or still owned by the Anglo-Irish ascendancy. Their modus operandi is to loot the houses of valuable *objets d'art*, before setting the houses alight. A post-mortem conducted by the State Pathologist Dr John Marsden concluded that Garda Larry Grehan died as a result of smoke inhalation. Garda Grehan was called to the premises by Lady Pat Dennehy after the burglars entered the house. Garda Grehan's widow Mary said she had no comment to make on Daniel Hall being jailed for burglary today. Mr Hall's brother Ray Hall remains under twenty-four-hour Garda surveillance. He exclusively told the *Sentinel* earlier about his hope for justice. 'My brothers and I have been victimised by Gardaí since we were old enough to walk,' he said. 'Let us hope today justice will actually be done, but I'm not holding my breath.'

The newsroom reeks of sweat, coffee and stale smoke. Has it always smelled like this, Nicoletta wonders, or has she only just noticed it, after being away for months on end? Nevertheless, the new odour makes a welcome change from dirty nappies and baby vomit. Every window is jammed shut, sealed by long-ago layers of paint.

She walks out to the kitchenette with her cup from earlier and when she comes back, Ann is at her desk, her coat on.

'Are you coming?' Ann indicates the stairs. 'Oh, by the way, someone just rang. They asked for you.'

'Who is it?' Nicoletta asks. 'Are they still on the line?'

Ann shrugs, her hazel eyes level with Nicoletta's. 'They'll ring back.'

She stands up and takes Nicoletta's arm. 'Come on, mixed grill in Clery's is calling. You're buying. I'm glad you're back.' The feathered bits at the front of her hair stick up in the heat. The gesture gives her a soft, endearing quality, like a baby chicken. Nicoletta wonders if this is a turning point; if they could actually become friends now that they are working so closely together, with Nicoletta as women's pages editor and Ann as her deputy.

Ann leads the way down the concrete steps, gliding out onto Burgh Quay. A dirty-looking sun persists. They're about to cross the street onto the bridge, when Nicoletta stops.

'Ann, maybe I should go back and see if the person is still on the phone. Did they ask specifically for me?'

Ann observes her with an air of detachment. 'They wanted the person who wrote the Julia Bridges stories. They were quite insistent about it.'

Nicoletta shifts her weight from foot to foot. 'Well, I'd better go. In case they don't leave a message.'

Ann leans into the wind to light a cigarette, her face half in shadow, dappled by passing clouds.

'Suit yourself. God knows you'd do *anything* for a story.' Nicoletta is about to ask what she means, but Ann turns on her heel and heads onward in the direction of the brass-trimmed doors of Clery's. Nicoletta makes her way back across the street, over the bridge and towards the *Sentinel* offices, a prickle of excitement needling her scalp. There's no one to see her at the door when she returns, and Noel the doorman says there have been no in-person or telephone callers since she and Ann have gone, so she slips back up to the newsroom and seats herself at her desk, waiting. For what, she doesn't know.

The minutes on the old clock above the door tick by in Roman numerals. Nicoletta's stomach gurgles and she thinks longingly of the mixed grill Ann is no doubt tucking into. Dermot stomps by for a chat, a sheaf of paper in his arms. She hasn't seen him in months, since her last day in the office when she'd been heavily pregnant and he'd organised a cake for her. He never visited when the twins arrived, she doesn't know why. She immediately feels lit by the spotlight of his personality. She's missed him.

'Well?' He pulls over a chair from the features desk, sliding the paper down on her desk. Ann always acknowledges Dermot with a huge smile. All the women in the office love him. Nicoletta frowns, wondering if Ann knows that her mild flirtation is water off a duck's back as far as Dermot is concerned. But Ann is a man's lady, and the only thing Nicoletta would have to do to earn her approval would be to maybe change gender, she thinks sourly. Ann sees most other women as surplus to requirements. Nicoletta shakes her head.

'How've you been?' she asks, cutting through the awkward silence.

'Ah, you know.' He smiles, meeting her gaze with his

usual glint, but she notices the grey-yellow under-eye pouches jaundicing the top part of his face. They make him look older. Wait, what age is Dermot? She can't honestly remember. But not old enough to look his age, that's for sure. She's aware of Brenda on the copy desk listening to every word. She doesn't care; she has nothing she could be bothered to hide anymore.

'No, I don't know, Derm.' She tries to soften the blunt response with a laugh. 'I haven't seen you since before the girls were born. I'm a mother now, remember?'

He scrubs at his right eye with the knuckle of his thumb, as though trying to expunge a swarm of insects. He has the good grace to look slightly uncomfortable.

'How are they?' He coughs into his hand. 'Twins, you had, right?'

She nods. 'Cara and Rosa. A handful each.' She laughs. He joins in, until they both trail off. She puts her hand on his arm. 'It's really great to see you.' She feels like crying. Dermot is her only ally in here. What the hell has happened? 'Come over to us one evening and meet the twins. We'll open some wine.'

His face crumples. It looks to her as though he might be the one about to cry. He scours both eyes this time with the back of his hand before answering.

'I'd love that,' he says. He seems sincere. 'Sorry I haven't been to see you yet. I'm not really a baby type of person.' He laughs, and she joins in. He surprises her then by enfolding her in a hug. She doesn't want to pull away before he does. He smells of perspiration and smoke. Usually Dermot smells of aftershave and soap.

'How's it been in here since I've been gone?' A nearby phone rings and no one answers it. She lets it ring, not wanting to break this moment with Dermot.

'You know. The usual.' He gives her a wry grin. Another phone starts up as though in harmony with the first.

'Any big stories?' She already knows the answer, but she's desperate to be back in the loop.

'Your fella's been busy with the Hall brothers, The Rook in particular,' he says. 'Every day of the trial and then some.'

'We went to his house earlier.' Nicoletta notes with some relief that the phones have stopped ringing.

Dermot raises an eyebrow. 'Really? I'd say the Rookster liked that. Barney probably didn't get a look-in.'

Nicoletta shakes her head. 'He didn't look at me once. He just wanted to make some sort of prepared statement and chat to Barney. Sounded pretty boring, if you ask me.'

Dermot looks thoughtful. 'Congratulations on your new gig, Miss Sarto. You're probably glad to be in features now. Away from gurriers like The Rook.'

'Maybe,' she grins. 'Did I mention I'm the women's pages editor?'

Brenda drops a pen and swears loudly, before picking it up. Nicoletta lowers her voice.

'This Rook guy really seems to enjoy the spotlight.'

'That he does,' Dermot says. 'Likes the sound of his own dulcet tones as well.' He guffaws. He's almost back to his ebullient self. But not quite. His face looks thinner, his cheekbones disrupting his face in sharp relief. Nicoletta observes him. She wants to ask him if he's all right, but now isn't the time. She resolves to try to catch him later in the week, to make time for reigniting their friendship.

She leans forward on one elbow, flicking a paperclip between her fingers. It lands on Dermot's sheaf of paper. 'He definitely loves the attention,' she agrees with a rueful laugh. 'Not everybody does, right?'

Dermot smiles and looks down at the pages. He picks them up. 'Don't I know it.' He puts a hand on her shoulder. 'You got a lot of flak for the Julia Bridges story, Nic. Are you okay now?'

She smiles, grateful for the old Dermot buzzing in across the connection they'd shared for so long. 'I guess so.' She shrugs. 'Tell you the truth, I'm never writing about myself again.'

'Never say never,' Dermot says with an explosive laugh, which sounds more like his old self. He stands up, enclosing the pages under his oxter once again, and stomps off, promising over his shoulder that they'll catch up later, before calling something to Brenda, who shouts something back in reply. At Dermot's retort, she throws back her head and laughs. Her smile seems to freeze when she catches Nicoletta's eye, and she quickly looks down, her fair hair curtaining her face. Dermot doesn't break his stride on his way to the case room. Nicoletta scrutinises him from behind. Maybe she's being over the top thinking there's something wrong with him since she's come back. When he'd presented her with the cake only six months ago at the start of December, he'd been his usual robust self. Now he looks thinner than he did before she went on maternity leave; thinner and more careworn. But surely so does she.

And maybe that's what happens when you view the world through sleep-deprived eyes. Someone breaks a cup in the kitchenette, and everybody cheers. The radio is tuned to the news, which is intoning about the recent nurses' strike. The broadcast gets mixed up with the jumble of background noise.

Nicoletta checks the clock. A half hour has passed since she sat back down at her desk. She should really go home. It's not fair on Joan. She's not due back officially until next week. She asks the switch if any calls have come in for her in the last five minutes, and the answer is none. She concedes defeat by standing up and putting her jacket back on. She's about to descend the stairs when Ann waltzes back in with a wriggle of her fingers.

'Have a nice lunch?' She yawns, displaying a bit of something red caught in her teeth. Tomato, maybe, from the mixed grill. Nicoletta wonders if the phone call actually existed. Or if Ann was testing her in some twisted way. She follows Ann back to her desk.

'Just caught up on a few things,' Nicoletta replies.

Ann sits down with a flounce. Nicoletta keeps her jacket on and continues opening the rest of her mail. She'll have to leave soon but can't quite bear to do so yet. An embossed card from someone called Louise Leonard, BL, falls out of a thick cream envelope, along with a printed postcard depicting a woman breaking free of shackles from her ankles and wrists. The handwritten note attached invites Nicoletta to a meeting of Irish Women for Choice that very afternoon. Nicoletta turns over the envelope. The postmark is dated from a couple of weeks ago. The note says: 'Please come along. We'd love to see you there.' The note has been signed in assured looping handwriting by Louise Leonard. The name sounds vaguely familiar, but Nicoletta can't quite place it.

She folds the invitation into her notebook without showing it to Ann and stows both in her handbag. She checks her face in the reflection of the grimy window. The river is low, as one with the sky, the same wispy blue. Barney is nowhere to be seen. He'll assume she's going home. She can't wait to get out the door, to have some time on her own, away from them all. Just to be.

She walks for a bit before checking her watch. There's twenty minutes until the meeting. Her feet start moving in the direction of a café on Hawkins Street, a well-known greasy spoon, run by an Italian family Nicoletta's grandparents used to know. On impulse, she opens the scuffed, slightly rickety door and orders a ham sandwich and a fizzy orange drink. The drink is served immediately in a tall glass, which she takes to a corner where there are two or three tables jammed in isolation. The ice clinks against the glass as she sets it down. Too late, she notices a man returning from the bathroom at the rear of the café, in shirtsleeves and blue trousers, his head bare. It's Garda O'Connor. She curses herself inwardly. Why did she have to choose this café? Or had she done it deliberately, in some deeply rooted subconscious way, hoping he'd be here?

'Good afternoon, Garda.' She speaks first, sitting down at her table, and boldly takes a sip of her orange. 'Good to see you.' She realises that she really means it. It is good to see him.

'And you,' he says with a smile. He sits down, turning his chair around to face her, his arms deeply freckled. 'How've you been?' The waitress delivers Nicoletta's sandwich, and he orders a pot of tea. Nicoletta declines his offer of anything else.

'I've been well.' She clears her throat. 'I had twins, baby girls, five months ago.' She takes a couple of bites of her sandwich.

He nods, his expression inscrutable. 'I heard.' He pushes back his chair and stands up, enveloping her in a hug. 'Congratulations,' he says, releasing her and holding her at arm's length. 'I'm delighted for you.'

She smiles and looks down at her drink. Garda O'Connor has been there through her worst moments, and she's been pretty honest with him. He knows more about her than Barney does.

'Are they sleeping for you?' His question lifts her out of her thoughts.

'Not a chance,' she says with a laugh. He echoes her laugh and then they settle into silence for a moment or two. She finishes her sandwich as people gravitate towards the tables and chairs assembled outside on the street: secretaries, businessmen in suits, uniformed kids on the hop from school. A newspaper seller struts past, his sandwich board proclaiming a conviction for Daniel Hall, aka The Wren. Nicoletta swallows the last of her lunch and takes a ruminative sip of her drink, the orangey bubbles hitting the back of her throat. She shouldn't be here. 'I'd better go,' she says suddenly. 'I've a meeting. But it was really good to see you.'

'You too,' he agrees, standing up and shaking her hand, perhaps thinking twice about another hug. When she tries to pay for her order, he won't let her.

'I'll get you next time,' she says, before regretting how forward it might sound to him. Did he think she was presuming there'd be a next time?

She wrestles with the door on the way out and she's faintly aware of his eyes on her as she passes to the end of the street and turns the corner. Something within her is telling her to pay attention, the way animals can recognise the precursor to a storm. She's come to listen to that voice when she hears it.

Chapter Four

Carlo's is a small Italian restaurant at the Stephen's Green end of Baggot Street, nestled among a row of shabby Georgian office conversions. It's covered by a red-and-white striped awning, but its windows are blank, and it looks closed. Nicoletta tries the door; it's locked. She lightly raps on the glass and waits until someone answers. The person who does isn't who she was expecting. It's a tall, fine-featured woman, wearing wide, dark slacks and a ruffled blouse. She's what Nicoletta's mother would have called handsome, rather than pretty. The thought of her mother makes her feel exposed, about to join this meeting of accomplished women feeling like a fraud. The woman's expression is as blank as the windows beside her, and she regards Nicoletta with ambivalence. Her hair is the most surprising thing about her. It's black and ironed dead straight, falling down her back almost to her waist, at odds with the staid office attire.

'Hi,' Nicoletta says, with a nervous upwards inflection. 'Nicoletta Sarto. I'm here for the meeting.' The woman doesn't say anything. 'I received an invitation from Louise Leonard?' Nicoletta adds. 'I work for the *Sentinel*.'

'Ah yeah, right.' The woman smooths an imaginary inky strand of hair out of her eye. She indicates for Nicoletta to come inside. The interior is cool and dark. A raucous peal of laughter erupts from a table in the corner, and the woman gives Nicoletta a meaningful look.

'Carlo gives us the whole restaurant for a lunchtime on Mondays once a month. He's closed on Mondays anyhow.' She raises her eyebrows. 'As long as we clean up after ourselves and keep the noise down.' She doesn't wait for Nicoletta to answer, weaving her way towards the place where all the noise is coming from. She stops at a curtain fringed with pale beading, jamming a finger in the air.

'You're the girl who wrote the Julia Bridges stories.'

Nicoletta nods. The woman inclines her head. 'Maureen French.' She holds out a large, cool hand, which Nicoletta shakes. 'Assistant news editor at the *Chronicle*. We're delighted you could join us. I know Louise is a big fan.'

Maureen beckons her through the curtain, which makes a faint jingling sound as they pass. Silence has fallen over the table at their arrival. Nicoletta feels several pairs of eyes appraising her. Maureen pulls over a chair from a nearby table, indicating for Nicoletta to sit.

'This is Nicoletta Sarto from the *Sentinel*,' Maureen announces to the group. 'The Julia Bridges story,' she says with a matter-of-fact nod, before Nicoletta can say anything.

She feels her cheeks burn through the pause that follows. A woman with ash-blonde hair piled on top of her head stands and extends her hand. 'Louise Leonard,' she says, lines fanning out from her eyes and mouth. 'That was a heck of a story.'

Maureen half sits, half leans in the space between Nicoletta and Louise Leonard.

'You're exactly the sort of person we want in the group,' Maureen says, more to the rest of the gathering than to Nicoletta. She seems to be in charge. A girl around Nicoletta's age, or younger, with a red headband holding back a shock of dark hair, nods uncertainly. A woman in the far corner stands up, revealing long tanned legs under a tiny skirt. She comes over to shake Nicoletta's hand. 'Billie Murphy from the *Evening Post*.' The rest of the women murmur friendly assent. Nicoletta relaxes slightly.

'What made you want to join?' Maureen looks down at Nicoletta from her vantage point half standing beside her, and Nicoletta feels as though she's pinned to the spot.

'I got Louise's invitation, and, I guess, curiosity got the better of me. It always does.' Her laugh is wry, and Billie smiles at her. Another woman, who Louise addresses as Jean, nods. 'It'll be all of our undoing,' she says, blowing smoke out her nose. Nicoletta must have given her a quizzical look, because she goes on to explain. 'Six of our twelve members are journalists.'

'I see,' Nicoletta says, feeling her scalp prickle with the heat, and the scrutiny.

'Have you read *The Feminine Mystique*?' Maureen is so close Nicoletta can feel her breath ruffle the top of her head.

'No, I'm afraid not.' Nicoletta shakes her head vigorously; aware she is possibly failing another sort of test.

Billie mouths her agreement.

'But I've read about it,' Nicoletta says, looking into all the faces around the table. Some are blank, most friendly.

'And what do you think?' Maureen presses, and Nicoletta wishes she'd just get a chair like a normal person.

'I think it's time for . . .' Nicoletta exhales slowly, desperate for some fresh air.

'Time for change! So do we,' Maureen pronounces, smiling broadly at Nicoletta. 'So do we all. And now it's time for some refreshments.'

Maureen glides back through the fringed curtain with a word. Louise pats her arm. Nicoletta finds herself shrinking away from the touch. 'Maureen can be intense,' she says into her ear. 'But you'll find as you go along that she's a sweetheart all the same.'

Maureen comes back with two silver urns filled with tea and coffee. There's much grumbling from someone in a green dress, whom Maureen calls Phil, who wants a cold drink, but accepts a cup of coffee. Nicoletta gathers that she works for the *Irish Independent*.

'What are you working on at the moment?' Phil asks Nicoletta. She frowns when she takes a sip of her drink.

'I'm starting back next week after maternity leave.' Nicoletta pauses uncertainly. 'Recipes are top of my remit at the moment, by all accounts.' She takes a scalding gulp.

Phil furrows her brow. She has shapely, drawn-on eyebrows, which Nicoletta can't stop looking at. 'Well, there's plenty more interesting stories out there than how to make jam buns and roly-poly pudding.'

Maureen makes a conspiratorial face at Nicoletta.

Louise drains her coffee. 'Right, let's move on to the next item on the agenda.' She nods at Maureen. 'What is it?'

'Repealing the contraception laws,' Maureen says. 'Louise is currently taking a case to the High Court pro bono, on behalf of a woman whose doctor advised her not to have any more children, but who can't access contraception in the Republic of Ireland. Louise is arguing that it's in breach of her constitutional rights.'

Nicoletta nods slowly, hoping she looks suitably awed.

'Who's taking minutes?' Louise asks with a brisk glance at Maureen.

Nicoletta raises her hand. 'I will,' she says, for want of anything else to do. She infinitely prefers to be writing than speaking. She spends the next hour scribbling so fast her hand feels crabbed from holding the pen.

Louise ends the meeting with a gasp at the time. She gathers up her things. On her way past Nicoletta, she almost shouts into her ear.

'Can I speak to you for a moment, please?'

Nicoletta's shoulders shoot up, startled. She hastily says goodbye as the women around the table drift away. Louise indicates the door, and they step out into the street.

They fall into step, crossing Baggot Street Bridge. Louise stops walking, almost colliding with another pedestrian.

'Thanks for coming today.' She emits a loud sigh, hefting a large leather satchel higher on her shoulder.

'Thanks for asking me. It's a great thing to be a part of,' Nicoletta murmurs, feeling like words are failing her, as a woman on a bicycle jogs her elbow. They round the corner, and Louise indicates a mossy-looking bench at an overgrown spot beside the canal.

'Let's sit here a moment. There's something I want to talk to you about.'

They sit down and Nicoletta wonders what's coming. Hadn't Louise been in a hurry to leave? Louise lights a cigarette with a shaky hand, scrunching her fingers to her mouth. She doesn't speak until she's blown out a pensive stream of smoke.

'We're on the lookout for a new secretary of the group. I can't do it anymore, just too busy. Would you be interested?'

Nicoletta shivers, remembering her feeling of earlier. Trusting her inner voice and accepting Louise's invitation has led her here. Where will it lead her now?

'All right,' she says. The sun has gone behind a cloud, and a breeze whips in over the sludgy water. A trio of mallards peck at the crusted bank. She hugs her bag for comfort and observes Louise. Her leather satchel is wedged upright between her ankles. Louise keeps smoking, avoiding Nicoletta's eye.

'Are you all right?' Nicoletta ventures.

Louise shakes her head, tossing the cigarette butt onto the towpath. It stays lit, smouldering dangerously until Nicoletta can't bear it anymore. She stands up and extinguishes the glowing tip with the heel of her shoe.

Louise looks at her in astonishment.

'Sorry,' Nicoletta says. 'I had to do it.'

The worry on Louise's face dissolves and she laughs. 'Okaaay,' she says, drawing out the word.

Nicoletta sits back down and places her bag between her ankles, mirroring Louise's position. She doesn't take her eyes off Louise's face. The ash-blonde hair is escaping from its knot, loose strands making her seem younger and less fierce than she had earlier.

'I've a lot on my plate at the moment, Nicoletta,' she says, lighting another cigarette.

'Tell me,' Nicoletta says with a careful smile.

Louise sighs a stream of smoke. 'My aunt is being exhumed next Wednesday. It's taken me months to make it happen.'

'Why?' Nicoletta asks uselessly, with a small gasp. This is not what she'd been expecting.

'I believe she was murdered. And I want them exposed.'

'Who do you want exposed?' Nicoletta frowns, confused.

'The nursing agency,' Louise continues. 'They're taking advantage of vulnerable elderly people.'

'Which nursing agency?' Nicoletta fits as few words as possible into curt frames; Louise appears to be talking in riddles.

'Nurses Direct. I believe the owners to be criminally negligent. And now my aunt is dead. She was murdered, I'm sure of it.'

'Who do you think murdered her?' Nicoletta asks.

A young man walks by with a rolled-up newspaper under his arm, whistling. Louise waits until he has passed before she shifts in a little closer to Nicoletta, their knees touching, an oddly intimate gesture.

'A nurse we hired to care for my aunt killed her, I believe. She was using a false identity. She gave her name as Barbara Highfield, and my aunt has left everything to this Miss Highfield in her will. Not that it matters. Miss Highfield simply doesn't exist.'

'I'm sorry,' Nicoletta says, grabbing her bag and digging around in it. 'Can I take some notes?'

'Sure,' Louise says with a wave of a ringless hand. 'For all the good it'll do.'

'Okay.' Nicoletta sits back, chastened.

'What was your aunt's name?'

'Helen Leonard,' Louise says, resuming the brisk, businesslike air of earlier. 'Miss. She lived at Seaview Terrace in Sandycove. Was born there, in fact. And she sure as hell died there.'

'Hold on,' Nicoletta breathes, remembering the tough old bird she'd interviewed when investigating the Julia Bridges story. 'I met your aunt. I'm so sorry to hear she's died.'

'I know you did,' Louise says with a cough, which she stifles with the heel of her hand. 'She told me you exposed that whole rotten business, and you didn't care who was collateral.' She gives Nicoletta a look. 'Though I suspect that wasn't easy.'

'No,' Nicoletta replies, feeling a tightening behind her eyelids, thinking of her mother. 'It wasn't. And I'm still feeling the fallout from it.'

Louise stands up and brushes down her trousers.

Nicoletta puts her notebook away and they start walking slowly along the narrow path, Louise leading by a stride or two. When they've reached the end, which widens out into a trio of saplings, Louise squeezes Nicoletta's elbow. She flinches.

'Forget about what I've said about Helen. Don't put yourself out. It's a matter for the State Pathologist and then the Gardaí.'

Louise raises a hand in salutation behind her as she dashes up through a gap in the low stone wall, towards the street. 'Have to get back to the Law Library. Stay in touch.' She stops and turns her head. 'And thank you for coming on board as secretary.'

Nicoletta follows her. She scuffs her elbow on a low hanging branch from a gnarled old tree, its roots extending to disrupt the pavement beyond.

'Wait,' she says, rubbing her elbow. 'You can't just leave like that.' A thin smudge of blood comes away on her finger. Louise starts walking again, as Nicoletta quickly covers the wound with her sleeve.

'When did Miss Leonard die?' Nicoletta asks, falling into Louise's slipstream.

'Three months ago.'

'Who found her body?' Nicoletta digs a pen out of her bag.

'Sadie Duggan, her housekeeper of many years. Lives locally. She then called the local priest, Father Farry, who administered the last rites. Don't try and talk to them. He certainly won't speak to you.'

Nicoletta scribbles the names on her arm. Louise looks

at her again with that amused, barely credulous look. Nicoletta blushes.

'Why isn't Maureen, or one of the other journalists in the group, looking into this?' It's Nicoletta's turn to shift from foot to foot, her full bladder making her departure a matter of urgency.

Louise sighs, swatting a tiny fly with the back of her hand.

'To be perfectly honest, Nicoletta. All right. None of them would touch it, if you really want to know. Too much to lose. They're not young and hungry.' She turns and starts walking away at a brisk pace.

'Like me? Is that what you mean?' Nicoletta calls, feeling ridiculous as she clutches her scratched elbow, the need to urinate taking over all other thoughts.

Louise pauses, raising a hand behind her in a mock salute.

'I'm not that bloody young,' Nicoletta mutters, half to herself, as Louise rounds the corner onto Lower Mount Street. The young man with the rolled-up newspaper under his arm walks back in the other direction and gives her a curious look, then averts his eyes and walks on, as if to say, *nothing to see here*. There's no wolf whistle, no admiring glance.

She starts walking the way Louise had gone, back in the direction of town. She spots a pub on the corner and sprints towards it, making a beeline for the Ladies' toilets at the back. She walks purposefully past a padded leather banquette on which a pair of office workers are lingering over cold soup, whispering to each other while the barman clatters around, running a brush around their feet. The lunchtime rush is over; this is a time for regulars and habitual drinkers only. She bites her lip and appraises herself in the grimy mirror as she washes her hands.

She has a bleeding elbow, her hair is an untidy mess, scraped back on top of her head, and she could do with about a month's sleep. She hadn't had time to apply make-up that morning. She dries her hands with a wad of rolled-up tissue and inspects her elbow, dabbing at the scratch. She needs to get back to the twins. She walks out, back on to the quiet street, and no one looks up.

She'll have to think carefully about whether or not she wants to get involved with the Leonards and Helen Leonard's death. It could well be a blind alley. And she has enough to be going on with. An image appears in her mind's eye: old Helen Leonard, with her overheated kitchen and her unfashionably long skirt, telling Nicoletta the unvarnished truth because it was the right thing to do. And now, had poor Miss Leonard been murdered in her own bed? Nicoletta is surprised to feel the once-familiar pinprick of emotion pop the weary bubble she seems to inhabit these days. She can still trust the voice that led her here. It's her one constant, a heartbeat.

Chapter Five

Nicoletta doesn't go home to Joan and the twins, as she'd planned. Instead, she returns to the newsroom and drinks two cups of instant coffee. She sits hunched over her desk, pretending to sort through her in-tray, while Ann rummages in far-off, dusty cupboards for recipe pictures of every iteration imaginable. She's aware of Ann's eyes boring into her back as she hefts bulging files stuffed with pictures of long-ago apple crumbles and rhubarb tarts back to her desk. She waits until Ann is engrossed with a bulging file before she stands at the high telephone table and picks up the receiver, asking for Father Farry, the Catholic parish priest for Seaview Terrace in Sandycove.

There are a few clicks on the line as the operator takes an age coming back to the phone. Nicoletta hears a distant, echoey peal of laughter, then several more clicks. She taps a pen against her teeth. She could just go out to Sandycove and see, but she doesn't have the time or energy required to just wing it anymore.

The operator comes back with a squeal of triumph. Nicoletta holds the receiver away from her ear. 'I've found him for you,' the girlish voice says with glee. She sounds very young. 'It's Father Matthew Farry, with an address at the parochial house in Glasthule.'

Nicoletta mutters her thanks. She scribbles down the name on a torn-off corner of newsprint from that day's city edition when Barney appears beside her.

'What're you doing, Nic?'

She snatches at the flimsy piece of paper before he can read it.

'Checking an address,' she says, reaching for her jacket and putting it on. 'Remember Helen Leonard? The old lady who lived beside the Creightons? Well, her niece told me she thinks she was murdered.'

Barney frowns. He leans forward, his shirt open at the neck, his tie discarded.

'Wait, are you thinking of writing something on it?'

'Maybe,' Nicoletta bristles. 'It sounds like there's more to it than meets the eye.'

Barney rests an elbow on the high table, casting a glance at the ebbing activity of the newsroom. 'Duffy will never allow it.' He shakes his head with finality. 'Helen Leonard was the half-sister of Lady Pat Dennehy.' He puffs out his cheeks in frustration at her ignorance. 'Wife of Sir Ken Dennehy, the owner of this newspaper?'

Nicoletta's mouth forms a tiny 'o'. 'The owners of Fairfax House, where Garda Larry Grehan died during the burglary?'

'The very one,' Barney says, his voice low, but making her feel about an inch high nonetheless.

'Why?' Nicoletta picks up her bag.

'He has his reasons.' He leans against the table, rolling a tiny ball of paper between finger and thumb, as though considering her.

'Did you hear about the Creightons?'

'No,' she says, her tone flat.

He smiles, his eyes crinkling his face – the smile that once undid her. 'Sally Creighton is flogging the house, along with all its contents. She's having an open house tomorrow and Duffy wants you to go. Get some colour on it. *How do you feel eighteen months after the events that occurred*, all of that.' He winks. It's the wink that sets her off.

'I'm the women's pages editor now.' Nicoletta's voice rises an octave, and a few curious glances are thrown her way.

'You won't do Creightons, but you want to go off on a whim about Helen Leonard?' Barney scuffs the already scuffed felt carpet with his toe. He's already bored of this conversation, she can tell.

'That's different,' she protests, trying to keep her voice on a moderate level. 'Helen Leonard was a defenceless old lady whose niece thinks she was murdered. Sally Creighton is a whole different ball game.'

He half turns. 'I'll tell Duffy you won't do it. He'll understand, I'm sure.' He tosses this over his shoulder like a grenade.

'I'm not writing about the Creightons anymore,' she says, clenching her jaw.

'Just go up there, Nic. Go and see what's happening. Then see how you feel.' His wheedling is tentative, but it works.

'Right.' She tries to soften her voice, to ease this deadlock they're in. 'Want to walk home together? It's nice and bright out.'

'It's roasting!' Barney turns away. 'I'm heading to Cassidy's. You coming?'

'I've to head back to the girls and your mother.'

He doesn't seem to hear her.

The sun is still blazing in the sky when she walks up the narrow, shaded path to Joan's house and lets herself in. The hallway envelops her in its dark, stuffy embrace and she sets down her bag and takes off her jacket. She can hear Joan feeding the girls from the kitchen. One of them gurgles and Nicoletta realises she doesn't know which twin it is. Did she ever know? Joan mutters a reply, her voice tender. She's never heard Joan use this tone before – certainly not on her. She wonders if Joan is currently speaking to her. Only one way to find out, she decides.

The kitchen is bright and messy, strewn with all manner of colourful baby detritus. Joan is sitting with both babies under the crook of each arm in the rocking chair. The radio blares from behind her, a popular quiz show with an annoying catchphrase. Nicoletta smiles.

'It's only me,' she says.

'I can see that,' Joan answers, standing up and handing her a baby, before brushing imaginary crumbs off her apron and untying it at the waist. Both babies immediately start to cry, and Nicoletta looks back to Joan. She's helpless, even with her own children. Anyone can see it.

She can see the scorn in Joan's eyes as she calms the babies down by rocking them against her. Joan sinks back into a chair.

Nicoletta takes a seat at the kitchen table, feeling every inch the unwelcome guest. This is not my house, she reminds herself. The situation is only temporary. She hears the thwack of Liam's football against the side of the house and feels another pang of guilt.

'I've been asked to go in tomorrow,' she says in a rush. It's not a lie, exactly. She'll go to Creightons, aware that no matter which way she glosses it, everything she says is going to be unsatisfactory.

'I see. And the day after that?'

'And the day after that, and the day after that. It's my job.'

Joan bristles at her flippant tone. 'Your job is to mind these little créatúrs.'

Nicoletta rubs her temples. She's not going to win this argument. 'I'm expected to do my job. It pays the bills. And then we can move out and buy a new house of our own.' She smiles hopefully.

Joan lowers the babies into a small circular playpen in the corner of the room and crosses back to snap off the radio.

'You're their mother. If they haven't got you, who have they got?'

Nicoletta stands up and retreats into the hallway. On second thoughts, she pokes her head back in the door, which she's left slightly ajar. 'I'll stay here tomorrow. And I'll make alternative childminding arrangements from now on. You don't have to mind them. It's not fair on you.'

Joan considers this for a moment.

'Good,' she says finally, and stands up, facing Nicoletta, her grey eyes sparking with intent. 'He'll never marry you. He never can. He's got a wife, doesn't need another.'

Nicoletta starts to speak but Joan puts up a hand to stop her.

'Marie will be back, you mark my words, and that'll be it for you and these two.' She gestures towards the playpen. 'The same way it was when he took up with you and Marie came back, all too briefly. Don't think if she clicked her fingers he wouldn't go running again.'

'How dare you?' Nicoletta croaks. 'Leave my children out of this.'

'You couldn't just have your little thing with Barney, no. You had to bring two innocent little babies into the equation.' She tuts. 'Children don't ask to be born.'

Liam enters through the back door which leads onto the garden, a football under his arm, his face flushed. He grins when he sees Nicoletta, but his expression crumples as he takes in her face.

'What's wrong?' he asks, stepping towards her. He looks uncertainly between her and his grandmother.

'Don't get muddy shoes on my clean floor,' Joan says.

Liam obediently takes off his football boots and lines them up on the mat at the door. He fills a glass with water and drinks it while the two women watch. He turns around, self-conscious.

'Did I miss something?'

Nicoletta ruffles his hair. 'Give us a hand with this stuff,' she says, indicating the Moses basket and the two girls in their play pen.

Joan sits back, apparently satisfied, and switches on the radio, this time at an alarmingly high volume. Nicoletta crosses to the playpen and scoops up both girls, handing their basket to Liam on the way out.

He places it at the bottom of the stairs, biting his lip.

'Are you going to leave?'

Tears fill Nicoletta's eyes, but she manages not to let them spill.

'Of course not,' she says, not letting him see her face as she places both babies in the basket, top to tail. They don't protest. She ruffles Liam's hair again.

'I just have to make a quick phone call. Why don't you go back and keep your gran company?'

As soon as he's back in the kitchen, she picks up the phone and dials the number she's known off by heart since she was a child.

Her mother answers briskly after two rings. 'Sarto's Newsagents?'

Nicoletta holds the phone against her ear, as Daniela repeats, 'Hello? Anyone there?'

She waits until the line goes dead before she accepts defeat and slams the receiver down into its cradle.

Chapter Six

After hours spent trying to settle both babies, who keep setting each other off in a chorus of colicky protest, Joan takes them both into her room. Nicoletta gratefully falls into an exhausted, dreamless sleep. When she wakes, she checks beside her, but the babies are gone. Then she remembers. Her eyelids itch. Barney's side of the bed is smooth and unruffled. He hadn't come home. She lies there for a minute, wondering what to do, before sitting up and checking her watch, the one that hangs on a bangle her parents gave her for her twenty-first birthday. Six thirty. She's only been asleep for two hours.

She yawns and wraps the comforter tightly around her shoulders.

'*He was working late,*' she says aloud. Her voice resounds in the still empty room, sudden as a gunshot. By the time she has made tea, drunk it, and brought the girls back into her room so Joan can sleep on, the thought of escaping for a few hours has brought heat to her bones.

Mid-morning, she tells Joan she has to go out for a while. She simply can't bear to stay here any longer.

Joan doesn't say anything, disapproving or otherwise. Curiosity compels Nicoletta to combine the story about the Creightons' estate sale with a visit to anyone who'll answer questions about old Helen Leonard. The train journey to Dun Laoghaire takes an age. Passengers jostle each other for space, many of them young people dressed in shorts and summer dresses, carrying bags with rolled-up towels poking out. Nicoletta observes their excited chatter with envy.

When she alights at Dun Laoghaire, she strides along the coast road she'd got to know so well during the Julia Bridges story, enjoying the sun's warmth on her face. Couples stroll along hand in hand, with the same idea as the youngsters on the train, many holding ice-cream cones and wheeling small children in pushchairs. Nicoletta takes the familiar turning onto Seaview Terrace, past Helen Leonard's house. When Nicoletta had met her eighteen months previously, Miss Leonard had seemed far from the archetype of a frail old lady who needed a live-in nurse. What had changed? On impulse, Nicoletta walks up the path. Miss Leonard's house has a secretive, hidden-away air, despite the bright day, its windows swaddled in heavy curtains. She raps lightly on the freshly painted green door, but no one comes. Reluctantly, she walks away and continues further down Seaview Terrace. It's a long way to the parochial house in Glasthule, and she stops at the Catholic church and asks a woman dusting statues for directions. She is overheated by the time she knocks on the door of the priest's house, asking for Father Matthew Farry. A young, good-looking housekeeper with strawberry-blonde hair tied in a messy chignon, with plump, rosy cheeks answers the door. The woman looks surprised to see her, as though she's dying to ask Nicoletta's business but manages to stop herself.

'He's just popped out,' she says. 'But you're welcome to wait for him to come back, if you'd like.' Nicoletta gratefully sinks into a comfortable armchair and accepts the woman's offer of tea.

'Thank you,' she says, the woman's kindness oddly touching.

She waits while the woman trustingly leaves her behind so she can fetch tea. When she carries it in on a tray, Nicoletta introduces herself. 'My name's Nicoletta Sarto. I was ... a friend of Helen Leonard's.'

'God love her,' the young woman says, her eyes dancing.

'Did you know Miss Leonard?' Nicoletta asks, pouring tea, using real tea leaves, through a strainer into a delicate china cup.

'No, not really,' the girl pauses, then appears to think better of it. 'She wasn't a regular Mass-goer.'

She walks back out, leaving Nicoletta to observe her surroundings. The room is sparsely furnished, with just a couple of straight-backed armchairs side by side at the fire. A framed, orange-toned print of the *Sacred Heart of Jesus* adorns the wall above the mantlepiece, sitting a fraction of an inch askew on the wallpaper, patterned with a busy motif of entwined bluebirds, which Nicoletta finds slightly dizzying. A small turf fire burns in the hearth, despite the day's high temperatures. Nicoletta leans into the chair. She leaves the tea untouched. She can feel her eyes closing in the heat. When she opens them again, a young man wearing a cornflower-blue sweater, with a priest's collar visible over the neckline, is sitting in the chair beside her, reading that day's *Sentinel*.

Nicoletta's hand flies to her mouth before she can begin to work out where she is. The man inclines his head to one side.

'I'm so sorry, Father,' she says, instantly mortified. 'I'm afraid I must've fallen asleep. I have two small babies at home,' she babbles by way of explanation.

The priest raises a hand and smiles, opening a wide mouth. He has very white teeth, and a smooth, tanned face with a slightly blank, beatific quality. The gesture reminds Nicoletta of the image of the Sacred Heart on the wall. 'Not at all, Miss Sarto,' he says, slowly closing the newspaper. 'I can imagine how it must be at the start of a child's life. Let alone two. These things happen.' He stands up and extends a hand. Nicoletta takes it, enclosing hers around the soft white fingers. 'Father Matt Farry. I'm the parish priest here in Glasthule. What can I do you for?'

Nicoletta blinks, trying to rouse herself to some semblance of alert professionalism. She yawns before she can stop herself.

'I'm sorry, Father Farry,' she says, covering her mouth with her palm. 'To intrude like this.'

To her surprise, the priest leans in and cups her elbow. 'How old are your babies?'

'Five months,' Nicoletta says with a small smile. 'They're identical twins. Girls. Rosa and Cara. They don't let me sleep a wink,' she says with a laugh.

'Beautiful names,' he murmurs, squeezing her elbow. 'Are they baptised?'

'No,' she says, trying to stand up, but he keeps on holding her arm. 'I haven't got around to it yet.'

The priest doesn't answer as she escapes and goes to stand beside the fire. Her clothes cling to her back and shoulders; it's like walking into a furnace.

'That's not why I'm here, Father,' she says, discreetly wiping her palms on her dress. 'I'm a reporter for the *Irish Sentinel*.' She glances at the newspaper in his lap with Barney's byline on the front page again. A knot squeezes her heart. The twins' birth has knocked her sideways, while Barney has continued on oblivious, with his big stories and front-page splashes.

'I was wondering if you'd have a few moments to speak to me about Helen Leonard.'

'What do you wish to speak about Miss Leonard for?' The priest stands up, leaving the paper behind on his vacated seat, walking around the small room as though he's exploring it for the first time, seeing it through her eyes. He crosses to the picture of the Sacred Heart and appears to examine it for a moment before turning, his hands folded at his navel.

Nicoletta hesitates. But she does what she always does: takes a deep breath and dives in. 'I understand you administered the last rites to Helen Leonard.'

Father Farry blinks. 'So? What does that have to do with a reporter? It's a private family matter for the Leonards.'

Nicoletta swallows, deciding how much to give away.

'I have reason to believe that there may be more to Miss Leonard's death than meets the eye.'

She takes a step forward, to escape the raging heat at her back. It feels hotter than the fires of hell. Father Farry reseats himself in his armchair, placing the newspaper on a small occasional table at his elbow. He indicates for her to sit beside him, which she does, reluctantly.

'What exactly are you saying, Miss Sarto?'

'Miss Leonard's family suspect she may have been murdered.' Nicoletta crosses her arms and observes his reaction. The priest blanches, his delicate features paling in alarm.

'Surely not,' he says. 'Who could possibly want to do something like that?'

Nicoletta deflects his question with one of her own.

'Do you know of anyone who may have wished harm on Miss Leonard?'

He rubs his chin. 'I hardly knew Miss Leonard. I can't say.'

Nicoletta pauses, unsure how to phrase the next question. 'How did Miss Leonard seem when you got to the house?'

'She was already gone,' Father Farry says simply. 'She was at peace. Tell me, Nicoletta, where are you from?'

'Fairview,' she says lightly.

She knows what he's getting at. The unusual, foreign-sounding name. He wants a potted history with all the salient details included regarding her background information. Well, she's not in the mood for the *quid pro quo* of social niceties today.

'Ah,' he says, by way of answer, closing his eyes briefly, as though conceding defeat.

'Thank you for your hospitality, Father Farry,' Nicoletta says quietly, eager to step out of this boiling room and into some fresh air.

The priest opens his eyes wide. 'I'm just sorry I couldn't be more helpful.' She's about to demur, but he continues. 'Miss Duggan got my housekeeper on the telephone just after midday that afternoon. I was in the middle of Mass. I finished up and went as fast as I could, but it was clear that Miss Leonard was already gone.'

'Miss Duggan?' Nicoletta is aware she sounds slightly breathless.

'Sadie Duggan. Miss Leonard's housekeeper for many years. A regular at Mass.'

'Did anything strike you as being off about the whole situation, Father?' Nicoletta takes another step away from the heat.

'No.' Father Farry frowns. 'An elderly woman went to sleep and, unfortunately, she didn't wake up, it would appear to me. As straightforward as the departure from this life gets, in my experience.'

'Thank you, Father,' Nicoletta says, making a break for the hall.

Father Farry walks Nicoletta to the front door. Despite the heat of the sitting room, not a bead of sweat has broken over his smooth features, somehow adding to the otherworldly effect. Trivial, earthly matters like perspiration just don't seem to concern him. He rests another hand on her arm, just as she lays her hand on the doorknob.

'I'm loath to just give out advice unasked, you know,' he says with a wry smile. 'But those children of yours need you. More than poor Miss Leonard ever did.'

She turns her head at the last moment, so the final few words are uttered as a reproach into the brisk sea air. Before he can say any more, Nicoletta is out the door, striding back towards Miss Leonard's house on Seaview Terrace.

She taps on the door and waits. A bird trills from deep within an overgrown hedge dividing the postage-stamp-sized front garden from the road. The persistent birdsong competes in futile stereo with the nearby drone of a hoover, from somewhere inside the house. She wonders who is here. Sadie Duggan? Hopefully someone who'll be inclined to spill the beans on Helen Leonard and her mysterious carer over the last number of months. She taps again, then a louder rap. The hoover stops, and the bird sings the same three notes over and over in a victorious riff. The door opens with a bang, revealing a woman, her small stature almost dwarfed by the doorway. She has short, closely cropped grey hair, and is carrying a rag streaked with dirt.

'Yes?' She clutches her chest, as though she'd just been undergoing extreme physical exertion, in a dramatic attempt at regaining her breath. She gives Nicoletta a curious look, eyes the colour of the overcast sky. She releases her chest and stands up straighter.

'Hello,' Nicoletta begins. 'I'm here about Helen Leonard.'

The woman dangles a dirty white plimsolled foot onto the top step, as though testing it against her weight.

'Haven't you heard? She died some time ago.'

'I heard,' Nicoletta says quietly. 'I'm very sorry. I'm a reporter from the *Irish Sentinel*. I'd like to ask you a few questions, if that's all right.'

The woman narrows her eyes. 'And your name?'

'Nicoletta Sarto. I'd like to speak to Sadie Duggan, or you, or whoever, about poor Miss Leonard and what's happened with this nurse of hers. Can I come in?'

The woman does a mock double-take and clutches her heart. Her skin is clear and unlined, and she is younger than she first appeared.

'*That's* how I know you.' The woman withdraws her foot from the step and opens the door wide.

'You're that girl who wrote the exposé on the Creightons.' She chuckles. 'I suppose you'll have to come in.'

Nicoletta doesn't know what to say as she follows the woman down the dark, narrow hallway towards the kitchen at the back of the house, which she'd visited only once before, when Helen Leonard was alive. However, whereas then it had been overheated and stuffy, now every available window is flung open, creating a chilly draught through the small room. The woman sits and takes out a pack of Woodbines. She indicates for Nicoletta to take a seat, before lighting her cigarette.

'I was about to take a break anyway,' she says, in a conspiratorial tone. 'This place needs a damn good clean.' She blows out a stream of smoke. 'It'll take another week or so before it's even fit for purpose.'

Nicoletta slides her notebook out of her bag and

uncaps a pen. 'Can I ask your name, please?' She's aware her voice sounds timid. The woman takes a long drag from the cigarette, slanting a glance at Nicoletta, before exhaling.

'I'm Sadie Duggan,' she says finally. 'D-U-G-G-A-N.' She peers at Nicoletta's notebook, as Nicoletta writes down the name. 'Please don't use my name in anything you write. I was Miss Leonard's housekeeper for years. There's something very off about this whole business with the nurse.'

Nicoletta underlines the name. She's beginning to feel goosebumps form on her arms. The room has been aired to the point of freezing. She smiles at Sadie, weighing up what she's going to say next.

'Miss Leonard's niece Louise thinks Helen was murdered,' she says boldly. 'What do you think about that?'

If Sadie is surprised by this turn in the conversation, she doesn't show it. She stubs out the cigarette with a brisk movement in a china ashtray shaped like a black-and-white dog. 'Miss Leonard was her own worst enemy, sure. But it's a bit late for them to make a fuss now.'

'Who's them?' Nicoletta asks with a mild tilt to her chin.

'Oh, Louise, and Tom, her father.' Sadie stands up. Nicoletta thinks she's been dismissed but an electric kettle is flicked on, and two mugs are filled. One is placed in front of her in silence.

'Mrs Duggan . . .' Nicoletta begins.

'It's Miss,' Sadie says, lighting another Woodbine with a snap of the lighter.

'Do you think Miss Leonard was murdered?'

'I don't know. I haven't the foggiest. I'm not the Garda.' Sadie taps ash into the ashtray and takes a swig of scalding tea, eyeballing Nicoletta. 'But my guess would be no. I think Louise's reaction now has more to do with guilt than anything else.'

Nicoletta holds her gaze, before breaking it to look back down at her notebook.

'Guilt? About what?'

'Oh, never visiting her aunt, getting a nurse from some Mickey Mouse agency who wasn't vetted properly. Poor Miss Leonard was hearing voices in her final months. Did Louise tell you that?'

'No.' Nicoletta shakes her head. 'I believe you were the one who found her. That must've been incredibly upsetting. Would you mind telling me about that?'

Sadie grinds the cigarette into the china dog's open mouth and grimaces. 'The Leonards might kill me if they found out I'd been speaking to a newspaper.' Her hand flies to her throat with the realisation of what she's just said. 'Not literally,' she says, recovering herself, as Nicoletta takes a sip of the too-milky tea.

Sadie tilts her chin on her palm, as though considering. Nicoletta glances out the open window. A jungle of bushes, greenery and unbridled growth comprise the back garden. A bird trills the same three notes somewhere in the dense foliage and she wonders if it's the same bird from out the front a few moments ago.

'All right,' Sadie says with a deflated finality. 'But you can't let on you've been talking to me. I've got a lot of work to do,' she adds, catching Nicoletta eyeing the layer upon layer of dust that coats the sideboards and cupboards. Nicoletta sneezes, as if on cue.

'Can you tell me what happened on the morning you found Miss Leonard?'

Sadie shifts in her seat. 'I popped in on the Monday morning to do some cleaning. And she was gone,' she says in a rush, her voice breaking on the last word.

'Gone, how?' Nicoletta writes the word out and underlines it.

'How'd you think, gone? Cold,' Sadie says with a sniff.

'How did you find her?'

'I called for Miss Highfield, but she was nowhere to be found.'

'Miss Highfield was Miss Leonard's nurse?'

'Yep,' Sadie scoffs. 'Barbara Highfield. If that was even her real name. I thought it was odd, her not being there. It was as if I already knew. I went up to Miss Leonard's bedroom and stuck my head in the door. It was dark. And she was lying in the bed. Her eyes were closed. She looked peaceful. I thought she was asleep.'

'What did you do then?' Nicoletta takes another sip of tepid tea.

'I tiptoed back down the stairs. And started cleaning. I thought maybe Miss Highfield had popped out, which she shouldn't have done. I was going to give her an earful when she came back. But she never did.' She pauses, looking directly at Nicoletta.

'When did you realise she wasn't coming back?' Nicoletta almost whispers.

Sadie sighs. 'I finished my cleaning at lunchtime. Threw

the mop, bucket, hoover, floor polish and rags back under the stairs. I noticed the painting was missing, from the place it was usually kept. There'd been no sound from Miss Leonard, so I thought I'd better tell her I was going. She really was as quiet as a mouse, so it wasn't that unusual.'

'I see. Wait, which painting might that be?' Nicoletta sits forward, gripping the edge of the plastic-coated tablecloth, which is greasy to the touch.

'Oh, this painting Miss Leonard had. Given to her by her father, Tom Leonard Senior. Her sister had the other one, apparently. *Among the Ruins*, it was called. She hated it, like she hated him, so she kept it under the stairs.'

Sadie looks down at her hands. 'They say it was worth something. But it was nothing to look at, just a creepy picture of a house and two children outside it.'

'Was it insured?' Nicoletta asks, splaying her fingers on the greasy tablecloth.

Sadie frowns. 'Don't think so. I doubt it. I think this Barbara Highfield took the painting. Is it true that Miss Leonard left her everything else?'

'I think so,' Nicoletta says as calmly as possible. 'But there's no sign of her. She seems to have vanished. What did you do then?'

'I ran up the stairs and into Helen's room. I don't know why I didn't notice it before. I touched a hand to her forehead, and she felt cold. God love her. I'd only glanced at her when I stuck my head in a few hours before, so I was kicking myself then. I ran downstairs and called Father Farry, as maybe something could be done.'

'You didn't call a doctor?'

Sadie shakes her head. 'Father Farry came quickly and did the necessary, but it was far too late. Then I called Miss Leonard's brother, Tom Junior, and her niece, Louise.'

Sadie stands up abruptly, gathering up the cups and dumping them in a clinking heap on the draining board. 'I'd best get on,' she says, her mouth a straight line.

She walks Nicoletta to the door without another word. Nicoletta stands in the tiny front garden for a moment, contemplating what just happened. The bird starts trilling its cheerful riff again, reminding Nicoletta of its presence, but the faraway drone of the hoover stays silent.

Chapter Seven

The now familiar sight of Seaview Terrace's squinting windows face her, but she can't face them, not yet. Instead, she slips through the concrete snicket which divides the terrace with the main coast road. The words BRITS OUT have reappeared in even bigger spidery black letters, so huge that they seem to obscure all the other graffiti: so-and-so loves so-and-so; such-and-such is a slut. When she passes through the other side, the breeze whips up her dress so that it balloons around her waist.

She retraces the steps that she and Barney took a year and a half before, down the coast road, along the stone wall dividing Seaview House from the rest of the world. She expects the side gate to be locked, but it opens with a tentative push. To her surprise, she sees dozens of people milling around the garden. It is magnificently in bloom, showy peonies and roses where once the cold, fissured earth was excavated for human remains. The peacocks she remembers from before, Antony and Cleopatra, mill around too, and the male fans his feathers as he's chased by a small boy across the lawn. Someone – who looks like they might be a professional photographer – pops a flash on a camera. Nicoletta makes her way into the centre of the lawn and stands for a moment, as the mother of the small boy retrieves him from the other end of the garden. Duly admonished, he hangs off his mother's arm.

'Has bidding started?' Nicoletta addresses the question under the woman's enormous floppy hat.

She peers out from under it. 'Yes. Better get in if you want the good stuff!'

'What sort of things are on sale?' Nicoletta asks, swatting a fly away. The woman angles her face to get a closer look at Nicoletta, and in the act of doing so, the sun catches her in the eyes. She shields them with the back of her hand.

'Sally's flogging everything, every last knife and fork. It'll be worth having a look, sure.'

The small boy takes the opportunity to break away from his mother's grip and run diagonally across the lawn towards a small hut at the back of the garden, near the mews, where Delia and John Dawkins live. Though John is now in prison. Nicoletta remembers the hut was used as a shelter by Sally's beloved peacocks. She wonders if she'll take them with her, wherever she's going. Or are they part of the estate? The woman runs after the small boy, holding on to her hat as she goes, and Nicoletta drifts around the side of the house, towards the front door, still feeling charged with the freedom of being out on her own, unencumbered by small babies, for the first time in months. The front door is wedged open, for anyone to traipse in and out as they please. The house has been thrust into the glare of publicity once again.

She climbs the granite steps and stands in the open doorway for a moment, seeking the solidity of the burgundy-papered wall to her left. She notices the door is fastened to the wall by a new-looking brass hook screwed into the wood. Everything looks the same as it did that Christmas Eve, only completely different. The chessboard tiles gleam, the pictures on the wall shine expectantly. Nicoletta stops at the 1916 Proclamation of Independence, which Barney had examined the last time they'd been here. It has a red dot in the bottom right-hand corner. She wonders who's bought it. Perhaps Sally Creighton wants to be rid of all memories. Anything that ties her to this place. Nicoletta makes her way alongside a small table, on which rests an old-fashioned black Bakelite telephone. Even this harmless household item has a red sticker affixed. The chestnut table gleams, like a prize racehorse's coat, and Nicoletta's moves over to a longer table beside it, festooned with photographs. Remnants of presumably happier times. A couple of sepia wedding portraits, an older man in tennis whites holding a silver cup. Her eye is immediately drawn to a photo of a man leading a little girl on a fat pony. The man is squinting into the camera, the girl is scowling and the shutter is overexposed, but she can see straight away that the man is Charles Creighton, and the girl is his daughter, Delia. Her throat tightens and she coughs to clear it. Once she starts, she can't stop. She almost doesn't notice the light footsteps on the tiles behind her.

'That's a nice one, isn't it? Shame it must go, all the same.' The woman's voice at her shoulder is low, melodious.

'How much are they charging for the photo?' she asks, without turning around.

'You put in a bid. Don't you know how auctions work?'

Nicoletta turns with a start to see an ash-blonde woman at her elbow, her eyes creased with amusement. *Sally has what they call a weak constitution.* She remembers the face from the New Year's Eve she and Barney had got engaged.

'Not really,' Nicoletta replies, looking Sally Creighton dead in the eye. 'No shame in that, is there?'

'None at all,' Sally replies, with just the smallest trace of irony.

Nicoletta turns around to face her and takes a step forward, onto a black tile. Sally mirrors her movement, moving opposite her, her eyes as heavily kohled as she remembers, her hair slightly more ash now than blonde. There are questions Nicoletta wants to ask her, but her mind is now as blank as Sally's expression. She wants to run, yet she remains rooted to the spot.

'I'm sorry,' Nicoletta says, though the words sound as meaningless as the nursery rhymes she sometimes sings to the twins.

'For what? Writing all that drivel about us?' Sally's face creases in amusement.

Nicoletta bows her head. 'No. What I wrote was the truth.' She stands, waiting for a response, but none is forthcoming. Sally has moved to stand under the skylight, to make way for a gaggle of women and children crowding the hallway, including the woman and little boy from outside. A stream of pale sunlight beams one side of her face into stark relief, leaving the other in muted shadow.

She feels like an animal in a zoo. Is she being watched? The woman steps forward to examine each photograph on the table, and Nicoletta jumps. Her little boy squirms out of her reach, taking in Nicoletta's bare legs revealed by the green maxi dress fluttering in the breeze from the open window with unashamed curiosity.

'I have to go,' Nicoletta calls to Sally Creighton, wending her way among the crowd.

The door is blocked by a glut of people, spilling all the way down the granite steps. Nicoletta mutters something about needing the bathroom. She imagines that she can feel Sally's eyes boring into her as she retreats, but when she looks back, Sally is laughing at something the woman in the floppy hat is saying, who is pointing helplessly to her son, running towards an adjoining door. Sally's wide mouth is tilted in mirth. Is she laughing at her?

Nicoletta flees into the tiny WC she remembers from the last time, tucked away in a recess at the far wall. When she's locked the door, she leans against it and takes a breath, though the air feels thick as soup. She washes her hands and dries them carefully on a damp towel. Why is she here? The face looking back at her is pale, deadened by exhaustion. *Because you were asked*, she says to her reflection. *But since when do you have to do everything that you're asked? The women's editor job is yours now. No more of this.*

The hallway is still crowded when she emerges into the half gloom, but Sally Creighton is nowhere to be seen. Nicoletta looks around. A wide staircase curves upward to the next floor. Curiosity spurs her on. She may never have another chance to see the rest of this strange house.

At the very least to lay a few ghosts to rest. As she puts her weight on the bottom step, it creaks in protest, and she momentarily stops, as though someone may be about to apprehend her. But no one does, and she keeps going. As she ascends the staircase, she feels as though she is embarking on some sort of grotesque pilgrimage. The top step squeaks as she springs onto the parquet landing beyond. A huge gold and orange ornamental vase filled with large drooping grey feathers sits on a table at a window overlooking the garden. A guide price on a tiny plaque resting in front of it advises a starting bid of £30. Nicoletta stands before it. She can see the tops of people's heads as they roam around like the peacocks pecking the ground in high expectation. What are they hoping to find? Nicoletta wonders if they even know themselves, and if she's any better than them, feeding on the spectacle of the whole thing. She bows her head, feeling slightly ashamed by her part in all this. All those old things give her the creeps. She gazes around at the giant feathers, the antique clocks, the expensive-looking furniture. It reminds her of a twisted Disney fairy tale. She expects one of the clocks to turn back into a pumpkin, or for a woman wearing a coat made out of dogs to appear. Nicoletta shudders involuntarily, a shiver running the length of her spine. Give her a nice new house with clean, white tiles, and all mod cons, any day. Old houses have too many secrets for her liking.

'Disgusting, isn't it?' a woman's voice says from behind her. The voice carries; it belongs to someone used to saying what she has to say, when she has to say it. And what's more, someone who's used to being listened to.

Nicoletta jumps. 'I . . .' Her cheeks redden as she turns around, as though she has something to hide. The voice belongs to a tall, thin woman in a long, shapeless red tunic. Her hair is also long and reddish brown, almost bronze-coloured, reaching down her back, nearly to her waist. Nicoletta wonders if it's dyed. She wears a lot of jangling rings and bracelets, and no make-up. Her eyes are small and brown, though bright as pennies. Nicoletta finds it difficult to put an age on her.

The woman appears to be referring to the nearest orange and gold vase, and the feathers.

'I wouldn't thank you for a present of this monstrosity.'

Nicoletta observes her as she bends over the vase. Her bracelets jangle. She sets a glass of wine on the table so she can examine the object from every conceivable angle.

'Dreadful,' she pronounces, picking up her wine and turning to Nicoletta at the window. 'I expect Charles picked it up on his travels. He never did have any taste.'

Nicoletta's tongue feels glued to the roof of her mouth. 'How do you know the Creightons?'

'I'm in the art business. I sold Charles the only nice things among this crap,' she says airily.

'Nicoletta Sarto,' Nicoletta holds out her hand. 'I'm the women's pages editor at the *Sentinel*.'

'Celine Rault,' the woman says, taking her hand and then dropping it to give the vase another look.

'Sit with me for a minute, will you.' It sounds like an order. 'I'll grab you a glass.'

Celine picks up a wine bottle from a small circular table in the corner and empties its contents into a single glass beside it. She hands it to Nicoletta. It is darkly sedimented, like damp earth. Nicoletta switches her focus to her surroundings. A squat carriage clock on the mantelpiece ticks away self-importantly. There's a red dot stuck on the bottom of it. Nicoletta takes a tiny sip of her wine. Celine follows her gaze and gets up to scrutinise the guide price. She exhales noisily.

'The amount people will pay for absolute shite.'

'It doesn't look exactly like shite,' Nicoletta says, after another sip of wine.

Celine laughs, a delighted sound. 'How do you know the Creightons?'

Nicoletta takes a deep breath. 'I, ah, knew Charles professionally.'

Celine laughs again. 'A bold little thing, aren't you?'

Nicoletta lets a long pause elapse before she replies. She shrugs. 'It's an open house.'

Celine spins around. 'Very true. I can't say I think much of their décor. Do you?'

'It doesn't float my boat. I don't like old houses. Too much history.'

Celine laughs again, her hand rising to her throat, the row of bangles tinkling against each other.

'Believe me, good taste is something you can't buy.'

'Is that so?' Nicoletta gives a polite cough, followed by a slurp from the glass. 'Then how do you acquire it?'

'You're born with it, of course. Then you develop it. I'm lucky, in that regard, being half French on my father's side. And in the art business.'

'Oh yes?' Nicoletta stretches her stockinged feet. 'What

does your father think of all this?' She indicates the breadth of the room.

Celine examines the clock. 'He died in February.' She turns back to Nicoletta with an impatient glance. Before Nicoletta can offer stuttered condolences, Celine's bangles tinkle with purpose and she strides over to look at something behind a wooden Chinese screen.

Nicoletta reluctantly steps back into her shoes when she hears light footsteps resounding from the corridor. She takes another furtive sip of wine before an elegant woman is framed by the doorway.

'Delia,' Nicoletta says, with mild surprise.

'Enjoying my mother's wine? Or have you come back to finish her off?'

Nicoletta holds Delia's gaze. She somehow looks older than Nicoletta remembers from their brief meetings a short time ago: there are now lines on her face thrown into relief by the sun blazing through the window behind her that hadn't been there when Delia was the carefree party girl from a previous life.

'How are you?' Nicoletta asks quietly.

Delia laughs hoarsely. 'Get out,' she says, as though emboldened by Nicoletta's voice.

Nicoletta bristles, horribly aware of Celine standing beside her with an amused look on her face.

Delia points to the door. 'She's a reporter,' she says to Celine, by way of explanation. 'Don't trust her an inch.'

'I didn't mean to intrude,' Nicoletta says, her voice still quiet, not wanting to draw any more attention to herself than necessary.

'Oh, I bet you didn't. Your type never does.' Delia points down the corridor. A group of middle-aged women hover outside, their voices hushed, as though they're in a church. Nicoletta's scalp tingles with a claustrophobic sense of horror. She knows they can probably hear every word. Delia clearly knows too and raises her voice to match. 'You're not welcome here, Nicoletta Sarto. Get out, or I'm calling the Guards.'

Nicoletta makes her way downstairs, away from Celine Rault and her wry wine-swigging, past Delia and her quiet fury, and out of the house. When she's on the street, she takes a breath. She realises she's shaking. She thought she'd swept all those feelings away, with the vigour with which her mother used to tackle dust on one of her early morning cleaning sprees when Nicoletta was a child. There was always something to do. No time to be idle. The thought of her mother scorches her skin like a naked flame as she marches down the coast road, looking for a way out of here. By the time she reaches the train station, boards a train, and gets back to the twins, to Joan, to the relentless drone of domesticity, the fury and humiliation has settled down to a hum and she resolves to banish Seaview House from her memory; it never happened. She'll have to tell Duffy that she never went to the Creightons' open house at all.

Chapter Eight

On her first official day as women's editor at the *Irish Sentinel*, Nicoletta has a sinking feeling that she's in the doghouse with Duffy for not filing any story on the Creightons' estate sale, and she's hardly seen Barney since they doorstepped The Rook a week ago. She'd spent the week listening to the radio with Joan in the kitchen and going on endless walks with the girls in the double pram, and she couldn't wait to get back to work. But now she feels a gossamer web of misery descend as she spends the morning up a ladder flipping through dusty folders, trying to identify faded pictures of puddings and Sunday roasts, the recipe pages curled at the edges, the paper yellowed, waiting for the axe to fall.

Ann wanders past with her bag over her arm and Nicoletta grasps at a chance for distraction.

'Ann! Fancy that lunch in Clery's?'

Nicoletta catches up to Ann at the top of the stairs and they walk down in almost companionable silence. When they get to the street, the sun is blazing in the sky, the seagulls are cawing lustily to each other, and the newspaper sellers are competing with each other about who can scream the headlines the loudest. She immediately feels safe here, in these familiar surroundings. The misery lifts. She was being silly. It's all a part of the job.

They're about to cross the road when she feels a hand on her shoulder. She spins around in fright. It's Dermot.

'Jesus, you're jumpy. Duffy wants a word,' he says in her ear. 'Now.'

'I'll catch up with you later,' she calls to Ann with an apologetic shrug, following Dermot back into the building and up the steep stairs. Her legs feel like lead as she climbs each step. The distinctive smells of metal and newsprint, and rooms that have never been aired, seem to catch at the back of her throat. She can't remember noticing them before. When she swings the door open, a couple of heads are bent over typewriters dissolutely clacking away, but other than that, the floor is silent.

'We'll catch up later,' Dermot mouths as she walks towards Duffy's closed door. The closed door indicates his being in situ. Nicoletta traverses the room, her eyes adjusting to the glare, which is too bright. Someone has switched on the fluorescent overhead lights, and they flicker on and off, a bulb needing to be replaced somewhere. The effect is disconcertingly akin to an uneven pulse. She puts down her bag and coat and crosses to the smudged plate-glass door. She takes a deep breath and knocks. A gruff voice commands her to enter. She waits a beat before pushing open the door and stepping into the room.

The light is off, and the room is in shadow. Duffy is

seated with his back to Nicoletta, gazing out the window at the static river below. When he turns around, he looks momentarily lost, as though he finds Nicoletta hard to place.

'Nicoletta,' he says finally, swinging his meaty frame under the desk. 'What can I do for you?'

Nicoletta sits down without waiting to be asked. 'You asked to see me?'

'So I did,' he says, rubbing his chin. 'So I did ... I still don't see any story filed about the Creightons' estate sale. Did you go?'

Nicoletta nods miserably. 'Yes. I got thrown out.'

Duffy rubs his hands together and emits a raspy guffaw. 'It's not too late. When are you filing?'

Nicoletta feels her chest tighten. 'I'm not going to file anything further on the Creightons.'

Duffy returns her steady gaze with a blank look. Nicoletta shrugs helplessly. She's about to stand up, before she sits back down again.

'But I think I have a story.'

Duffy's eyes focus. 'Go on.'

'Helen Leonard, an old neighbour of the Creightons', is being exhumed in two days. Her niece believes she was murdered.'

Duffy's blank look returns. 'I know. How'd you know?'

Nicoletta allows herself a rueful smile. 'Louise Leonard, Helen Leonard's niece, spoke to me about her aunt's death. Her paid carer is missing. It's all very suspicious.' She coils her hands in her lap.

Duffy claws at his beard. 'Right. So, where do I come

in? Or where do you come in, I should say? How're the women's pages coming on, by the way?'

'Okay,' Nicoletta says, the uncertainty returning. Duffy has gone back to staring out the window. 'They're fine.' She sits back down again. 'As I've said, Louise suspects Helen was murdered.'

Duffy blinks. 'Why'd you talk to her?'

'She spoke to me. Because she believes the circumstances surrounding her aunt's death are slightly off.' She pauses to give weight to the mild euphemism.

Duffy snorts. 'Ah, Helen Leonard. A larger-than-life local character, you might say. She was in the Wrens during the war. Doesn't make her too popular around here.' He steeples his hands behind his head, looking at Nicoletta like he doesn't know why she's still there. 'I'd tread very carefully on this, Nicoletta.'

Nicoletta clears her throat. 'But what if she was murdered?'

Duffy raises an eyebrow, seemingly bemused by her boldness. When he speaks, he lowers his voice, though Nicoletta is sure no one can hear them. 'Sir Ken Dennehy.' His voice rises an impatient octave on the last syllable. 'Self-made captain of industry and the owner of this very newspaper? The man who pays our bills? His wife, Lady Pat, is Helen Leonard's half-sister.'

Instead of making the appropriate impressed-sounding response, Nicoletta uncrosses her legs. 'So?' The word is out of her mouth before she can put a cork in it.

Duffy buries his face in his hands. When he emerges, he's scrutinising her as though observing a caged animal.

'There was some bad blood there,' he says finally. 'Helen didn't speak to her half-sister, or much of her family. Not for years.'

'She must've been on speaking terms with her niece, Louise. Otherwise, I wouldn't know about her death and subsequent exhumation.' Nicoletta starts as something buzzes from the windowsill, possibly a dying insect in a desperate bid to escape. She feels inexplicably protective of Helen Leonard. 'Well, maybe she had good reason to be estranged from her family,' she says lightly.

Duffy gives her a look. 'Helen's father, Tom Leonard, was a republican, one of the old guard. Went to South Africa in the twenties and made a lot of money in mining. Manganese, I believe. His first wife, Helen's mother, died while they were there. He remarried when they came back to Dublin. Helen wouldn't leave the house she'd been born in. A stubborn woman. She also defied her father's politics to fight for the Brits in the Wrens during the war.' He shakes his head.

'Families are complicated.' Nicoletta ventures a smile.

Duffy gives her another look, as though she's a simpleton. 'Don't go involving yourself in this, Nicoletta. Don't mind Louise Leonard. She's one of these women's libbers.' He puts air quote marks around the words. 'She probably feels guilty now because no one in the family gave a damn about her old aunt Helen when she was alive. Bit late now to care, I would've thought.'

The bluebottle buzzes again and Duffy casts it an irritated look. 'This weather,' he mutters darkly, 'brings out every manner of bug there is. Give me a nice cold day over this wretched heat any time.'

Nicoletta doesn't say anything. She's waiting for him to say it. To tell her what to do. And he doesn't disappoint.

'Be a good girl now and go back to the women's pages. There's plenty for you there. You don't want Ann to wipe your eye, do you?'

Nicoletta stands up and walks to the door. She presses down on the handle but can't bring herself to open it. 'Helen Leonard's housekeeper, Sadie Duggan,' she blurts out, 'said there was a painting missing. Her description of it sounds very like the one stolen from Lady Pat by The Rook. *Among the Ruins*.'

Duffy turns around and squints at her as though through a fog. 'What on earth are you talking about, girleen?'

Nicoletta sinks back down in the chair. 'Lady Pat's painting was part of a diptych, wasn't it?'

Duffy blinks. 'One of a pair,' Nicoletta explains. 'The other one has been missing for years. But what if it was never missing at all? Pat's sister Helen had it the whole time. Sadie said Helen kept it under the stairs.'

Duffy grunts, so she takes it as a sign to continue. 'What if someone knew that Helen had the missing painting? And now they've killed Helen and stolen the painting.'

Duffy sucks in two pockets of air, eyeballing her. He stands up, exhaling through his nose. 'Go back to the women's pages, Nicoletta. Tell Price or Barney about this if you must, but mark my words, they won't do anything about it. Leave it all alone now.' He moves out from behind the desk and crosses to open the door, holding it open for her. 'My door's always open for you, you know,' he says with a wink as she crosses back into the newsroom, and he shuts the door with a bang behind her.

She scans the room, shading her eyes against the early afternoon sun dipping through the blindless windows. In her peripheral vision, she sees Robert Price, the deputy editor, glued to a sports broadcast of some sort, nursing the radio in his lap like a favourite pet. He studiously ignores her as she approaches his desk, until she hovers in front of him.

'Robert?' She forces a confidence into her voice.

He flicks a glance over her, from her feet right up to her face. His eyes don't quite find hers, and instead he engrosses himself in fiddling with a dial on the radio.

'Robert?' she says again.

'What is it?' he says with a flash of irritation, finally looking up.

She takes a deep breath, before forcing a smile. He doesn't return it, instead lighting up a cigarette from a pack on the desk behind him and blowing the smoke above his head, giving the unfortunate impression of a turkey sticking its neck out.

'The thing is,' Nicoletta begins in a faux conversational tone, grabbing a nearby chair and pulling it opposite him, though she hasn't been invited.

'The thing is?' He raises an eyebrow. The sports commentary has reached a dramatic crescendo and he holds up a finger for Nicoletta to be quiet. She waits as the announcer babbles on breathlessly. When the commentary finally runs out of steam, it's Nicoletta's turn to raise an eyebrow.

'Who won?' she asks innocently.

'We did,' Price mutters, flicking the radio off. 'Go on. Spit it out. I'm on my way out the door, as it happens, so make it quick.'

Nicoletta doesn't bother with a smile this time.

'Helen Leonard, an old lady who lived in Sandycove, is thought to have been murdered. Her grave's being exhumed on Wednesday,' she says briskly. 'I'd like to be there to cover it for the *Sentinel*.'

'Helen who?' Price stows the silent radio in a drawer and stands up, retrieving his coat from a hat stand in the middle of the room. When he comes back, popping up the collar and smoothing back his straggly hair, he gives Nicoletta a nod. She runs after him.

'Helen Leonard was a lady who lived beside the Creightons in Sandycove. I met her during the Julia Bridges story.'

'Ah yes,' Price says, walking towards the door. 'Your big shot at fame. How's that going?'

Nicoletta trots after him. 'Miss Leonard's niece thinks she was murdered,' she says quietly.

Price holds open the door for her and they stand shoulder to shoulder at the top of the stairs. Neither makes a move to go either backwards or forwards.

'I'm guessing Duffy told you that Helen Leonard is this newspaper's owner's sister. Or was.' Price cups his jaw and edges to the top of the stairs like a runner waiting for the sound of the starting pistol.

'He did,' Nicoletta answers smartly.

'So, the answer is no,' Price says with a smirk, descending

the steps. He half turns when he's partway down. 'You already made a name for yourself with the Julia Bridges story. Now, go and do the women's pages job you wanted so badly. And stop annoying me.' He mutters the last bit under his breath.

Chapter Nine

Nicoletta swears inwardly as she hears his footsteps descend to the ground floor and then he's gone. She marches back into the newsroom and grabs her coat and bag. Instead of the familiar threat of tears, she feels pure, white-hot rage, which makes her oddly calm. She looks up the business address of Leopold Slift, whose personal ad promises that he is busy 'Reuniting friends and loved ones since 1919'.

She strides all the way onto College Green. Her feet find their way down Grafton Street until a light drizzle mists her face, and she's climbing two flights of stairs up to an office above a dressmaker. She raps sharply on the door. Leopold Slift appears after a long few moments in shirtsleeves, rubbing his eyes. If he is surprised to see her, he doesn't show it.

'Miss Sarto,' he says. He indicates for her to close the door behind her, before neatly folding a woollen blanket at the end of a low leather couch and sitting down at his desk.

'I closed my eyes for a minute after lunch,' he says, seeing her clock the blanket. 'I find it makes me more productive.

What must you think of me.' He laughs, but it comes out more like a grumble than a sound of genuine mirth.

'I'm sorry for barging in like this,' Nicoletta says, taking the seat opposite him. 'I've been meaning to visit you for ages.'

'Oh, yes?' Slift shuffles some papers on his desk and peers over horn-rimmed spectacles. He then closes the window.

'I wanted to thank you and your wife for being so kind to me that time.'

Slift and his wife had been there when Nicoletta had miscarried during the Julia Bridges story. Slift acknowledges the memory with a slight nod, walking over to a kettle on a table beside the sofa and flicking it on. 'It was traumatic for you, I'm sure. The truth doesn't always set us free, I'm afraid, as I recall you wrote in one of your articles about the Julia Bridges case and the circumstances surrounding it,' he says, carrying two cups of milky tea over to his desk and setting one down in front of her. She takes a sip, and it scalds the tip of her tongue.

There's an awkward pause before Nicoletta speaks. 'I have to tell you, Mr Slift, I'm interested in the kind of work you do. Is it still all "reuniting friends and loved ones"?'

'No, in a word. That was my father's game. I've branched out into investigating some select projects. Suspected insurance fraud, missing persons – mainly due to emigration – marital surveillance, that kind of thing.' He raises the corners of his mouth in a mournful smile. 'The latter is big business, as I shouldn't have to tell you.'

Nicoletta roots in her bag for her notebook. 'What about

missing paintings?' She writes down the words AMONG THE RUINS, underlines them, and rips the page out.

'I don't know anything about art, Miss Sarto.'

'Who does?' she says brightly, sliding the page across the desk to him.

'Quite a lot of people, actually,' he says, tucking the sheet into what looks like a small, blue, leather-bound diary. He gives her an amused look, then rubs his eyes. 'How've you been since . . . our last meeting?'

'Good, good,' Nicoletta replies. 'I live in Ringsend with my fiancé and his mother. And our twin baby girls. And my stepson. And I'm women's pages editor at the *Sentinel*.' She waves away his murmurs of congratulation.

He takes off his glasses and polishes them against the front pocket of his shirt, before replacing them at the end of his nose and sitting back. Nicoletta feels him taking everything in – her bedraggled appearance, the suitcase-sized dark shadows under her eyes, her brittle, bordering on manic, demeanour.

'Where do I come in, Miss Sarto?'

She holds his gaze, though she can feel the artificial fizz brought on by the rage begin to dissipate. 'I wanted to say thank you. For telling me the truth when no one else would. And for being so kind to me when . . . I had that accident.' She can feel the breath leave her lungs, like a punch in the stomach, as though in sympathy with the muscle memory.

He sits back, cradling his cup against his chest like a baby. 'Come now, Miss Sarto. Why are you really here? I don't know much about art, so I can't help you there, I'm afraid.'

'Surely you have contacts all over the city.' Nicoletta bites her lip, willing herself to come back to the present. The whir of sewing machines from the dressmaker below must have started up again after the lunchtime lull, and she finds the noise grounding. 'You say you handle missing persons cases,' she continues slowly.

'Most of the missing people I'm tasked with finding simply don't wish to be found,' he cuts in, raising his palms to the ceiling.

'What if they didn't exist in the first place? And it's a simple case of fraud.'

'Oh?' He raises his voice by a semitone, but Nicoletta knows she has his interest.

'I've been asked to look into a story where an old lady's paid carer has gone walkabout with a valuable painting. The name the nurse gave was Barbara Highfield, but no one seems to know anything about her. It's like she doesn't exist. This painting is one of a pair. The other part was stolen by The Rook earlier this year.'

Slift blinks heavily. 'The Rook?'

'Ray Hall. The Birds? They rob stately homes.'

'Are they affiliated with any, ah, political organisation?'

'No. Just organised crime,' Nicoletta says with a wry laugh.

'Ah, well there's plenty of that about these days.' He takes off his glasses.

Nicoletta leans forward. '*Among the Ruins* is one half of a diptych, as I've said. The other painting was owned by Lady Pat Dennehy, of Fairfax House, which has been missing since January of this year when The Rook and his associates cleaned out Fairfax House, relieving it of some of its most valuable artworks.'

'So?' Slift shrugs and puts his glasses back on.

'So, Lady Pat Dennehy and Helen Leonard, the old lady whose paid carer went missing, were sisters. Half-sisters, I believe. Their father, the late Tom Leonard Senior, a well-known barrister, gave them the paintings.'

Slift steeples his fingers together. He hesitates for a moment. 'Miss Sarto, if I may ask, why are you getting involved with this particular story? You say you have your new position at the *Sentinel* to think of, and two small babies. That all sounds promising. Do you really want to start unravelling something which may put you, or your family, in quite considerable danger? It hardly seems worth it.'

Nicoletta sighs, an involuntary gasp which seems to release something hard in her chest.

'I could have minded my own business, of course,' she says, 'when Miss Leonard's niece told me about it.' A shaft of sunlight casts an uneven glow over Leopold Slift, with half his face in shadow. 'Maybe I was looking for a distraction. I don't know if that makes sense.'

Slift frowns and stretches out, his fingertips splayed across the desk, giving the temporary impression of reaching towards her, as though to save her from herself. He straightens up and looks her straight in the eye. 'I would tread very carefully, if I were you, Miss Sarto. This fellow isn't like you or I.'

Nicoletta gives him a smile. 'We're all more alike than we'd care to think.'

Slift raises a corner of his mouth. 'Didn't this fellow kill a Guard?'

'He was acquitted,' Nicoletta answers simply.

'He wouldn't hesitate if it came to harming you, Miss Sarto. Or a member of your family.'

Nicoletta acts as though he hasn't spoken. She waves a hand grandly and stands up. 'Accidents of birth are all that separate us. I'm sure he's not that bad.'

Slift furrows his brow, as though perplexed, but not wanting to contradict her. 'I'll find out what I can about the provenance of *Among the Ruins*,' he says thoughtfully. 'But I can't promise anything. I'm sorry I can't be more helpful than that.'

Nicoletta puts her notebook away. They shake hands across the desk, and he takes hers with both of his. 'Take care of yourself, Miss Sarto,' he says. 'And get some rest before you think any more about getting involved with any of this.' He gives her a wink.

She turns on her heel, the fizz of excitement making a tentative return. She trips lightly down the stairs, and before she can stop herself, she enters an empty phone box at the corner of South Anne Street, where it meets the main shopping thoroughfare of Grafton Street. She inserts a coin into the slot and takes a deep breath, dialling Pearse Street Garda Station before she can stop. Garda O'Connor takes an age to come to the phone. She's considering hanging up before the pips go on the call, when she hears the familiar gravity of his voice.

'Garda, it's Nicoletta Sarto.' A shrill little beep sounds in her ear, and she knows she has to speak quickly. 'Meet me at Ricci's, in ten minutes. If you want, of course. My shout this time.' The line goes dead before he has time to reply.

She feels like a balloon that's been pricked as she walks down Grafton Street, towards Ricci's on Hawkins Street. What if she's made an awful mistake? She wants to ask O'Connor about The Rook. But if she's honest with herself, she also wants to see a sympathetic face. He's never judged her. She knows how far-fetched it sounds, but she feels as though he understands her, in ways no one else could.

Ricci's is half empty when she pushes open the door. She scans the room. He didn't actually agree to meet her. She might have made a giant fool of herself for nothing. But O'Connor is sitting by the window, his arms folded on a corner table, in the seats they'd occupied before, albeit by chance that time, his face in profile. He doesn't see her until she's right beside him. He stands up, pulling out a chair for her. She sits down opposite him, her back to the window, setting her bag at her feet.

'Thanks for coming,' she begins, sounding somewhat formal to her own ears. If he notices, he doesn't say anything.

'It's no hardship,' he replies, his voice a little gruff. 'I come here all the time anyway, sure.'

She folds her hands on the table in front of her. His fingers riff on the speckled Formica edge on his side. They are as freckled as his arms, she notices.

She clears her throat. 'You're probably wondering why I asked you here.'

He raises his eyebrows with a small smile. They hush as a waitress takes their orders, then bustles away.

'I'm presuming you wanted to ask me about The Rook.' He raises his eyebrows again, his eyes dancing with a rare playfulness.

'How'd you know that?' Her throat feels blocked; her voice sounds small.

He shrugs. 'After seeing you beyond at his house in Rathmines, I was thinking it might be something you'd developed an interest in. You couldn't ask Barney, no?'

He holds her gaze with frank curiosity. Eventually she looks down at her hands. The waitress delivers their drinks and when she's gone back to the counter Nicoletta finally answers. 'I'm not supposed to get involved with all this. I'm the women's pages editor now.'

He regards her thoughtfully. 'There might be something in that, you know, Nicoletta. If you don't mind my saying.'

'Something in what?' She answers a little more sharply than she intended. 'It's Barney's story,' she explains, in an attempt to sweeten the sharp response. She twists her hands in front of her, the pot of tea untouched. O'Connor pours out for them both and she adds a splash of milk and takes a scalding gulp. 'You don't have to do this to yourself anymore.' His words are gentle, but she finds herself blushing, nonetheless.

'I know I don't have to do anything. It's in the public interest,' she says, a little defensive.

'So, what's in it that's captured *your* interest?' The playful look is back, and she grins despite herself.

'Helen Leonard, an old lady from Sandycove, is being exhumed tomorrow,' she says.

He picks up his cup. 'I'm aware of that. I don't happen

to think she was murdered, but the Leonards are very influential. I think it's a whole lot of bother for nothing.' He puts down his cup. 'What's Helen Leonard got to do with The Rook'?

Nicoletta bites her lip. 'What if she had a painting that he wanted? That's now missing. And her paid nurse is also missing. Isn't that strange?'

O'Connor shakes his head. 'What if, indeed. I'm sure The Rook wants a lot of things, Nicoletta. But he's not in a position to get them anymore. We're on his back round the clock.'

'I know, I know.' Nicoletta holds up her hands. 'But it's a possibility all the same.'

O'Connor doesn't say anything. He looks at her across the table. She bites her lip and hastily picks up her cup.

'Ah, maybe I should go,' she says finally.

'Nicoletta, don't take this the wrong way,' he says, patting her lightly on the back of the hand. 'But maybe you should drop this story. As I've said, you don't have to do this to yourself anymore.'

She frowns, and he swallows, as though regretting what he's just said. 'How're the twins?' he asks, changing tack.

'They're fine,' she says airily. 'Loud. Sleepless. There are two of them!' She laughs. It must come off as slightly unhinged, because O'Connor frowns at her.

'Are you all right?' He pushes his cup aside. 'Tell me to mind my own business, but after everything that's happened to you, maybe you need to mind yourself.'

She finds the relief soften the pressure in her chest, at the prospect of talking to someone who understands.

'I'm fine,' she says, pushing back her chair, overwhelmed at the kindness in his face. 'I'm so sorry, I have to get back to the office. I'll get these,' she babbles at the waitress, who comes with their bill.

She turns around. O'Connor is sitting with his chin in his palm, not facing outside. He looks contemplative. On impulse, she gives him a sideways hug across the table. He looks surprised, as she squeezes his hand. He smells of soap and the outdoors. 'Thank you,' she says over her shoulder, before fleeing onto the street.

Chapter Ten

The next day passes in a hum of repetition as Nicoletta is carried along by the rhythm of her new job. Come evening, after Barney and his cronies have disappeared to the pub, she backs out, through the noisy newsroom, keeping her head down. There's only one place she can go where she knows she won't be bothered for a few minutes. She climbs a short flight of stairs and emerges into an oasis of cardboard.

The *Sentinel* library is a cramped warren of two rectangular interconnecting rooms piled floor to ceiling with clippings from all editions of the newspaper catalogued in a mysterious system penetrable only by the librarian Dolores, who seems quite ancient to Nicoletta and everyone who works there. Her age is unknown but the subject of much speculation. Dolores sits on a high stool listening to classical music on a tinny transistor radio and simultaneously sorts through a mountain of clipped newsprint, firing each disconnected article into an assortment of boxes spread on a high-topped table in front of her where they sigh like discontented leaves. There's no one else in the warm, airless room. She's wearing a blue woollen twin set, despite the heat, and her hair is set in a complicated knot at the top of her head, bedecked like a wayward tiara by pince-nez which hang from a chain around her neck. Dolores doesn't look up. She knows her territory is often used as a respite from the bustle of the newsroom, and she doesn't mind as long as everyone minds their manners. Nicoletta leans against a stepladder on wheels at the furthest wall, praying she doesn't send all Dolores's hard work teetering over like paper dominoes. She sits down on the bottom rung of the stepladder, planting her feet on the worn felt tiles. When she straightens up, she senses someone standing over her. She jumps. She hadn't heard anyone walk over.

Nicoletta snaps her head up with what she hopes is a winning smile. 'Dolores, I was wondering if you could do me a favour. I came to ask you to find me everything you have on a set of two paintings called *Among the Ruins*, and the Hall family. Also known as The Birds.' She tilts her chin in defiance towards the towering cardboard stacks.

'The Birds ... That's going to take quite a while,' Dolores says, with a brisk nod.

'Don't worry, I have all night.' Nicoletta sinks with a defeated clunk on the bottom rung of the ladder and waits for Dolores to scuttle back to her station at the back of the room. She stretches and yawns, the overhead fluorescent lights stinging her eyes. She's wondering if she should go home, to Barney's mother's house, if it can be called her home. She glances at Dolores, who's crouched over a corner shelf, rummaging in a deep boxed file. Nicoletta ducks through the low doorway, lingering on the landing, when she hears heavy footsteps. The familiar gleam of Dermot's fair head rises to meet her, as he mounts the summit of the steep flight of wooden steps.

'Well, now,' he says, concern quickly furrowing his brow. 'Just saw you running for your life through the newsroom.' He jingles his pocket. 'I've the car with me. Give me ten minutes to finish up and I'll drop you home. We can catch up. Haven't seen you properly in ages.'

Nicoletta exhales a shuddery breath. She could just tell Dolores she'll be back tomorrow for the cuttings. But Dolores is sitting on her high stool, her hands folded over a large file in her lap, which she brandishes at Nicoletta.

'I thought it was going to take a while,' she says with a breathless flourish. 'But your Barney requested them earlier this week and he kept them for days.' She wrinkles her nose. 'I hadn't put them all back yet.' She holds out the file and Nicoletta cradles it against her chest, rage like a lump of unchewed meat sitting at the pit of her stomach.

'Thank you,' Nicoletta says solemnly. 'I'll get these back to you quickly. I just want to have a quick look.'

She sits down on the floor, while Dolores glides back to her stool, and rifles through the worn manila file.

Most of it is stuff she already knows. About the robbery at Fairfax House, Ray Hall, aka The Rook, his brothers Danny and Ronan, how they'd all been acquitted of murdering Garda Larry Grehan, though Danny had been jailed for his part in the robbery they committed. About how their modus operandi was to burgle and then set fire to stately homes. *Among the Ruins* was listed as one of the paintings stolen in the robbery from Lady Pat Dennehy, who is, it now turns out, Helen Leonard's sister. But something jumps out from an article Nicoletta hasn't seen before. It concerns a robbery and arson attack on Holloway House, a stately home in Donabate, dating from the previous year, for which Ronan Hall received two months in prison.

HALL JAILED FOR BURNING OF NORTH COUNTY DUBLIN MANSION
By Barney King
26th March 1969

Ronan Hall (40) with an address at Grosvenor Avenue, Rathmines, Dublin, was jailed for two months today for his part in an armed robbery and arson attack on Holloway House, a stately home just outside Donabate in January of this year. Hall, also known as 'The Magpie', is a member of the organised crime gang nicknamed The Birds, along with his brother Daniel Hall, also known as 'The Wren', and his brother Ray Hall, also known as 'The Rook'. Other senior members of the organisation's identity are unknown. Their modus operandi is to burgle stately homes around the island of Ireland, and latterly to set fire to them in an echo of the civil war of 1923. Some of the artwork believed to have been stolen from Holloway House was allegedly found at an auction house in Dublin and the owner of Rault's Gallery, Antoine Rault, was fined in the District Court for possession of stolen goods.

Ray Hall and Daniel Hall were not charged with any crime in the Holloway House robbery. The owners of the house, Mr and Mrs Ted and Eliza Field, have lived there since their marriage in 1939, and inherited the property from Mr Field's parents. Mr Field told the Sentinel that a great many priceless artworks were looted from Holloway House, some of which may never be recovered ...

Nicoletta stops reading and memorises the names. Holloway House of Donabate, owned by Ted and Eliza Field. Antoine Rault, art dealer.

'On second thoughts, can I take these away with me?' she calls to Dolores, who raises a hand in acquiescence. Nicoletta places the file in her bag and trips lightly down the stairs to meet Dermot at the security desk by the front door. He's tapping his foot waiting for her. He eyes the file sticking out from her bag but offers her his arm and they walk out onto Burgh Quay. She forces her mind to go blank; not to think about Barney or the children, or Joan, as they stride purposefully along Westmoreland Street. Dermot grips her arm ever tighter, as they duck behind another pub to where the car is parked down an alley beside Pearse Street Garda Station. Nicoletta wonders if Garda O'Connor is inside, working away at his desk, his hat on the chair opposite him, the window wide open to circulate some air, or if he's already gone for the day. She wonders what he's doing now, if he's at home. She shakes off the thought.

'I thought no one'd be stupid enough to rob it if I left it beside the cop station,' Dermot says, extracting the key from his pocket and inserting it into the driver's door.

'People are a lot stupider than you give them credit for,' Nicoletta says with a chuckle. 'Present company excluded, of course,' she adds, as Dermot revs the engine higher than is strictly necessary and inches out at a crawl.

'All right, smart arse,' he mutters, swearing at a man on a bicycle dashing across the neck of the alleyway without looking. Dermot swerves and they fold into the traffic heading out of town. Nicoletta throws her bag into the front passenger footwell. Dermot glances down at the file wedged into it.

'What's that?' His eyes flick back to the steady traffic.

'Clippings about The Rook, and the Hall family in general. Oh, and a missing painting called *Among the Ruins*. Which may or may not have belonged to Helen Leonard. That old lady from the Julia Bridges story? Her death may or may not have been murder. Throw in what sounds like a crooked art dealer, Antoine Rault, and it's a tangled web.' She smiles at him. He puffs out his cheeks and doesn't smile back. He swallows, as though he is choosing his words carefully.

'Antoine Rault was a good guy. He's not long dead, Nic.'

Nicoletta keeps her eyes on his face. He doesn't look at her. 'Oh, you knew him?'

'Not really,' he says gruffly. 'I met him maybe once.'

'How did he die?'

He doesn't answer her. She presses on.

'What do you know about him? He definitely seems to be part of the puzzle.'

'What do you mean, "part of the puzzle"? For God's sake, Nicoletta, not everything has to be about your big opportunity to be the next Nancy Drew. These are real people you know nothing about.'

'It's just a story I'm working on,' she says, a bit taken aback, taking it down a notch.

Dermot frowns. 'Isn't that Barney's story? The Rook thing. What's that got to do with the women's pages?'

'It's a story about a woman, as I said. A woman being murdered is a story for the women's pages, right?'

'You said yourself, Helen Leonard may not have been murdered. Why don't you just take your beak out.'

They're at the end of her road now. Dermot is still talking, and she can see his mouth moving but can't quite make out the words above the roaring in her ears. Two young girls play hopscotch on the road in the quivering dusk, and a young man walks past with a guitar case slung over his shoulder. It's a beautiful summer's evening, but she can't bear it. Her own two girls are inside waiting for her. Her stomach grows tight. He's looking at her, waiting for her reaction to something or other, she guesses. It's her turn to speak.

'I can't go in,' she says, suddenly, in a small voice.

'Nic,' Dermot's tone changes. He bites his lip as though considering his words carefully. 'I'm sorry if I came off a bit harsh. The Rook is a dangerous beast. Besides, it's Barney's story. This is your job at stake. Duffy won't thank you for muscling in on it and ignoring the women's pages gig. Focus on that.'

She knows he is right. And yet. She unrolls the passenger window, breathing in as much of the night air as she can.

'What if we were to work together on this? You and me,' she says quickly, in case he thinks she means Barney.

He doesn't say anything, and she keeps talking. 'I'll go

through this file tonight and maybe tomorrow you could drive us to Fairfax House?'

'Fairfax House? In Blessington? At the weekend? Nic, this isn't a game,' he says, a little more sharply. He lets the engine idle, then cuts it. When he looks at her, there's a determined set to his jaw. But she is shocked by how gaunt he has become. Not even the shadows of the evening can hide it from her.

'A game? What do you think I am, a child?' A fleck of warm, angry saliva lands on her chin. She wipes it away, ashamed.

He sighs, turning so that he's looking straight ahead, at the road, the hopscotch, the horizon. 'No, of course I don't think you're a child, Nic.' But his voice is tight and compressed. Not like the Dermot she knows, who's always up for everything. Who laughs at her jokes, accompanies her on various capers, listens to her. Something has changed. He finally turns to look at her. 'I think you should go home to your children. They need you far more than dead old ladies and criminals missing paintings ever could.'

The fury rises through her windpipe like a gas leak. 'Don't you dare talk to me like that. Don't say the same thing, just like everyone else. Don't you think I know that?' Her eyes fill with tears. 'I have to go in,' she says finally, ducking out of the car before the tears can fall.

Dermot hangs on while she walks up the short dark path and lets herself in. She's no sooner in the hall, than she picks up the phone and dials her parents' number. No one answers. She wonders where they are. They must be in bed, the shop closed. They rarely go out. She can hear the twins from the kitchen; she knows she has to face the music.

She bites her lip in frustration, putting the phone down slowly and quietly, loath to draw Joan on her. She contemplates picking it up and dialling her mother's number again, when it peals twice. She retrieves it on the third ring and answers with a hesitant 'Hello?'

'Nicoletta?'

'Yes, this is she. Who's this?'

'Hello, Nicoletta, it's Leopold Slift. I have some information for you. It's not much, but I thought you might be interested to know that both parts of the *Among the Ruins* diptych were bought by Tom Leonard Senior from Antoine Rault, a Dublin-based art dealer, in August 1951. I don't know where they came from before that, but I'll try to find out.'

'Thank you,' she says, the handle slipping down her damp palm. 'I believe Mr Rault is dead?'

She hears a hiss of breath. 'That's right. Mr Rault died in February, by suicide.'

Chapter Eleven

Long after the twins have settled that night, Nicoletta is still awake. Barney's side of the bed is empty. Eventually she gives up on sleep, dressing in yesterday's clothes, tying the belt of a huge coat around her waist in a rigid knot. There is light coming from Joan's room; she raps gently on the door.

'I have to go out early today,' she says apologetically.

Joan is sitting on the bed, over the covers, in a housecoat, her hair in curlers, listening to the radio. She peers at Nicoletta with suspicion.

'What do you mean, early? It's still late, the middle of the night.'

'It'll be bright in an hour. The dawn chorus will start soon.'

Joan snaps off the radio. 'Did my son come home?'

Nicoletta shakes her head with feigned nonchalance.

Joan heaves herself upright with a creak of the mattress springs. 'Well, going chasing after him isn't going to bring him home, let me tell you.'

'I have to go out on a job.' Nicoletta shifts her weight

from hip to hip, hoping Joan won't ask her about exactly where she's going.

'Right.' Joan crosses to the vanity table and sits down. Her reflection gives Nicoletta a pitying look as she begins to take out the curlers.

Nicoletta shifts her weight again, and the floorboards creak. Everything creaks in this house. 'Thank you. The girls love you.' *They're indifferent to me*, she feels like saying.

The pins clatter into a china cup on the vanity table one by one with a dainty *plink plink* sound.

'Never chase after a man. It's something I've always lived by.'

Nicoletta is practically jogging on the spot. Joan looks up.

'Go. But don't say I didn't warn you.'

Nicoletta is down the stairs and out the door without a backward glance.

The air is cooler than yesterday or the day before; the breeze hisses in her face, blowing skittish patterns with her fringe. Wind riffles the leaves on a clump of hedges at the end of the road, and a lone magpie flies off with a screech, as though outraged at being disturbed. Nicoletta shivers, despite wearing the thick coat. The sight of the magpie feels like a portent of something bad, though she doesn't consider herself to be superstitious. She picks up the pace, her aimless trot turning into a beeline towards town. It feels more like dusk than the hour before dawn. A plane drones from somewhere overhead, and she longs to be on it.

A girl and a man in dishevelled evening dress walk by. The girl is carrying her shoes, a pair of gold platform sandals. The man's shirt is unbuttoned to his waist. They are swaying and laughing together, and the man cups the woman's hip and pulls her in for a kiss. Nicoletta wonders if they're on their way home from the Trinity Ball. Fingers of pink and gold begin to creep through the clouds as the couple break apart, and Nicoletta walks on, hoping they haven't noticed her observing them.

She looks at her watch. It's coming up to four. There's about half an hour to daybreak proper, when the exhumation would most likely begin. She's not going to make it at this rate. The warnings from Dermot, Barney, Price and Duffy about not reporting on Helen Leonard's exhumation ring in her ears, and she thinks about turning back. She wonders why it is that now she has the women's editor job she coveted so badly, she doesn't seem to want it at all. The same with her relationship with Barney. She stops, a thought alarming her. Maybe it's her. Something wanting in her, a sign it wasn't meant. But then what? A single taxi waits in the line outside Amiens Street Station, the end of the driver's cigarette an ember in the gloom. Nicoletta charges forward, her hand out, before another wretched thought can drag her back someplace she doesn't want to go.

By the time they reach Deansgrange Cemetery, the sky is a haze of palest blue. Nicoletta is just in time to see a coffin making a reverse journey. The space at the back of the hearse is blank and impersonal, instead of bedecked with the usual floral tributes. It is also flanked by several

Garda cars. Nicoletta hovers for a moment or two, getting her bearings. A small crowd has gathered at a respectful distance. A couple of other reporters are there from rival newspapers; she doesn't see anyone from the *Sentinel*. Eventually, the hearse inches towards the entrance at the front, a gate is opened, and after consultation with several uniformed Gardaí, it begins to move out.

A gleam of red flashes across her path, and O'Connor dashes out from where he'd been obscured by a huge Celtic cross, to get into the driver's seat of a nearby Garda car at the rear of the spectacle. He is accosted by a reporter, a small fellow with a bristly moustache and a fidgety appearance. O'Connor stoops to answer him. Nicoletta puts her hands in her pockets. She feels ridiculous, like the world's worst rubbernecker. She wonders why she's come, and if she can break away from the group without being noticed. But she stays. She owes it to Helen Leonard, who had been kind to her once, and surely didn't deserve this indignity. She scans the crowd but doesn't see Louise Leonard. She scuffs her toe on the ground. The grassy earth underfoot has a tender quality, and she wonders how she's going to get home. It had been a mistake telling the taxi not to wait for her, but it cost a fortune as it is. The man with the bristly moustache gives her a curious look, as O'Connor breaks away from him, and she digs her hands deeper into her pockets, buffering herself against his gaze, and from the chill wind.

The crowd is beginning to disperse. O'Connor is about to get into his car when someone else calls him over, a tall man with a beaky nose. Nicoletta recognises him as being from the *Press*. O'Connor's eyes meet hers, and spark with recognition. She manages to smile and give a small wave. She is all too aware she has no right to be here, and he has every right not to give her the time of day. He raises his hand in mock salute and his mouth in an uncomplicated smile. Her heart cranks into life like a motor being sprung. She's glad she stayed now. She waits, with the patience of a child waiting her turn at musical chairs, knowing he'll be at her side before long. He hears a call from behind and the hearse at the entrance to this section of graveyard begins its not-quite-final journey back to front, to the city morgue. O'Connor races back to his car and opens the driver's door at last. Nicoletta and the tall reporter with the beaky nose are the only people left on the fleshy verge. O'Connor mouths something at her. She can't quite make it out. He beckons her towards the car.

'Do you want a lift?' he comes over and says in her ear, and she nods mutely and gets into the back seat. The man with the beaky nose gives O'Connor a wave and they move off, after the hearse.

'You could've got into the front.' He unscrews a steaming flask and takes a swig.

'I don't want anyone to get the wrong idea about me.'

O'Connor swivels his head around to look at her. Nicoletta colours.

He twists the stopper back in the flask one-handed and replaces it between the front seats.

'I'm surprised to see you, actually,' he says, finally, wiping his upper lip with the back of his hand.

'Why's that?'

'Ah, you know. Duffy not wanting anything to do with this story and that. But maybe I shouldn't be too surprised.'

'What do you mean?' she asks cautiously.

'You're determined,' he says with a smile.

The suburbs of South Dublin start to whiz past: washing lines cast over neat patchwork gardens silvery in the early morning light.

'I'm not here for Duffy,' Nicoletta says.

'Oh yeah? Who are you here for, then?'

Nicoletta shakes her head. 'I wanted to pay my respects to Helen Leonard.'

O'Connor raises an eyebrow in the rearview mirror. 'Don't trust us to do our jobs, is that it?' She looks away. They're on the coast road now, waves foaming against the rocky shore. She looks longingly at the bubbly mass. She'd love a bath, with a whole bottle of foam emptied into scalding water, an hour of relaxation all to herself. She forces herself to focus on the conversation.

'Of course I do. Just, I suppose, I wanted a distraction from everything.'

O'Connor chuckles. 'Most people don't chase after criminals and potential murder stories for a distraction.'

'I guess I'm not like most people,' she shoots back.

'You're not like most people I've ever met – that's for sure.' He smiles at her in the mirror, and she colours again, before sliding her notebook out of her bag. 'Do you think foul play entered the equation with Helen Leonard's death?'

O'Connor shakes his head. 'I wouldn't like to speculate. But no, in answer to your question. All this fuss now, I'd say the family feel horrible guilt. We'll see what the pathologist says.'

Nicoletta remembers Louise Leonard's haughty pronunciation about pressuring the Minister for Justice for an exhumation licence and she wonders what Miss Leonard's brother, Louise's father, feels about it. She vaguely recalls a mention of Tom Leonard Junior as being a well-known barrister. She'll have to visit them.

'Who's the new State Pathologist?' Nicoletta asks, feeling hopelessly out of the loop, wishing it were still Professor O'Malley, whom she had grown very fond of in the space of a week before he retired.

'Dr Marsden. A young fellow. Over from London. I'd say we'll have an answer on poor Helen soon enough.'

The city spreads out before them, the usual low grey sprawl of the Dublin skyline. The time that's gone by feels like none at all, and Nicoletta doesn't know how much longer she can keep sidestepping what she really wants to say. If she doesn't say it, she'll always regret it. But it's too soon, and not the right time, and possibly not the right person. She clenches her teeth as they pass through the village of Sandymount, as indicated by a painted sign surrounded by neat flowerbeds planted with bluebells, primroses and cowslips, colourful row upon colourful row, neat and suburban, the furthest thing imaginable from being threatening. Nicoletta inhales a big gulp.

'About that missing painting from Miss Leonard's house.'

O'Connor gives her a sideways glance.

'It's extremely valuable. Called *Among the Ruins*. The

other part of it is owned by Lady Pat Dennehy of Fairfax House. Who was burgled by The Rook earlier this year.'

O'Connor takes a sip from his flask. 'What are you getting at, Nicoletta? The Rook isn't responsible for every stolen painting in the city.'

'What do you know about Antoine Rault?' She closes her notebook and drums her fingers on the plastic laminate cover.

O'Connor turns around to look at her. 'A well-respected art dealer. Until we caught him moving stolen paintings for The Rook. He died in February. Suicide. A bad business.'

'Do you think it really was a suicide?'

He gives her another long glance. 'Yes. And don't be going talking to his family, upsetting them. They all work in the art business. It's still very raw, I'm sure.'

'What are their names?' she asks, idly tossing her notebook into her bag.

'The wife's name is Agatha. The son's name is Louis, and the daughter's name is Celine.'

Nicoletta remembers the woman at the Creightons' estate sale.

'Ah yes. I've met Celine already.'

A cyclist attempts to overtake them and O'Connor's brakes screech in protest.

Nicoletta takes a deep breath. 'I'm going to put a note under The Rook's door asking for an interview.'

'That is a very unwise thing to do, Nicoletta,' he says, changing gear in an effortless motion. 'You don't want to be on his radar. He's a nasty character. You don't want him to even know your name, believe me.' He turns to look at her.

Nicoletta looks him full in the face, taken aback by this relatively long and impassioned speech. She chews on the end of her pen. 'Maybe I already am on his radar,' she says.

His eyebrows hit his hairline in the rearview mirror. 'What do you mean by that?'

'Barney has written plenty about him. He probably already knows where we live.'

O'Connor exhales slowly, his hands gripped straight in front of him on the wheel.

'I'm not just saying this as your colleague, but also as your friend. The Rook is highly dangerous. Back out of this story now. Go home to your kids. Your new job. Enjoy your life.'

Her throat tightens. 'Maybe I can't.'

There's silence as he parks the car. When he's levered up the handbrake, he turns around and looks at her, scanning her face. She blinks, as though feeling the beam of a spotlight.

'You've lots to be delighted about,' he says gently.

She thinks of Barney's empty spot beside her in the bed and puts her hand on the door to open it. 'Thank you, Garda,' she says, aware her tone is formal once more.

She takes her leave of him with an awkward handshake, self-conscious after sliding out of the back seat, all unsteady limbs. The sun is beginning to warm the pavement in a hot burst. She doesn't wait until he goes back through the doors of the station, all too aware of unseen eyes catching her emerging from his car in plain view. She knows she should be beyond caring what people think at this point. But she has her job to think of. And the girls. She starts walking, enjoying the breeze on her face as she crosses O'Connell Bridge, pausing to watch a fleet of rowers as they glide through the sludgy water, like exotically coloured swans. A man throws a bucket of steaming soapy water down the steps of a pub, while barrels of Guinness are rolled through a service hatch below. She huddles into her bulky coat, walking at a brisk pace, savouring the sounds of human life going on around her regardless. The man with the bucket doesn't give her a second glance.

Chapter Twelve

Nicoletta walks as far as she can. The streets are almost empty, save for the odd newspaper seller strutting their stuff with placards boldly declaring a heatwave for the next week. She squares her shoulders and keeps walking, towards Townsend Street, in the opposite direction to the newspaper offices at Burgh Quay. A taxi passes, and she keeps walking. She needs to think. She had looked it up in the telephone directory the night before. Louise Leonard's father, Tom Leonard, lives in Donnybrook. There had been no mention of his wife. Another taxi zips by but doesn't stop. Nicoletta is almost at College Green before she hails a car.

She pays with a regretful last fistful of change, outside the Catholic church in Donnybrook. She'd mentioned it as her destination because it's the only Donnybrook landmark she knows and she feels like a walk to get her bearings. The driver skids off, leaving a trail of dust behind him; he hadn't asked what her business was: a rarity. Perhaps he presumed she was part of the growing crowd that seemed to be gathering outside the church for a wedding. A young man in tails paces anxiously between a row of ancient gravestones while another man, perhaps the best man, paces two ineffectual strides behind him. *A nice day for a wedding*, Nicoletta thinks, then shakes her head. Is it really? It's unbearably hot with no sun.

She walks across the small bridge back towards the village, the air stifling around her, the sky heavy with distended clouds. They look swollen, and helpless, the way she had when she was expecting the twins. The way she'd been feeling swung between hopeful – that things with Barney mightn't be the huge mistake she was suspecting they might be – and her natural state of pragmatism, to which the pendulum always returned.

She remembers the address from the telephone directory. Mr Thomas Leonard BL is listed as living at 3 Victoria Terrace. Nicoletta doesn't recognise the name of the street, and it takes a while of walking and asking people for directions to find it. She's hot and bothered by the time she knocks on the door of a smart, red-brick Edwardian House just off Donnybrook's main street. A neat lawn gives way to a row of rose bushes growing close to the house, and Nicoletta can see her reflection in the brass knocker shaped like a griffin, its hideous teeth bared. She bares hers back just for devilment, and to check for rogue lipstick marks. Then she knocks; there's no doorbell. She raps again this time, a big booming sound that seems to reverberate throughout the core of the house, tipping the rose petals outside and giving them a nervous tremor like an old man with the shakes. Nicoletta is surprised when Louise Leonard eventually answers the door. Her face is completely bare, and she looks older, and paler, than she had previously. Nicoletta shuffles her feet on the doorstep. But Louise gives her a thin smile.

'Nicoletta? What a surprise.' Her tone is flat.

'I didn't see you at the exhumation earlier,' Nicoletta says before she can stop herself.

'I didn't go.' Louise dabs her mouth with the back of her hand distractedly. 'I stayed here with Dad. Look, why don't you come in?'

Nicoletta follows Louise into a large kitchen drenched in sunlight, which filters through two enormous picture windows taking up an entire wall. Louise raises a hand to shield her eyes.

'I've just sent several reporters away. There's nothing to tell them. The results of the post-mortem aren't back yet.' She indicates the kettle. Nicoletta nods and Louise bustles around as tea things are produced from a stacked dresser made of smooth blonde wood with moulded plastic handles. She doesn't offer Nicoletta a seat until the tea is made and she indicates an ornate high-backed chair jammed against a small plastic-topped breakfast table.

Nicoletta accepts her tea gratefully. 'I thought your parents lived here?'

'My mother's dead. I'm staying with Dad for a while.' Louise's tone is still flat.

'He must be very upset?' Nicoletta presses, cupping the tea between both hands though it's burning her palms.

'He blames me for stirring things up. He doesn't think Helen was murdered and he has no idea why I got the exhumation order. I blame myself too, if you really want to know how I'm feeling,' Louise says with a brusque shrug.

'Why does he blame you?' Nicoletta places the cup on the table and casts a discreet glance around her. This table is piled high with books, papers, letters and magazines. A pile of papers spill onto the floor. A squashy-looking low couch upholstered in blush-coloured fabric faces the windows into the garden, which is alive with wildflowers of every variety in a riot of colour, with no apparent order to its sequence.

Louise pushes her tea away. She hasn't touched it. 'It was my idea to hire the carer. Picked a place that obviously wasn't too stringent about references, didn't I? I didn't know the nurse would disappear.'

Her eyes search Nicoletta's face. Nicoletta responds carefully. 'Do you think your aunt Helen was targeted because of the painting, *Among the Ruins*?'

Louise gives an imperceptible nod. 'Undoubtedly. We'll never see it again.'

Nicoletta stays silent.

For one awful moment, Nicoletta thinks Louise might be about to cry. Then she recovers, shaking her head as though allowing the unpleasant emotions to fly from her face.

Nicoletta takes a long swallow of tea, which has cooled down to a barely drinkable temperature. She brushes imaginary lint off her sleeves and prepares to stand up. 'I'm going to talk to the nursing agency. Expose their shoddy practices in caring for the elderly.'

Louise nods. 'Nurses Direct on Dame Street. I don't

know what good it might do. But they need to be answerable.'

'My editor doesn't want me to report on this at all, due to your aunt Helen being the half-sister of Lady Pat Dennehy,' Nicoletta says suddenly.

Louise waves a hand in dismissal. 'They didn't speak for years and years. That's the terrible irony of it all.'

She rests an elbow on the table and presses her knuckles into her cheek. 'Aunt Helen was an awful hoarder. Before we got the carer in, I cleared out a pile of old newspapers from her bedroom, some of them going back years. She'd clipped out all your reports on the Julia Bridges story.' She gives an abrupt, dry laugh. 'She hated those Creightons. Do you believe in signs?'

Nicoletta thinks for a second or two. 'No,' she says.

'Neither do I,' Louise shoots back. 'But Aunt Helen was always going on about signs, and visions, and angels, and the importance of dreams. Did you know she spent a fortune on a psychic in her final months?'

'No, I didn't know.' Nicoletta pauses. 'Do you know the psychic's name?'

Louise shakes her head with a sniff.

Nicoletta scrapes back her chair. 'I've intruded on you for long enough, Louise. I wondered if your father's here? If I could speak to him. About Helen.' She tries to gauge the expression on Louise's face.

Louise surprises her by standing up suddenly, slopping a puddle of tea onto the table. She doesn't seem to notice, and guides Nicoletta by the elbow through a connecting door into what looks like a small breakfast room set up with the same style of furniture as the cosy sofa in the untidy kitchen.

'He's terribly upset about Helen,' she says into Nicoletta's ear. They're already in the centre of the room before Nicoletta notices a man slumped into a large armchair, leaning against an overfilled bookcase. An unattended cigarette burns itself into the ashtray. He jumps when he sees them. It looks as though he's been asleep.

'Louise,' he says in a low voice. 'Who's this?'

'Nicoletta Sarto from the *Irish Sentinel*,' Nicoletta says, sticking out her hand. The man doesn't take it.

'Louise, why have you let a reporter into the house?' He rests his head on the edge of a shelf.

'This reporter is writing a story about the nursing agency and their failings,' Louise says, indicating Nicoletta but looking straight at the man. She turns to Nicoletta. 'This is my father, Tom Leonard.'

He sits up and stretches, yawning in a noisy display, like a gorilla beating its chest, before appraising Nicoletta.

He indicates a stool for her to sit on. 'Please. Take a pew.' To Louise, he waves a hand and says: 'Any chance of a coffee?' He mimes drinking out of a cup and Nicoletta shakes her head with a smile.

When they're alone, he rests his elbows on the table and scrubs his eyes with the back of his hand. Nicoletta has a chance to observe him. He is tall and thin, with a long rectangular face and hangdog pouches under his eyes. His age is hard to determine. Though if Louise is close to forty, he must be at least sixty.

Nicoletta perches on the stool, a little unsteady. 'I'm so sorry about your sister.' For a moment there's silence.

Tom Leonard sucks in a sharp intake of breath. 'There's nothing redeeming about the situation,' he says, his head bowed. There's a pause as Louise comes back with his coffee.

Leonard doesn't elaborate, but catches her eye, as though daring her to contradict him.

He snatches a cup from Louise. 'We should have just put Helen into an old people's home, a nursing home or what have you. That would've been the kindest thing.'

'Why didn't you?' Nicoletta glances from father to daughter. She keeps her own features soft, but she's aware of every muscle in his face, angled tensely at her, and ready to snap.

'Hindsight is a wonderful thing, isn't it?' he says a little gruffly. 'The truth is, Miss Sarto, that Helen was difficult. She wouldn't have been able to cope outside her home.'

'Really?' Nicoletta asks with mild surprise.

'Louise didn't think it was a good idea,' he says quickly. 'My sister loved her home. She'd been born there. She wanted to die there.' He takes a gulp of coffee.

Nicoletta remembers the spry, alert woman she'd met eighteen short months earlier. Had it been the case that her family was simply waiting for her to die? She faces down Tom Leonard with a brisk nod.

'Do you think your sister was targeted for her half of the *Among the Ruins* diptych?'

Tom shrugs. 'My sister was … a difficult character, as I've said. She'd refused to speak to me on and off for the last year of her life, for example. I don't know. Then she becomes very fond of this nurse, who walks away with the painting. It's all very odd.'

'Why didn't you speak in that final year?' Nicoletta looks over at Louise, but she's scanning the bookshelves, lost in her own world.

'That's the way she was. I can't pinpoint one particular reason.' Tom swipes at the air with his hands as though with a blade. His meaning is clear: that's the end of it.

'I see,' Nicoletta says uncertainly. 'The painting, of course, is missing. *Among the Ruins*. It's very valuable. How did it come into Helen's possession?'

Tom swallows the rest of the coffee, slams the cup down and stands up.

'I don't know how valuable it really was,' he says. 'And it wasn't much to look at.'

Nicoletta makes a polite noise, while thinking.

Louise hovers behind her father's chair, wringing her hands, as though she's been dragged back to the present.

'My grandfather, Tom Leonard Senior, gave the painting to Helen,' Louise says. 'He gave its other half to Helen's half-sister, Patricia.'

'Ah yes, Lady Pat,' Nicoletta murmurs.

'From my father's second marriage,' Tom says, standing up and opening the door to the kitchen, indicating for Nicoletta to follow him through the hall and out to the front door. 'There's thirteen years of an age gap between the two sisters. My father thought it might connect them forever.' He opens the front door, but Nicoletta stands on the threshold, not ready to let go just yet.

'And did it?'

Tom shakes his head with a humourless laugh. 'They barely knew each other. I don't think Pat ever visited Helen once in her final days.'

He continues holding the door, looking at her expectantly, before sighing and leaning forward. 'This is a very delicate family matter, Miss Sarto. Leave any mention of this conversation out of your investigation into the nursing agency, if you please.'

Nicoletta doesn't budge an inch. 'What about Ray Hall? Also known as The Rook.'

A muscle pulses in Leonard's jaw. If he could pick Nicoletta up and place her back on the pavement like a rag doll, he would. 'What about him?' His tone is less than friendly.

'He's already believed to be in possession of Lady Pat's half of *Among the Ruins*. Doesn't it stand to reason that he may now have Helen's? That he may have killed her in order to get it?'

Tom puffs out his cheeks with a scoff. 'Miss Sarto, that's a bit of a stretch.'

'Is it? I'm beginning to think it may be a very real possibility.' Nicoletta stops. She realises she is babbling.

'On what basis are you coming up with these findings?' Leonard's voice is soft, and dangerous, an apex predator ready to pounce.

'I don't have any solid proof yet. But my instincts haven't let me down before,' Nicoletta says, aware she sounds a little breathless.

'Your instincts. I see.' Leonard takes a deep breath as

though doing so causes him immense pain. 'Miss Sarto, my sister was a very difficult woman. That's a fact. The post-mortem results haven't come back yet with conclusive proof that she was murdered. Until then, we'll leave the fanciful theories to your colleagues in the popular press.' He begins to close the door, and Nicoletta ineffectually pushes it with her palm, but she's no match for his strength.

The door closes in her face with a soft click, and there's silence. After a moment, she admits defeat and walks back onto the main road.

Chapter Thirteen

Nicoletta is at her desk two days later when a call comes through from Garda O'Connor. The newsroom is quiet, the sounds of concentration rattling Nicoletta's nerves: typewriter keys clacking, biros clicking, the sound of Barney's knuckles cracking.

'There was no sign of foul play in relation to Helen Leonard,' Garda O'Connor says quietly, as though sensing she might have an audience. 'We've closed the inquiry.'

When he's rung off, she scrapes back her chair and heads over to the row of typewriters where Dermot's brow is furrowed in concentration.

'Fancy a sandwich?' she says in a low voice, aware of all the eyes and ears in the room.

He doesn't look up; nor does he miss a beat. 'Let me finish up here. See you in the Bailey in half an hour.'

She launches herself into the cool stairwell before anyone can ask her anything. When Dermot finally arrives at the Bailey, just off Grafton Street, over an hour has passed.

He gives her a hug and sits down; his forehead still creased with tension. 'Sorry, Nic. Got delayed.'

They order their food and drinks. While they're waiting for them to arrive, they sit in silence.

'Helen Leonard wasn't murdered after all,' Nicoletta says finally.

'I heard.' Dermot rubs his jaw. 'Maybe it's time you finally focused on the job you actually have.'

She bristles, not saying anything when their drinks arrive.

His face relaxes slightly. 'Look, I suppose just leave it now. It's done and dusted, right?'

'Not quite,' she says, taking a slug of her white wine spritzer. 'There's still the missing nurse, and of course the missing painting.'

Dermot frowns again, his face settling into a stony scowl. 'Nic, just drop the whole thing. I'm begging you.'

Nicoletta takes another gulp of her watery wine. 'Why? It's harmless.'

'It's far from harmless.' Nicoletta can see a faint pulse in Dermot's cheek.

'There's something else I came across.' Nicoletta fiddles with the stem of her glass. 'Antoine Rault, the art dealer you'd met. He was the one who sold Tom Leonard Senior the paintings originally.'

Nicoletta looks up. Dermot's face has gone puce. 'What the fuck are you talking about, Nic? Who's Tom Leonard Senior? And who the fuck cares?'

Nicoletta blinks, taken aback by his outburst. 'Tom Leonard, Helen Leonard's father. He gave a painting each to Helen and her half-sister, Lady Pat Dennehy. The Rook already has one. Or does he have both?'

Dermot pushes back his chair. 'Look, I have to get back. Do yourself and everyone else a favour, Nic. Come back to reality and go look after those children of yours.' He puts some money down on the table and walks out, just as the waitress arrives with their food.

After she's sent Dermot's food back with apologies, and picked at her Niçoise salad, Nicoletta ruminates on what's eating Dermot. She resolves to talk to him later. She wanders on to Dawson Street, dodging a throng of people gathered around a man busking with a guitar.

Rault's Gallery stands in a narrow Georgian building on Kildare Street, its name and purpose picked out in small gilt letters on the fanlight. Nicoletta rings a doorbell and waits as the shrill *bing-bong* reverberates through the silence. No one comes. A dull picture of people on horses with dogs out hunting in muddy greens and browns stands on an easel in the window, in front of a blue velvet curtain. It doesn't look like the sort of place to have sold a couple of multi-million-pound paintings, or to be connected to criminal activity. Nicoletta sighs and rings the doorbell again. But, then, how would she know what sort of gallery sold *Among the Ruins* to Helen Leonard's father? Or what a valuable piece of art should look like, for that matter? She presses the bell one last time and waits, attuned to every sound. She listens. She can finally hear a tread, very faint, but there's someone behind the door. She presses the bell again for good measure. A lock slides back with a click, and the door opens a few inches. A slight, middle-aged woman with dark hair in a chignon peers at Nicoletta with disdain.

'I thought you were a delivery driver. Are you?'

'I'm not.' Nicoletta smiles. 'Are you expecting one?'

The woman looks Nicoletta up and down. 'Yes. Which is the only reason I answered the door. Why the hell did you ring so many times?'

Nicoletta talks fast. The door hasn't closed yet. 'I'm looking for Celine Rault. Do you know where I could find her?'

The woman frowns, as though in pain. 'Why do you wish to know about *Dr* Rault?'

Nicoletta's cheeks ache from smiling. 'I'm a reporter for the *Sentinel*. Nicoletta Sarto is my name.'

The woman frowns again. 'What business could a reporter possibly have with Celine?' She starts tapping her foot, and the door begins to close.

Nicoletta steps forward, peering into the dark space beyond. 'I'd like to speak to Dr Rault about the *Among the Ruins* paintings.'

The woman's jaw is set. 'Well, she won't speak to you.'

'How do you know that?' Nicoletta smiles again. 'Have you asked her?'

The woman exhales through her nostrils as though such impertinence is beyond her. 'Because I'm her mother. That's why.' The door starts to close.

'Agatha? Agatha Rault?' Nicoletta speaks into the diminishing gap.

The door opens a crack. 'How do you know my name?'

Nicoletta bites the inside of her cheek. 'I'm sorry about your recent loss.'

The woman blinks. 'What?'

'Your husband. It must have been a terrible shock.'

The woman doesn't answer. An engine purrs in the background and a car door slams. The woman peers out. Nicoletta takes it as her cue to peer in. She catches sight of a plush blue carpet. The woman is staring at her all this time, her dark eyes boring into Nicoletta's face, as though memorising it.

'Can you tell me about the missing paintings, *Among the Ruins*?'

'No, I cannot,' Agatha Rault snaps, her lower lip trembling.

Nicoletta is almost knocked off her feet by a man carrying several rectangular-shaped parcels on his shoulder climbing the steps. He greets Mrs Rault with a grunt.

The man is admitted, and the door is slammed behind him. Nicoletta tries the doorbell again, before conceding defeat.

She ducks across the road onto Nassau Street, hoping she melds into the late morning stream of shoppers, sure-footed as a line of ants. She looks behind her a couple of times, the unsettling feeling of thinking she is being followed like some half-remembered dream. But there's hardly anyone down this way. She drifts towards Dame Street, passing a small newsagent shop at Andrew Street. She fancies a man with a wide-brimmed brown hat pulled low over his eyes reading a newspaper from the rack outside shoves the paper back into the pile when he sees her and starts walking behind her. She begins to stride so quickly she almost breaks into a run, but he turns left onto Exchequer Street, his pace slow, seeming to barely notice her, while she continues towards the newsagent's where she grabs a local phone directory. Nicoletta finds a listing for Nurses Direct easily enough. Mr and Mrs N. Ramsey are listed as the proprietors, with an address given around the corner on Dame Street. She doesn't have much time, and a vague plan has already formed in her mind, though she knows she has to wing it, like she generally does.

She smiles her thanks at the proprietress and exits the newsagent's with a jangle of bells. The skittish breeze from earlier has worked itself into a bluster. The nursing agency is at the top of Dame Street, in the opposite direction to which she'd come, behind a nondescript unvarnished street door. Nicoletta gains access by ringing an electric bell. A woman comes down and opens it, half a sandwich in one hand, a look of annoyance on her face.

'We weren't expecting anyone,' she wheezes, as Nicoletta follows her up a narrow stairway to a dusty, two-roomed office above. There is no one else around.

'Who's "we"?' Nicoletta asks, boldly.

The woman swallows the remainder of what she'd been chewing and swivels around to take a good look at Nicoletta.

'My husband. And co-proprietor of this operation.' She waves a hand without any apparent irony to indicate the grand vista of operations at Ramsey headquarters.

Nicoletta smiles. She's aware she should go on a charm offensive, but she's not sure yet if she can be bothered.

'Thank you,' she says, sinking down into the white plastic fold-up chair indicated by Mrs Ramsey, who huffs into place behind the desk opposite her.

'You're here now, pet,' Mrs Ramsey says, with a businesslike uptick in mood. 'What can I do you for?'

Nicoletta hesitates. She's not sure how to play it. But if she pretends to be a potential client looking for a carer for an elderly relative, Mrs Ramsey will give her the hard sell, and if she can just get her talking, she might be able to find out something worth knowing. She takes a deep breath and picks a lane.

'I'm looking for a carer for my uncle. This agency came recommended.'

Mrs Ramsey smiles, showing a smudge of lipstick on her front teeth. 'That's what we like to hear, lovey.' She grabs a piece of paper from underneath a magazine and writes something at the top. Nicoletta nonchalantly tries to see what it is, but Mrs Ramsey covers it with her hand.

'How old is your uncle?'

'Ninety-six.' Nicoletta gives a number at random. She remembers reading about an outbreak of influenza earlier in the year affecting the elderly. 'He had bad flu a few months ago and now we think he needs a bit of help, poor thing.' She volunteers the information while running her eye over her surroundings – discreetly, she hopes. A couple of black office chairs line the furthest wall. Two narrow windows open onto the street, their panes smudged and dirty. An electric kettle rests on the floor beside a wet patch on the carpet behind Mrs Ramsey's desk, beside which is a low metal filing cabinet. Mrs Ramsey herself doesn't seem to notice Nicoletta's surveillance, or if she does, she doesn't seem bothered.

'Indeed,' she says, looking up. 'That seems to be the way.

There was a vicious outbreak of influenza this winter. A few of our elderly clients were left in a bad way.'

Nicoletta smiles politely. 'We're looking for someone trustworthy to check on him every day, cook meals and do some light housework. They don't necessarily need to live in,' she improvises.

Mrs Ramsey writes some more and shoves the piece of paper loose into a manila folder, before taking out a few sparsely typed sheets stapled together. She swiftly closes the folder. She's wearing spectacles dangling on a long chain, Nicoletta notices, which she props up on her nose.

'Let's do the paperwork now, shall we?' She thrusts the stapled pages at Nicoletta and rolls a pen across the table. 'A form to fill in, and be signed, if you please.'

Nicoletta coughs softly. The room is chilled, despite the heat of the day. She folds her hands in her lap.

'We can do that later,' she says easily. 'Can you tell me a bit about your agency?'

Mrs Ramsey lights a cigarette from a pack in her drawer without offering Nicoletta one. She narrows her eyes through the smoke. 'I thought you said we came recommended.'

'Yes, that's right.' Nicoletta goes to stand up, her bag on her arm. Time is running out. 'I just wanted some more information. I am, after all, entrusting you to find someone to care for a beloved family member. But I can come back another time if now isn't convenient.'

The sound of the door below opening and shutting, and a tread on the stairs, stops Mrs Ramsey in her tracks. She stubs out the cigarette in a saucer and shoves the whole lot into a drawer, standing up and wrenching open a stiff metal-framed window overhead, fanning the air.

'You've got company,' Nicoletta murmurs, fascinated by this change in Mrs Ramsey.

'Neill,' she cries, smoothing stray strands of wiry hair from her face and sitting back down. 'I have a client.'

Nicoletta half turns as a man with a hangdog expression and sacks of excess skin under his eyes approaches the desk. Ignoring Nicoletta, he slams down a sheaf of papers on the desk. 'Waste of time,' he mutters. 'The bank is closing soon for lunch, and the manager wouldn't see me.' He storms off into a back room and slams the door.

Mrs Ramsey pushes back her chair and stands, giving Nicoletta a sheepish smile. 'My husband,' she says, in a loud whisper. 'He's been under a lot of stress.'

'I see,' Nicoletta says, though she doesn't at all.

The door behind them opens and Mr Ramsey comes out. 'I'm going out,' he snaps, grabbing the sheaf of papers, before hurrying down the stairs. The front door shuts with a slam.

Nicoletta coughs politely and walks slowly towards the stairwell. 'We can talk another time,' she says, nodding in Mrs Ramsey's direction.

'My dear, don't go just yet?' Mrs Ramsey says with a hopeful inflection. She sounds on the verge of tears. She hovers at the top of the stairs, her hand flying to her throat. 'I'll be back in one moment.' She follows her husband out onto the street. The door closes with a desultory thud. Nicoletta stands poised between wanting to go and wanting to have a poke around. She takes a step towards the filing cabinet when Mrs Ramsey charges up the stairs wringing her hands in apology.

'There you are, dear,' she beckons for Nicoletta to take a seat. 'My husband can be awkward. Now, you were saying something about your uncle?'

Nicoletta stays standing. 'Is Barbara Highfield available?'

Mrs Ramsey colours. 'No. Why do you ask?'

Nicoletta swallows. 'An acquaintance of mine recommended her.'

Mrs Ramsey cocks her fingers in the air for a moment, as though about to fire an imaginary gun. 'I'll have to come back to you on that. Miss ... ?'

Nicoletta hesitates. 'It's Sarto,' she says. 'Nicoletta Sarto. I'm a reporter for the *Irish Sentinel*.' Mrs Ramsey takes a step back. Nicoletta clasps her hands in front of her.

'Miss Highfield was Helen Leonard's paid carer, who came through this agency. Miss Highfield has vanished, along with a valuable painting.'

Mrs Ramsey flaps her hands. 'That can't be right. I told Miss Leonard's niece that she seemed like a highly competent young woman. She came with references.'

'Who interviewed Miss Highfield?'

Mrs Ramsey hesitates. 'My husband.'

'And what about these references you mentioned?'

Mrs Ramsey blows a stray wisp of hair out of her eyes. 'That's confidential.'

Nicoletta takes a step towards the stairs. 'Mrs Ramsey, I'm going to write about Miss Leonard's circumstances. She was a vulnerable elderly woman, who was open to being exploited. It's hardly a coincidence that this Barbara

Highfield and this painting going missing at the same time is a coincidence. You can co-operate, or not. But it might be more to your advantage if you do.'

'Very well.' She rubs her eyes. 'The reference just said Mrs something. It wasn't legible. Number three Chesterfield Buildings, Rathmines.'

'And did you speak to this Mrs something?'

Mrs Ramsey lowers her eyes. 'There wasn't time.' Her voice breaks and Nicoletta is horrified to see several fat tears roll down her cheeks in quick succession.

Nicoletta concedes defeat. She's not going to get much more information here. She hastily descends the stairs and when she's at the bottom step, she pauses. Mrs Ramsey is still sitting in the same position, sobbing silently into her sleeve.

Chapter Fourteen

Nicoletta walks briskly down Dame Street, before she can change her mind. She knows she doesn't have long. She digs around in her bag and finds some change, hailing a bus heading to Rathmines at College Green. She'll figure out the rest when she gets there.

The bus deposits her outside Rathmines library. A pub on the corner is rammed, people trailing onto the pavement. Music with a heavy bassline seems to vibrate from the very centre of the low building. A man leaning in the doorway wolf-whistles as Nicoletta picks her way past, and she brushes against the wall, feeling its calloused surface chafe uncomfortably against her bare skin. She jumps, feeling foolish, as a girl with dark hair swinging around her face walks into the pub. He wasn't whistling at her. The man laughs, whether at her or something else, and goes back inside, tossing a cigarette butt into a nearby flowerpot.

Nicoletta steels herself for what she's about to do. She goes into the pub and orders a lemonade. A tiny detail pops into her memory like an errant bubble of air. A story, in the *Sentinel*, she can't remember exactly when, about Chesterfield Buildings in Rathmines, a well-known block of flats belonging to the local authority. She breathes in, tucking in her stomach and filling her chest with air. She's probably mad, seeking out trouble, instead of minding her own business. She should've stayed home with Joan and the twins. But everyone is acting strangely towards her, including Dermot. Something compels her to down the lemonade, keep walking, past the man who wolf-whistled, and out onto the street. The sun is high, and a recent sprinkling of rain has washed away any residual ennui. Everything looks brand new: the road shines, the leaves glitter, the birds chirp with feverish excitement.

She keeps going until she reaches a triangular junction. She's almost at the end of the road, where pristine new-build bungalows and haughty Victorian mansions are mixed up together in untidy harmony. A narrow street juts abruptly to her left. It's more of an alley than anything – dark, unyielding. Nicoletta is glad it's broad daylight. Building work is taking place somewhere nearby but out of sight, and the noise goes through her head like a chainsaw. Out of habit, she looks back, but there's no one behind her. A faded sign at the top of the wall says: 'Chesterfield Street'. Looks promising, she decides. She walks several paces, past a multitude of graffiti, until she reaches a bockety iron gate that hangs crookedly off its hinges. Part of the sign has been ripped off, but Nicoletta can see 'esterfield Buildings' legibly enough to know she must be in the right place. She looks straight ahead. A wrecking ball slams into the side of one block of flats with a sickening clatter as though in answer. Most of the site is a sea of mud, except for one shabby red-bricked, flat-roofed block at the far-right-hand corner. Nicoletta half turns. She's come on a wild goose chase, that much is clear. She's about to go, when a very young man wearing a high-vis jacket and yellow hard hat comes whistling around the corner carrying a rolled-up newspaper under his arm.

'How's it going?' he calls cheerfully. He doesn't seem surprised to see her there, an onlooker.

Nicoletta smiles her brightest smile. 'Hi,' she says softly. 'Is this all for demolition?'

'Yep.' He puts a hand on the gate and wrenches it open with a squeal of rust. 'End of an era. The residents are being rehoused in the suburbs.' He winks. 'But there were a few who were doing us dirty and were refusing to leave. A few in block three, over there, if you can believe it.' He jerks his head to the right in the direction of the flats she'd presumed were vacant pending destruction. 'A few of the older ones,' he says, with another wink, before stepping through the gate. He holds it open and Nicoletta steps into the sea of mud. The builder squelches ahead with a slight raise of his hand and Nicoletta is left sliding her way towards a sign that points to block three.

The front door is smartly painted a glossy crimson. She raps lightly. There's silence, until the crash of the demolition work rents the air with a wallop of noise. Nicoletta stands, hesitating for a few minutes. There's nobody stirring behind this door, not that she knows what to say or what she wants to find out if there were.

She leans on one foot, sinking deeper into the mud, and

knocks again, louder this time. She looks left and right, then cups her ear to the wood. All she can hear is the smashing and digging of whatever is going on behind her. She backs away; her hunches can't always be bang on. She blames the exhaustion.

She looks down. The mud has coated her shoes, and the platform heels keep getting stuck. Not the most suitable footwear for what's turned out to be a building site. That isn't right, she decides. Things are constructed on building sites, whereas this is a place of destruction. She starts trudging back to the gate, before stopping in her tracks, looking behind her, scanning the churned-up mud for anyone she can talk to. Anyone at all. The builder she'd passed earlier is sitting in a forklift, his feet up on the steering wheel, a newspaper spread in front of him. Nicoletta walks up as far as the forklift, stepping up onto some breeze blocks that are standing uselessly on their sides.

'Excuse me!' she shouts above the racket.

The man looks up in alarm. 'What are you doing up here? It's dangerous.'

Nicoletta smiles. 'I'm looking for whoever lives in flat number three.' She points over to the sole surviving block of flats. 'From over there.'

The builder shakes his head. 'You shouldn't be up this far. There's stuff flying around. You could get yourself killed.'

'Do you know who lives there?' Nicoletta asks hopefully, ignoring his warning.

He closes his newspaper with a sigh and swings his legs around so they're dangling out of the driver's seat, facing her. She looks down, shifting her weight on the breeze block, which acts as a solid platform, then hurriedly focuses on his face. She doesn't want to fall face down into the mud.

'An old bird,' the man shouts.

'Pardon?' Nicoletta yells back.

'An old woman,' he returns the volley. 'She died last week,' the builder tells her with an impatient flap of his newspaper. The digging starts again. 'Which is why we're starting work now. We're way behind,' he shouts.

Nicoletta can feel a film of dust collecting at the back of her throat. She coughs, then clambers down from the breeze block. Her heels sink back into the murk. She raises a hand of farewell at the oblivious builder, before inclining her head. She's about to say something else, but he tosses aside the paper and shouts something to a thickset man in a fluorescent flak jacket near the demolition site. The repetitive drone of the digging starts again, and Nicoletta decides to beat a hasty retreat back to the pub where she'd bought the lemonade.

She inserts a stream of coins into the payphone near the toilets and dials the *Sentinel* number. 'Copy, please,' she says in a cheery voice that belies her real feelings. 'I've something about current nursing shortages and elderly people and their families being let down by negligent nursing agencies.' When she's finished her piece, she puts down the phone and walks outside. The evening is still bright, but a chill has seeped through the summer façade. It occurs to her that she's finally out of leads, and she has to put this whole story to bed. The thought sinks to the pit of her stomach like a stone as she keeps walking.

Chapter Fifteen

When she gets back to the office the next day, she throws herself into work: her new position as women's editor. Planning pages, sorting through correspondence, retrieving bundles of fading stock pictures from old files. Ann is quiet, acquiescing to every task with barely a murmur of dissent. When the city edition of the *Sentinel* comes in, Nicoletta scours it, but there's no mention of Helen Leonard's exhumation and the pathologist's subsequent findings. She thumbs through all that day's papers but they're scant on detail about Miss Leonard's exhumation. Miss Leonard merits a brief mention in the *Chronicle*, saying that the inquiry has been closed, but there's more about Miss Leonard's family connections than there is about her. Nicoletta notes the byline: Maureen French, from the Women for Choice meeting. She feels a pang of guilt that she's completely ignored her new role as secretary of the organisation in order to go chasing after this story. By lunchtime she has a raging headache, and a yearning to see her children. She can hear Barney's voice from the back bench, joking, calling instructions, swearing, and she immediately feels as though she wants to put some physical distance between them.

'Ann, just going home for lunch,' she calls. Ann continues flicking through the city edition, as Nicoletta slides on her jacket and makes a quick exit before Ann can say anything.

The house in Ringsend where Barney's mother lives is part of an estate of grey, identical, double-fronted pebble-dash houses owned by the local authority and built around twenty years earlier. Many of the older inhabitants, such as Joan, have since bought their homes from the council. Nicoletta waits while her eyes adjust from the bright afternoon to the gloom of the hallway. She pauses at the pay phone Joan has installed in the hallway for the lodgers she usually takes. Nicoletta is aware their presence in the house has stopped Joan from doing this in recent months and thus deducted from her income. She extracts a sixpence from the depository at the bottom of the telephone and slots it back in, waiting for the dial tone. Nicoletta asks the switch at the *Sentinel* for Barney King.

When he comes on the phone, his voice is brisk. It doesn't soften when he hears her name.

'Nic, what can I do for you?'

'I . . . just wanted to ask if you'll be home later?'

Barney clears his throat. It sounds like he's moving further away. 'Of course,' he says, his voice slightly muffled. 'Like I always am.'

'Right,' she says, twirling the cord around her finger in an endless loop. 'Will you be home for dinner?'

'Don't know yet. Didn't realise I had to account for my

every move. Look, Nic, I have to go, but we'll talk soon. Listen, mind yourself, all right?' The call cuts to the dial tone and Nicoletta hangs up. The coin slides straight out of the shoot. The same sixpence is used for all telephone calls in the house as Joan never gets the machine emptied. She doesn't want her lodgers to think she needs the money.

Nicoletta pauses, savouring the precious silence. A plane drones from somewhere far away. There's a distant crackle, possibly from the house next door. Some jumbled words, the familiar riff of a pop song. Then silence. She tiptoes up the stairs and raps lightly on Joan's bedroom door. There's nothing but the hum of the next-door neighbour's hoover. Or is it the radio being switched back on? She turns the handle on Joan's door, and it gives easily. Nicoletta pushes it and it swings open against the threadbare carpet, the discoloured brass handle meeting the wall with a tap. There's no one in the room, the bed made, the window slightly raised, with sounds from the street leaking through. She closes the door behind her and pauses at the bedroom she shares with Barney. She opens it, her heart leaping into her throat when she catches sight of two mobile cots underneath the window, which is similarly ajar, the broderie anglaise flounce Joan had covered them with fluttering in the breeze.

She strides over, stumbling on her own feet, but there are two solid baby shapes occupying both, wrapped in pink and cream blankets respectively. She bends down, not wanting to disturb them, yet feeling like she wants to snatch them up, tuck them under her coat and run out of this house. Rosa's pearly pink eyelids are fluttering rapidly, and Cara's cheeks expand with air pouches every time she exhales. Nicoletta puts a finger to Rosa's palm; it's cool. She closes the window as quietly as she can and sinks down at the end of the unmade bed, clenching her shaking hands. After a minute she goes downstairs. She doesn't need to look to know that there's nobody in the kitchen or the front parlour, which is hardly ever used. She sinks down at the bottom of the stairs and waits. When Joan bustles back in through the front door, her hands full with groceries, she starts when she sees Nicoletta waiting for her.

'Wasn't expecting you,' she says, by way of greeting, shutting the door quietly behind her. She puts down the bags and divests herself of her maroon cowl-necked coat, which has reddened her face and is clearly too hot for this weather. Nicoletta stands and relieves her of the carrier bags. She walks ahead, carrying them into the kitchen. She sets them down on the floor in front of the sink before she meets Joan's eyes.

'How long have you been leaving my children alone?'

Joan shrugs, extracting a carton of eggs from one of the bags. 'It was only for a few minutes while I did some messages.'

'They're tiny! The windows were open. Anything could've happened.' Nicoletta's voice cracks, and Joan gives her a sidelong look, before busying herself with putting everything away.

When the empty bags have been deposited back in a cupboard, Joan sits down at the table. 'I think we could both do with a cup of tea. Put the kettle on.'

Nicoletta does what she's told. When she's made the tea

and brought it over to the table, Joan indicates for her to sit down opposite. They sip in silence for a minute or two. Nicoletta doesn't want to be the one to break it.

'I'm too old for this,' Joan says eventually. 'They're tiny babies. There's two of them, for Christ's sake. They need their mother.'

Nicoletta blows miserably on her tea. A drop or two sprays out onto the waxed tablecloth. It's a cheerful motif of cherries spilling out of baskets. She dabs at the splotch with her thumb, watching it spread.

'What are you saying? That I should quit my job?'

Joan takes a slug of boiling tea and swallows it with obvious relish. The heat has wilted her tightly curled hair somewhat to the consistency of cotton wool and softened her face. She smiles, and her eyes crinkle up her whole face, a look that is pure Barney. She surprises Nicoletta by reaching across the table and patting her hand.

'They're hard work at that age. You should know that. And I think you need to rethink this whole situation.'

'I would if I could,' Nicoletta says, the bitter laugh stinging her mouth as she thinks of Barney's empty side of the bed, their lack of communication, her feeling of being trapped; that she's made the biggest mistake of her life so far. This job is her only lifeline.

Joan puts her mug down with a sharp little rap, her eyes glittering. She doesn't spill a drop. 'My son deserves better,' she says, her mouth making an indignant little upside-down semi-circle. 'But I'm glad you think it's funny.'

Nicoletta shuts her eyes in frustration, hoping to make up for the sarcastic laugh. 'I meant, I'm sorry it's so much on you,' she says quietly. 'And you do so much. Thank you. I wouldn't be able to do my job without you.'

Joan shrugs, picking her mug back up with both hands. 'Is it worth it?'

Nicoletta's shoulders rise, surprised with the pointedness of the question.

'Yes, it is. And I'm doing it for all of us. Not just me.'

Joan takes a gulp of tea. 'I said some harsh things the other day,' she says, changing tack. 'About you and Barney. I shouldn't have.' Her chest constricts with the saying, as though she's been physically holding on to some sort of misplaced guilt. Nicoletta acknowledges the apology by clearing her throat, wishing she could be somewhere, anywhere, but here.

'It's nothing,' she says, standing up. With relief, she hears one twin roaring her head off from upstairs, swiftly followed by the other. She ascends the stairs two at a time.

She stops when she gets to the top of the landing, and looks back, realising, too late, that her hands are empty. Joan follows with two warmed bottles under her arm.

Together, they settle the twins, a baby each. Nicoletta sinks down onto the bed, while Joan perches on a chair beside the vanity table, which is strewn with clothes from every available angle.

'I won't go back to work this afternoon,' Nicoletta announces. 'I'll stay here where I'm needed.'

Joan's drawn-on eyebrows shoot up, but she doesn't make any comment.

With the weight of the child in her arms, Nicoletta can feel her eyes grow heavy. She yawns.

'I haven't really been sleeping,' she says by way of explanation.

Joan nods. 'It won't be like this forever,' she says, her tone kind.

Nicoletta blinks back to being alert. This unexpected tenderness is overwhelming.

'You know,' Joan says. 'I can give you something for your sleep. A tablet. Something the doctor gave me.'

'It's only at night I need it,' Nicoletta says with a laugh. 'During the day I could fall asleep on my feet.'

'Put your head down and have a rest now,' Joan advises, whisking the girls back downstairs, leaving Nicoletta to scoot under the covers and squeeze her eyes shut. But sleep still won't come. She's considering going down and asking Joan for one of her sleeping tablets, when she thinks about picking up the phone and calling her mother. If Nicoletta turned up with the twins, her mother would have to take her in. Just until she figured out what to do. The next thought floats across to her before sleep steals up and drags her down into its murky depths. Would her mother ever forgive her?

Chapter Sixteen

Nicoletta is at her desk at the end of the next day, feeling glum. She pretends to rummage for something in her bag, angling her face away from Ann's scrutiny.

Barney and Price drift about trying to round up people for the pub. Nicoletta is thinking of making her escape back to the twins when the phone goes and Ann answers.

Nicoletta stands up, a surge of claustrophobia scalding her neck.

'Can I take one of these?' She indicates Ann's open packet of cigarettes on her desk. 'And this?' She grabs the lighter before Ann can object and dashes to the door.

'Where're you going?' Ann ends the call and picks up the cigarette packet, coming after her.

'Clippings library,' Nicoletta says, taking the narrow stairs two at a time. 'Have to check something.'

She reaches the door of the small archive but doesn't open it, instead sinking to her haunches and leaning against the wall, sticking one of Ann's cigarettes into her mouth.

'I thought you didn't smoke,' Ann says, sinking down

beside her. 'How the mighty have fallen. Trouble in paradise? Hate to say I told you so.'

Nicoletta's eyes swim with tears. She clicks the lighter in front of her face, taking in several mouthfuls of smoke before releasing them into the jaundiced corridor where they colour the air. 'Hate to say fuck off and mind your own business, but I just did.' She takes another drag off the cigarette until water fills her eyes and nose, and she splutters like a spaniel underwater. 'These things are disgusting,' she says with a laugh, when she finally stops coughing. Ann takes the cigarette back and smokes the rest of it. When she's finished, she pulls Nicoletta to her feet.

'Let's go to the pub,' she says, her spiky eyelashes dancing.

Nicoletta shakes her head, the tiled floor dusty under her feet. 'I've to get home.'

'Suit yourself,' Ann replies, lighting a new cigarette from the butt of the old one, the smoke settling around her shoulders. Nicoletta stifles a cough, before returning the wave and heading back into the newsroom. It is much quieter now, with people already drifting off to after-work drinks. She launches herself into the cool stairwell before anyone can stop her.

The wind has picked up when she steps out onto Burgh Quay, and she pictures Price and Barney in the pub, a flurry of empty pint glasses in front of them. The sun is a bobbing orange in the sky as she turns the corner to Westmoreland Street and shoulders open the door of Cassidy's with unnecessary force. The pub is dark and shadowy, despite the bright summer's evening leaking through the open door. It swings shut behind her with a bang, blocking out the errant light, and Nicoletta allows her eyes a moment to adjust. The crowd from work are spilling out of the snug inside the door. When Ann sees Nicoletta, she waves.

Nicoletta stands at the gap in the wood-panelled square of coloured glass, depicting a toucan with a huge orange beak drinking Guinness, a frayed banquette that has seen better days running its length beneath. One of the subs takes a sloppy nip of his pint and doesn't acknowledge Nicoletta. She tries to smile. 'Do you know where Barney is?'

The sub smirks and looks down into his drink. Price does the same, saying something under his breath that Nicoletta doesn't catch. She ducks away from them and approaches the bar. A strand of wispy sunlight strikes a mound of sodden beer mats at her elbow. It reminds her of her first date with Barney, in this very pub. She'd spilled gin and soaked the carpet. She'd thought herself invincible, at the start of something important. How young she'd been, how foolish.

The barman doesn't flick her a second glance. She's about to say something but decides against it. She scans the room. There are more people here spread out through the room, plenty of them, but none she recognises. Faceless suits, with open-necked shirts, ties stuffed into their pockets. She almost takes a run for the snug at the back, guided only by the bristling hairs on the backs of her arms, and pure spite. She knows what she'll find before she sticks her head in. But later she'll envy the past version of herself who still didn't have a clue.

A rumble of murmurs, a laugh. And Barney's sandy head, bent close to Brenda's, the fair-haired new copy girl who'd only started the week before. They're having some sort of tête-à-tête. He looks from her to Brenda, like a dog that's been caught eating the Christmas ham. How had he slipped into old habits without her realising, or caring? Nicoletta backs through the bar, flinging open the double doors and emerging into a cacophony of familiar sounds: traffic, birdsong, evening newspaper sellers plying their wares. She rounds the corner and stands on Burgh Quay considering what to do. She doesn't want to go home, but she knows she should. She waits. And then she hears the unhurried *slap, slap* of footsteps on the pavement.

'Nic,' Barney calls. 'Look, it's not what you think.' He reaches for her, and she pushes his shoulder; he stumbles and for one horrible moment she thinks he'll fall, that he'll hit his head on the heavy flagstones, that he'll close his eyes and won't wake up. What would she tell his mother? Liam? The girls? Maybe she'd go to prison. But then he rights himself and smiles at her, the one that swallows up his whole face, the one that undid her at the start of their relationship.

'I'm going home,' she says wearily. 'I'm taking the girls and I'm going home.'

He holds up his hands. 'What do you mean, taking the girls? Your mother isn't even speaking to you,' he calls. The words bounce off the buildings beside them until they're swallowed by the creeping dusk.

She wheels past him, walking home in jagged fury. She's grateful for the sudden unseasonal chill wind and drizzle which have emptied the streets. She doesn't know how she'll go back to work the next day, and the day after that, and just keep going. She could do with talking to Dermot, but even he's been acting strange. She thinks of Duffy, and Price, encouraging Barney at every step, while she'd been at home half crazed from lack of sleep. Rage shoots through her veins. She can just imagine Duffy waving away Barney's new intense friendship with a copy taker with a meaty hand and a wink. *While the cat's away . . .* Rage rises in her throat like bile, and she swallows it down. Hadn't that been how they'd started? The worst part is that she shouldn't be surprised. She'd somehow thought things might be different, now that they have the twins.

Shadows are swallowing every familiar thing as she walks along and gets closer to her destination. A dustbin minus its lid, at the end of the road, a gate off its hinges, the parked car of a neighbour – objects she hasn't paid very much, if any, attention to in daylight are all imbued with a heavy dread she feels from the pit of her stomach.

The light has almost completely faded by the time she steps through the door and into the hallway, but all the curtains and blinds are still open. Nicoletta can hear Joan upstairs settling the girls and hopes she herself hasn't been heard. She creeps as quietly as she can to the kitchen, expecting it to be empty, but Liam is sitting at the table reading a comic in the gloom.

'Hiya, love,' she says in surprise, turning on the overhead light. 'You'll strain your eyes.'

He doesn't answer, and she leaves him to it, boiling the kettle, tiptoeing around in the guise of making herself a cup of tea when what she's really doing is gauging how much she needs to take. The double pram by the back door and the Moses baskets in the corner are the only bulky items she has to move. She considers this. She could come back for them, though after tonight she doesn't want to set foot in this house ever again. She nudges the unwieldy pram wheel with her toe.

'What are you doing?' Liam asks suddenly, closing the comic. He doesn't meet her eye, leaning in his chair, crouching over the table.

'Just pottering around,' she says airily.

'You're not leaving, are you?'

Nicoletta sits down on the long side of the rectangular table so that she's diagonally opposite him. They don't look at each other. She grips the weak tea she's just made, and he picks at his nails. They sit in silence for a few minutes. Nicoletta can't outright lie to his face.

'What made you say that?' she finally asks. The tea is the same colour and texture as dishwater and the look of it makes her want to gag. She puts down the cup and looks at him directly.

'You're restless, I can tell. Mam was like that before. Where's Dad?' He looks up for a moment, then goes back to his nails.

'He's working.'

Nicoletta's brusque response is followed by silence. She stands up, stepping across the pram, unlatching the back door. 'I need some fresh air,' she says, bringing the half-drunk cup of tea out with her.

In the garden she leans against the trunk of a gnarled

rowan tree in the middle of the grass, the damp petals from the white summer blossom tickling her face.

After a moment, Liam slips outside after her, leaning against the side of the house, one foot against the rough, pebble-dashed wall.

'You're not going to leave, are you?' he asks quietly.

Nicoletta looks over at his hunched silhouette. He is as tall as an adult, yet his shoulders are trembling in the cool night air. He's just a child, she thinks, with agonising clarity, yet you can already see the man he'll become. He'll be a different one to his father. He pays attention to people, to the world around him, the people closest to him. That's why she feels so wretched for what she's about to do. It would be easier if he had Barney's thick skin.

She exhales slowly. 'We can't all keep living here on top of your gran. It's not fair. The plan was always to move out.' She hopes she sounds reasonable, yet she feels like the biggest heel going.

'Right,' he says. 'I see.' She knows he does see. But he's too young to understand any sort of explanation; it wouldn't be right or fair.

She quenches the dry earth around the twisted roots of the ancient tree with her cooling half-cup of tea. 'I've to go back in. Relieve your gran from babysitting duties.' The words catch in her throat. He doesn't follow her back inside.

The hall is still empty when she pushes the kitchen door partially shut behind her, reluctant to draw attention to herself with a click or an inadvertent bang. She creeps over to the phone and dials the number she knows off by heart.

'Sarto's Newsagents?' Her mother answers on the third ring, sounding slightly breathless.

'Mam, it's me. Nicoletta,' she says with low urgency.

There's silence on the other end of the line, but there's no slam of the receiver, no shouted expletive, which she takes as a good sign.

'Me and the girls need somewhere to stay for tonight.'

'All right,' her mother sighs, and Nicoletta hangs up before anything's said that can't be unsaid. She needs to get out of here.

She's halfway up the stairs when she looks back and sees Liam slumped in the doorway. He's half standing, half sitting on the brown swirly carpet, his shoulders rounded self-consciously. His arms and legs look too long for his body. He seems to her in that moment little more than an overgrown child again. She knows she can't change her mind.

'Liam,' she calls softly.

But he stands up and backs into the kitchen, slamming the door behind him.

Chapter Seventeen

Nicoletta comes to in the single bed of her old room. For a moment she is caught behind the heavy caul of sleep, and she doesn't recognise her surroundings in the semi-dark, her mind weighted by what happened the day before. On autopilot, she checks for the babies, but they're gone. Then she hears noise from next door. Her mother has taken the girls into her bed. Her father is away for a few days, helping out in his cousin's shop in Clonmel after his wife died. She opens her eyes and tries to focus on the day ahead. Joan's voice resounds in her head, competing with the gurgling pipes. *It's not as though you can ask your own mother for help, is it?*

She had hurt her mother, she knows that. She had exposed them all. Not only the Creightons, and all involved, but her own parents, and herself. How could she have done it? Even Dermot told her it was a bad idea. But she'd listened to that inner voice, the one that never steered her wrong. Does she still trust it? She lies there until light floods through the thin curtain, the realisation of what she's done catching her like a blade. Her mother has been unexpectedly brilliant, under the circumstances. She opened the door to her last night, and they stood in front of each other in silence for a few moments, before Daniela started cooing over the babies and making an appropriate fuss of her new grandchildren. She didn't once ask Nicoletta what had happened with Barney. Nor did she pass any comment on their arrival, other than to say, in a low voice, once they were seated at the kitchen table, their hands wrapped around steaming mugs: 'I'm glad you're here.' Even though her mother has been understanding and supportive, she can't just expect her to disrupt her whole life and take sole charge of the twins so Nicoletta can return to work. She'll have to think of some alternative. But in the meantime, she has to make a phone call.

She hauls herself out of bed. The paltry few hours of sleep have nonetheless made the world sharper and less fuzzy at the edges. She taps on her mother's door and pokes her head in. Daniela is sitting up in bed, bleary-eyed, with a baby under each arm.

'Thanks, Mam,' she says. She pauses. She might as well say it. 'Would it be okay if we stayed here again tonight? Just until I figure things out.'

Her mother's face momentarily crumples. Then she smiles, which radiates genuine warmth across her whole face. 'Of course. This is your home.'

Nicoletta can't speak for a second. When she recovers, she excuses herself to go back down to the kitchen. She seats herself at the table and contemplates using the phone. Her mother enters the room with both girls attached to her chest. She doesn't say anything, stretching out a blanket on the floor for them to kick their legs on. Nicoletta hunkers down beside them, feeling self-conscious in her father's old flannel dressing gown.

Daniela busies herself at the sink. When she turns around, her expression is resigned. 'I can mind them for a few days,' she says carefully, not meeting Nicoletta's eye. 'Until you get yourselves sorted out.' When Nicoletta stands up, her mother gives her shoulder an unexpected squeeze.

Daniela goes back upstairs, leaving the twins on their makeshift playpen. Nicoletta basks in the noisy silence of these familiar walls, with their predictable murmurs and occasional flutters. She seats herself back at the kitchen table, the room lit only by a small lamp on the table, and flicks through her contact book, dialling Dermot's number. It rings several times before he answers. His voice is heavy with sleep. He perks up when he hears her.

'What's going on?'

'I've left Barney.' The statement is bold; bolder than she feels. She can hear Dermot putting the phone down and slurping something before picking it back up.

'Where are you?'

'We're at my mother's.' Nicoletta doodles a skeletal drawing of a house on the front of her plastic-coated address book.

'Well,' Dermot says after an awkward pause. 'How are the girls?'

'They're fine. Mam's looking after them for the next couple of days. Listen, Dermot. I'm not coming in today, and possibly not for the rest of the week.' She draws an upright rectangle for a chimney stack. It looks like a child's representation of a house.

'Is that such a good idea, Nic?'

'I'm spending time with my children. Just like you advised.' She adds two squares for windows. They look blankly menacing. She hastily grids them into picture windows.

'Come in and show your face, Nic. Keep Duffy sweet.'

'Tell Duffy I have the flu. And, Dermot, are you all right?'

'Grand,' he says. 'Never better.'

'Right, see you,' she says, ringing off.

That evening, she walks around for hours with the girls in the double pram, thinking about what to do. When she comes back, she sees Barney's unmistakable red rust heap with the missing factory badge parked in a zigzag outside Sarto's Newsagents. She opens the hall door and hears Barney's distinctive bark, followed by a murmur of female voices of a slower tempo.

'I'm not leaving without my children.' A rustle of paper. 'From my solicitor. I'll call the Guards if I have to.'

She stays where she is until the kitchen door opens and Barney stands framed in the doorway, flanked either side by Daniela and her sister, Rossella. Daniela nods at Nicoletta, calmly, as though Nicoletta might be in danger of bolting back through the door.

'You've got a visitor.'

Nicoletta can't help but smile. 'I can see that,' she says, kicking off her shoes. Her feet are bare, and she scrunches her toes. 'Hi.'

'I see you're still wearing your engagement ring,' Barney says, ignoring her greeting, sitting down at the bottom of the stairs, leaving a swathe of space between them, barely glancing into the pram. He's wearing new, flared brown trousers that she's never seen before, with a tan jacket and a wrinkled, open-neck shirt.

His long legs are sprawled sideways, so his head is angled back at her. 'That's something, at least. Will you come and sit beside me?'

'We're not engaged anymore, Barney. It was all a mistake. Why did you come?'

His eyes widen in disbelief.

'My children are not a mistake. And I did what any man would do.'

He looks back at Daniela and Rossella, as though defying them to question his logic.

'Now, if you don't mind, I'd like a word alone with Nicoletta.'

Nicoletta nods at Daniela, who looks at Barney thoughtfully, her pink tongue sticking out between the crowded rows of little teeth.

'Why don't you both take a seat in the kitchen?' Daniela puts her hand on Barney's arm, a grey-brown curl falling into one eye. She blows it out of the way. Barney nods, uneasy.

'We'll leave you alone.' Daniela indicates for Rossella to follow her upstairs, and they lift a sleeping baby each as they go.

The kitchen is dark and musty after the chilly lamplit street. Barney sits down at the table. Nicoletta doesn't sit. Barney clears his throat.

'How are the kids?' His long fingers are laced together tightly in his lap.

'Fine. The same as they always were, not that you've ever shown any interest in them up to this point.' She turns around but he hasn't reacted.

'Get them,' Barney says to Nicoletta. 'I'll be in the car. Enough of this nonsense. We're all going home.' He scrapes back his chair and doesn't look behind him before he slams the front door.

Daniela and Rossella appear in the hallway, as though by unspoken agreement. Rossella leans against the banister, which stretches right up to the eaves.

'What am I going to do?' Nicoletta stands beside the sisters, and they look out, at the quiet street, at the familiar beaten-up red car parked just under the sign saying 'Sarto's Newsagents'. Barney sits in the driver's seat, drumming his fingers on the wheel. Nicoletta knows that he's being his usual stubborn self. He expects this to be quick, and painless. He hasn't come all this way expecting to go home empty-handed.

'Let him wait,' Rossella says with a contemplative flick of her hand. 'There are no winners in this game.' She tucks a protective arm around Nicoletta, though she is much shorter than her.

Nicoletta looks down at her, smiling. 'How long have you been here?'

'Oh, all day. I came to help your mother with the babies. We thought you needed some time.'

Nicoletta feels weak with gratitude. 'Thank you,' she says. 'You didn't have to.'

Rossella squeezes her arm, and they look out at the dusky street. The streetlamps glimmer in front of their eyes with promise, though Barney won't do them the courtesy of looking their way.

'He's always been a proud man,' Nicoletta says aloud, feeling the need to explain him away, though they are far beyond that.

Rossella keeps looking out, into the encroaching night, her arm around her niece, while Daniela has gone into the kitchen to put on the kettle. 'He is, all right. Who does that remind you of?'

Nicoletta sighs. 'Me?'

'Indeed.'

Nicoletta's eyes fill with tears and Rossella slips her arm around her waist and pulls her close.

'Hey now. It's not too late to fix this, if that's what you want.'

Nicoletta shakes her head so vigorously she fancies she can hear her teeth rattle in her skull. 'I don't think there's anything there to fix,' she says with a whisper, afraid her mother might hear. 'We don't know each other. Not really. We never did. It was a crazy thing.'

Rossella puffs out her cheeks with a hiss. 'All right. Well, you're going to have to talk to him.'

They stand together, looking out as Barney stares straight ahead, his profile rigid, the constant glow of his cigarette the only outward sign that he's agitated.

'I guess you're right.' Nicoletta pulls away from her aunt and grabs her coat from a hook. She pulls on some old, too-big plimsolls lined up in a neat row by the door. 'I'll be back in a minute.' Her voice to her own ears sounds steady, but she feels anything but.

Rossella purses her lips. 'If you're not, I'm coming out to get you.'

Nicoletta leans against the outer door, facing the lengthening shadows. She knows he's going to react.

She approaches the driver's door, weighed down by the unfamiliar, oversized shoes. It feels like how she'd imagine walking through snow. She sees him from here, tightly coiled, as though observing a stranger, cracking his knuckles, his mouth a straight line, a muscle going in his jaw. He rolls down the window and flicks out a gleaming butt. She sees that he hasn't smoked it all the way. It's not like him to waste a cigarette. He leaves the window halfway open. She takes this as a positive sign, in consideration of her weak lungs.

'Can we talk?'

He indicates the passenger side. 'Get in.'

She slides into the car and glances sideways at him, but he's still angled straight ahead, looking out through the windscreen. She follows his gaze. There's nothing in particular to see. A pair of dustbin lids which have come loose from their respective parts are rattling in the breeze; a middle-aged man walking a dog comes into view. He shoots them a curious look, before zigzagging over to the far pavement where the dog, a shaggy spaniel of some sort, cocks its leg on a protruding dandelion growing through a crack in the concrete.

She fully turns around towards him, until he faces her. He lights another cigarette and closes the window.

'I've given you some space, Nic, but you didn't even have the decency to tell me what you were doing.'

'I did,' Nicoletta says, not quite sure if she's heard him correctly.

'My mother's raging. You didn't even tell her. Not to mention Liam.'

Nicoletta feels her guts twist with guilt at the mention of Liam. Would she ever see him again?

Barney cracks his knuckles again and Nicoletta winces, which turns into a cough.

He stubs the cigarette out in the overflowing ashtray. 'You can't just take my kids away from me, Nic. That's not fair.'

She clenches her fists in her lap. This conversation is almost over, she's decided.

'Since when do you give a shit about Rosa and Cara? Can you even tell them apart?'

Two spots of colour appear high on his cheeks. 'They're my children. Of course I give a shit about them.' Spittle flies out of his mouth and lands on her fingernail.

She takes a breath, letting it sit there, not reacting. Not yet. 'Look, Barney. We're finished. I'm not coming back. It was all a mistake.' She glances up at him. 'I'm sorry.'

He doesn't answer for a moment, his face expressionless. 'Is there someone else?'

'No, no.' She puts equal emphasis on each word. Her hand is on the door when he slams his fist into the steering wheel. The horn blares with a burst of fury, and Nicoletta jumps, as does the man and his dog, who are loitering by a tufty patch of grass at the opposite kerb. The dog whines and strains on the lead at the unexpected noise.

'You'll be hearing from my solicitor,' he says quietly, as she opens the door and lets herself out. The adrenaline propels her to hold herself ramrod straight until she's back inside the front door. Then she sinks onto the old brown carpet and a pile of shoes, and sobs. It doesn't feel good, but it's right. She knows that. His pride is hurt, and he won't go without a fight. But she knows she can never go back.

Chapter Eighteen

Nicoletta is in the kitchen with the twins next morning when the phone peals from the shop next door. Her mother appears in the doorway, a frown creasing her forehead.

'It's for you,' she says. 'A man.' She nods briskly towards the open door that connects the shop with the living quarters. By unspoken assent, Daniela sits down at the table where Nicoletta had been. Nicoletta wraps her father's flannel dressing gown tightly around her and belts it at the waist, before ducking behind the counter and picking up the phone.

'Are you coming in today?' Dermot says by way of greeting.

'I hadn't planned on it. As I told you,' she answers tersely, aware of Mr O'Brien, one of their regular customers, taking his time weighing three loose oranges on the scales which juts out at a right angle to the shop counter. He eyes Nicoletta's attire and selects an apple and two bananas to add to the pile, before putting the oranges back. Nicoletta puffs out her cheeks unselfconsciously, echoing the way the babies sleep.

'As your colleague, and your friend, I think you should come in,' Dermot says in a low voice. She can hear someone shouting in the background. His voice sounds muffled, as though he's cupping the receiver with his hand. 'People are talking.'

'What're they saying?'

'That Barney kicked you out, that you're quitting the *Sentinel*. Get back in here. Put the story straight.'

Nicoletta's chest fizzes. 'That's not what happened at all,' she says, trying not to raise her voice. 'That prick.'

Mr O'Brien looks up from his fruit and tightens his mouth with a moue of disapproval. Nicoletta drops on the dusty floor and drags the phone down beside her.

'You don't have to tell me,' Dermot says, speaking quickly. 'I know what Barney's like. But Barney's here, and you're not. Therefore, he's setting the record.'

She tries to slow down her breathing as Mr O'Brien carries his chosen produce under his arms and dumps it on the counter. He peers over at her.

'Are you all right there?'

'One moment please,' Nicoletta mouths furiously. 'Listen, Dermot, I've got to go. I'll be back in the office this morning.' She drags the telephone cord back over to the corner of the counter and looks helplessly at Mr O'Brien.

He winks at her. 'Are you back working here? I seem to remember you were a dab hand at fruit and vegetables.'

'No, I'm the women's pages editor at the *Sentinel*,' Nicoletta says firmly, ringing up his items. 'I'm having some time off, visiting my parents.'

'Of course you are,' he says, taking ages counting out

the exact amount of money. 'Your exploits made very entertaining reading.'

Nicoletta doesn't rise to the bait. Instead, she smiles sweetly and puts everything into a brown paper bag, handing it over while he goggles as the tie on her dressing gown unravels. She hastily reties it and nods politely, waiting for him to leave. He leans an elbow on the counter, his thread-veined nose sniffing the air, like a rodent considering the change in wind direction.

'I'm surprised Daniela took you back in after what you wrote.'

'I beg your pardon?' Nicoletta raises herself up to her full height, horribly aware for the first time that she is barefoot on the tiled floor. Mr O'Brien takes her in, all of her, and leans back as though admiring his verbal handiwork.

'Himself was prepared to forgive you, but he's always been soft where you're concerned. Personally, if you were my daughter, I'd consider that unforgiveable. Wouldn't you?' He rocks backward and forward, waiting for a reaction, but when none is forthcoming, he scrunches the bag under his arm and raises his other arm in farewell, before sidling out onto the street to the chime of bells.

'Who was that?' Her mother is on her feet when she comes back into the kitchen.

'A colleague.' Nicoletta sits down heavily at the table, scrubbing her face with her knuckles. She looks up, aware she has been too brusque. 'He was checking to see if we're all right.'

'And are you?' Daniela's tone is flat, matter of fact.

'Yes,' Nicoletta says, standing up, managing a smile.

She leans down, the tips of her fingers brushing Daniela's shoulders, but she turns at the last moment, picking up some empty cups and carrying them over to the sink. Nicoletta blinks away the hurt. Just because she's taken them in for a few days, it doesn't mean her mother is a completely different person. A leopard doesn't change its spots. She thinks of Barney, and the doubts that had sprouted in her head, the seedlings of unease in the days when they'd been sneaking around. Why had she expected him to be any different once he was officially with her?

She takes a shuddery breath and clears her throat.

'Mam, thank you for letting us stay here. It . . .' her voice wobbles. Her mother's face remains impassive. 'It means the world.'

Her mother busies herself pouring hot water and soap into the sink, and piling dirty dishes on top of each other, so that the water rises and splashes onto the floor. Nicoletta presses on. She knows she can't keep avoiding the things they don't want to talk about.

'Mr O'Brien said just now that what I wrote was unforgiveable. Is he right?'

Her mother turns around slowly. Her expression is unreadable. 'You hurt us,' she says at last. 'But if it were unforgiveable, I wouldn't have let you stay here.'

Nicoletta stands, picking up a tea towel and gingerly retrieving one of the dripping cups her mother is stacking on the draining board. She swirls the towel around its rim and puts it in its usual place on the dresser.

'What I wrote was the truth,' she says at last. 'Why is that so hard to take?'

Her mother exhales in what sounds like a long hiss. 'We could all go around telling the truth. But the world doesn't work like that.' She stirs the water with unnecessary vigour, and more suds slop onto the floor.

'I'm sorry,' Nicoletta says, her head bowed.

Daniela slams a cup onto the draining board in reply, and Nicoletta abandons the tea towel on to the counter. She crosses the room, picking up each twin in turn and kissing their perfect little cheeks, before making her escape upstairs.

'I have to go to work, Mam. I'll be back soon.'

Her mother doesn't answer. When she comes back down washed and dressed, she hears a brisk tread in the hall. Daniela appears in the doorway, dressed in the uniform of Sarto's Newsagents, a dark blue overall with Sarto's embroidered on the breast.

'Where are the girls?' Nicoletta blurts, pulling on her jacket.

'With Rossella in the kitchen,' Daniela says shortly. 'They're being looked after.'

She goes into the kitchen to say goodbye. Her aunt Rossella sits contemplatively at the kitchen table, with the girls asleep in their Moses baskets at her feet; Daniela must have gone back into the shop.

Rossella places a finger over her lips, before breaking into a smile. 'Time for a cup of something?' she whispers.

Nicoletta hesitates. 'I'm late for work.' But she nods and makes two cups of strong tea for herself and Rossella, squeezing the hell out of the teabags. She sits down opposite her aunt.

Rossella blows on her tea. 'You've been a busy girl, these past few years.' She gives Nicoletta a warm smile. Despite being two years older than Daniela, she doesn't have all the worry lines Daniela seems to have developed. Nicoletta feels the familiar pang of guilt.

'That's my life,' she says, a touch on the defensive. 'I'm a journalist; it's what I do.'

Rossella raises her face to the stream of light flooding through the back window, rendering her hazel eyes almost yellow, reminding Nicoletta of a cat's. Then she leans forward as though she's decided what she wants to say.

'Maybe ...' she begins, a little cautious. 'That's what your life was. Before the arrival of the twins. But now you're a mother. And you have to look after your children.' The look on Nicoletta's face is mirrored in her aunt's sudden wince, and she reaches out a beringed hand to cover her niece's. 'I'm sorry, that was clumsy of me.'

'It's okay,' Nicoletta says in a small voice, as much for her own benefit as for Rossella's. 'I know what you meant.' She musters up some enthusiasm. 'And thank you for helping out with the girls. Are you okay to mind them today while I go to work?'

Rossella gives her a brisk nod. 'Of course. But this isn't an indefinite arrangement, Nicoletta.'

Nicoletta scrubs at her eyes with the back of her hand. 'I know. I didn't exactly plan this. To be left single and homeless with two tiny babies.'

Rossella withdraws her hand and scoops up her cup. 'Enough of the self-pity. Look, you've got a lot going on at the moment. That much is obvious. What I'm trying to say is, your priorities should be with them.' A downward motion indicates the Moses baskets. 'Sorting things out with your man, finding somewhere permanent to live, putting down roots.'

'Did my mother put you up to this?' Nicoletta asks with a clench of her jaw.

'She doesn't have to put me up to anything. I speak for myself.' Rossella unconsciously echoes her niece's jutted jaw, and Nicoletta wonders if it's a shared family mannerism.

'What did she say?' Nicoletta drains her tea.

'She wants to know how long you plan on staying here, what your plan is in general.'

'I don't have a plan. And if I did, this wasn't part of it,' Nicoletta says miserably.

'Well, maybe it's time you got one – a realistic one,' Rossella says. This time it's her turn to drain her tea. 'Trust me from experience, your mother means well, but her patience can only stretch so far.'

She flashes Nicoletta a conspiratorial smile, and grabs her hand, squeezing it, perhaps aware she has sounded too harsh.

'Are you going back to Barney?' she asks in an urgent whisper, as though Daniela could walk back in at any moment.

'No,' Nicoletta says simply. 'No way.'

Rossella drops her hand and bustles over to the sink with the cups. Her hands full of suds, she places a soapy hand on her niece's cheek, patting it gently. 'You are angry right now, whatever happened. But don't do anything you'll end up regretting.' She turns back to the sink and Nicoletta makes her escape through the hall before the twins wake up.

Chapter Nineteen

When Nicoletta enters the newsroom door, as quietly as she can, there's an unwelcome hush. For a split-second, reporters stop typing, like orchestral conductors with their fingers poised mid-air; a copy boy freezes halfway through his journey to the case room; two copy takers glance up from the bank of telephones and give each other meaningful looks, their eyebrows in danger of climbing into their hairlines. Nicoletta zigzags over to the features desk, her head down, like a sprinter, and busies herself hanging up her jacket, sitting down, rummaging through her in-tray.

'Morning, Ann,' she says without looking up from a sheaf of memos and unopened envelopes addressed to her.

Ann swings her purple-clogged feet off the desk beside her and gives a little squeal, whether with excitement, or rage that she's back, Nicoletta can't tell.

'Afternoon,' she says, scrunching up her chair closer to Nicoletta's. 'How are you?' Her warm breath smells smoky and sweet, and she pauses for effect, lowering her voice to a scratchy whisper. 'Are you and Barney over for good?'

Nicoletta flicks a glance at Duffy's office. The grubby

glass cube looks impenetrable, and the door is closed. 'Have you got a minute, Ann, for a meeting?'

Ann responds with a giddy laugh and proffers her open cigarette packet from beside a blue plastic pen holder. She's already got a lighter in the other hand.

Nicoletta accepts a cigarette. This is what the last few days have driven her to.

'Let's go up to the library,' she says, leading the way. 'We can talk there.' She nods at Duffy's office door. 'That could open at any minute.'

They're at the door when Barney pushes past them. He doesn't stop, closing the door behind him with a click.

'I'm just going to have a quick word,' Nicoletta says to Ann. 'Why don't we go out for a coffee? Wait for me in the Ha'penny café. I'll follow you down in a minute.'

Ann narrows her eyes speculatively. Or it could be against the smoke. She then retreats down the stairs at haste and Nicoletta knows she has offended her. But she's worried about Barney, despite everything. Guilt pools in her stomach like acid. Ann has reached the bottom of the stairs before she raises a hand without turning around.

'Don't stand me up this time,' she calls, passing back into the newsroom and banging the door behind her. Nicoletta goes after Barney, following him into the cardboard-lined room, her eyes and ears taking a moment to adjust to the peculiar monotone colour and quiet of this space. She finds him leaning against a rickety ladder in the adjoining room, inhaling deeply on a cigarette.

'You okay?' She crosses the room quickly. 'What's happened?'

'Oh, nothing.' He taps ash into an empty cigarette packet. 'Just came in here for a quiet moment. You know yourself.'

'I do, as it happens.' Nicoletta sits down on the floor. She's tempted to curl into the foetal position and catch twenty minutes' sleep while she's at it.

Barney cracks his knuckles and grinds out the cigarette, tossing the butt into the empty packet before putting the whole lot into his pocket.

'You sure that you're okay?' she asks, worried now.

He looks at her, an incredulous smile playing around his lips. 'You've got some nerve,' he says, spitting out the words, syllable by syllable.

'Some nerve, what? For showing my face in here? Is that what you mean?' she asks.

He doesn't answer.

She leaves the smoky room behind her and gratefully escapes to the Ha'penny café for a catch-up with Ann, a raucous hour of planning pages and stepping around the subject of Barney with the stealth of burglars in the night. After her meeting, she returns to her desk and sits there quietly for the rest of the day until it's time to go home. Then she walks to her parents' house on Richmond Road in Fairview. A place to which she never thought she'd be so grateful to return.

Her mother is sitting in an armchair in the kitchen, the girls playing with colourful plastic rings on a blanket on the floor, which must've been donated by Rossella and her many grandchildren. Nicoletta's guilt is compounded by two purple rings of exhaustion encircling her mother's eyes. A look passes between them, unspoken, though clear as day. *Get yourself sorted out.* There's only so much her mother can help her.

'There's dinner for you. In the oven,' Daniela says by way of greeting.

Nicoletta nods her thanks. She's so tired she can barely speak. She doesn't ask if Barney called; she doesn't want to know. She'll think about it all when she's had a chance to sleep. She picks up each baby in turn and holds them close. Cara grabs a fistful of her hair, and she closes her eyes and breathes in her clean baby smell.

'I'll put them to bed now, Mam. You have a rest.' She gestures to Cara, who is curled into her chest. 'Thank you for all this.'

'Have your dinner first,' Daniela says, waving away her gratitude.

Nicoletta walks over to the oven and takes out a plate covered by another plate, on which is piled a chicken breast dried out by the heat, some mashed potato and some shrivelled carrots. She sits down at the table and devours the meal, both from outright hunger, and partly because she's conscious that her mother needs an immediate break; she looks worn out.

She stands up and rinses the plate at the sink, before picking Rosa up and stroking her blonde downy head, while Daniela picks up Cara.

'I'll give you a hand,' she says, following behind.

They're halfway up the stairs when there's a short knock on the door. Nicoletta looks behind at her mother, whose face is lined with horror. 'Are you expecting anyone?'

Nicoletta suspects it might be Barney, come to make a last-ditch attempt to get her to come back. She passes her mother to go to the door.

It's Garda Peter O'Connor, looking shy and solemn as a little boy in his communion photograph on the doorstep. He's wearing dark corduroy trousers and a pale shirt. Nicoletta can count on one hand the number of times she's seen him out of uniform.

'Garda O'Connor,' she says with a stammer. 'What are you doing here?'

'Peter is the name,' he says with a slight wince. 'There's something I thought you might like to know.'

'Oh?' Nicoletta isn't sure what to do. 'Why don't you come in?' She opens the door to let him pass and leads him back into the kitchen. Daniela is rooted to the stairs, and more lines have joined the horrified expression to embed her face in a grid of disapproval.

She indicates for O'Connor to sit down at the kitchen table, which he does, with an awkward scrape of the chair. 'I'll be with you in a moment,' she says, darting back to the stairs.

'Who's your man?' her mother asks with pursed lips, as though the words themselves taste sour.

'Oh, just a colleague,' Nicoletta says with an attempt at being airy. 'He won't stay long.'

Daniela wordlessly takes Rosa and carries both babies upstairs. When she's reached the landing, she calls down, the words meant for Nicoletta's ears only, soft as eiderdown.

'Next time you make your bed, you'll damn well lie in it.'

O'Connor is sitting perfectly still at the table, his arms folded against his chest, waiting for her to come back. He doesn't give any indication of having heard what her mother said. He clears his throat, as though he's been mentally rehearsing what he's going to say.

'I'm sorry for intruding like this. But trust me when I say this couldn't wait.'

'I do trust you,' she says, simply. She hides her flushed cheeks by bustling around with the kettle and clattering tea things from the draining board. She finds some chocolate digestives in a cupboard and fans them out on a plate, bringing everything over to the table where O'Connor accepts a steaming mug with gratitude.

'Tell me.' She takes a bite out of one of the biscuits and lets it crumble in her mouth. 'What's going on?' She stands up again. 'Wait,' she says, grabbing her bag from the other side of the room. 'I've a feeling I'm going to need to take notes.'

She opens her notebook, pen poised.

He takes a sip of tea, without adding any milk or sugar. He places the mug carefully down in front of him before he answers.

'We've found Barbara Highfield, Helen Leonard's missing nurse,' he says.

The nib of her pen pierces the page. 'Where?'

'In the Dublin mountains. She's dead. She'd been shot once in the back.'

'Jesus.' Nicoletta takes another bite of biscuit, and it feels like dust on her tongue.

'She was also known as Meredith Field, aged twenty-one,

of Holloway House, North County Dublin. Her parents have identified her body, which is currently being held in the city morgue.'

'So, how do you know she was calling herself Barbara Highfield?' Nicoletta studies his face; she still hasn't written any notes. His eyes are clear grey pools. She thinks he's being straight with her; he's not playing games or deliberately hiding anything.

'Miss Field's parents had reported her as a missing person. Her description matched the missing nurse you'd been writing about, and Miss Louise Leonard, Helen Leonard's niece, has confirmed this was the same nurse who lived in Miss Leonard's home and was working as her paid carer. So did Mrs Ramsey, the owner of Nurses Direct, the agency Miss Leonard hired her from. I just wanted you to know.'

'This is a lot to take in,' she says.

O'Connor gives her a brief nod and cradles his tea in both hands. 'You'd better believe it, Miss Sarto,' he says. 'The other thing is that we've found one half of the pair of paintings. *Among the Ruins.*'

'Which one?'

O'Connor nods. 'Miss Leonard's half. It was found close to Miss Field's remains.'

The curtains are still open, and the light has faded to shadows. Nicoletta is horribly aware of how intimate this might look at a glance were her mother to walk in. She breaks the thread of the conversation by standing up to snap on the overhead light. Something tells her she'll have to visit Holloway House. The shadows recede and the new electric light casts a clinical, more businesslike glow over proceedings, banishing the intimacy of earlier.

'Why do you think Meredith Field was killed?' she asks, sitting back down, taking another biscuit.

O'Connor drains his tea. 'We think she was killed for the painting. She was a History of Art student at UCD. An heiress, one of these rebels without a cause. She even stole valuable artworks from her own parents, but they managed to keep it out of the papers.'

'Ted and Eliza Field,' Nicoletta says, remembering the news clipping. 'Was she linked to The Rook?'

'We think so,' O'Connor says.

Nicoletta sighs. 'I appreciate you coming to tell me. But where do I come in?' She's not sure if she detects amusement in his face at her resigned tone.

'That's not the Nicoletta Sarto we know and love,' he says with a laugh. 'This is your story, after all. I thought you'd be eager to get an exclusive on this. Before it leaks into all the morning papers.'

She can feel the familiar gallop of her heart racing under her clothes. She shakes her head. She doesn't know if she's able for this anymore, but she can't say that, not when he's come all this way to do her a favour.

'You don't have to do anything with it,' O'Connor says, standing up. 'It might be more than your job's worth. You mightn't want to ruffle Duffy's feathers anymore. But I know you cared about Miss Leonard. And I wanted you to be the first to know.'

Nicoletta follows him through the hall and out to the front door. She opens it and he turns to go.

'Why did you do this?' She stutters on the words like a stopped clock.

Their eyes meet for a fraction of a second before he turns with a wave. 'Because I trust you,' he says, stepping into the dusk and zipping up his jacket.

'Peter,' she calls into the heavy air. She's never called him that before. He turns around, his hands in his pockets. He doesn't move back towards her. She closes the door behind her and moves towards where he is. 'I'll walk you to your car,' she says.

He has parked at the end of the road, and they walk along in heightened silence. A football rolls in front of them, and O'Connor kicks it back to a trio of boys playing in the road. The sun has sunk below the horizon, and maybe Nicoletta feels emboldened by the cover of the smudged sky. He takes his key out of his pocket and unlocks the door.

'Good luck with the story,' he says, ducking into the car. He doesn't close the door or start the engine. On impulse, she gets into the passenger seat, and they sit in companionable silence for a moment or two before she breaks it.

'Why'd you really come and tell me all this?' She attempts nonchalance, but her hands are twisting in her lap. 'Why not just ring Barney or someone like that?'

O'Connor looks at her. His gaze is so direct, and clear. There's nothing hiding behind his eyes. 'Barney has his way, and I have mine,' he says, with a diplomatic cough. 'That's all there is to it.'

Nicoletta can't help but laugh. 'That's one way of telling me you don't like Barney.'

O'Connor closes the driver's door and turns right around to look at her. 'Do you?'

Nicoletta places her hands on the dash in front of her. 'What sort of question is that? He's the father of my children.'

He places his hands on the steering wheel, averting his gaze from hers. 'And yet, here we are.'

'Yes,' she replies. 'Here we are.' She clears her throat. 'In answer to what I think your question was, my life with Barney is over. I'm not going back.' She looks at him. 'But I have to figure out my next move. Especially as I have the twins.'

'I understand,' he says. 'I think.'

'So.' Nicoletta crosses her arms and looks straight ahead. The football players are right in front of them. Their ball hits the windscreen with a thwack and O'Connor mutters under his breath. 'Are you here because you trust me? Or are you here because you like me?'

He surprises her then, turning right around to face her, and grabbing her hand in his. 'Can't it be both?'

She smiles, and her smile mirrors his. It lights up his entire face, as though he's been spotlit from within.

'I'm glad it's both,' she says.

He doesn't let go of her hand. 'I'll be patient,' he says quietly. 'Because I understand it's not as simple as it might've been previously. But I want you to know that I'm genuine.'

'I know,' she replies. 'I've always known that, from the first moment we met.' She trails her fingers against his smoothly shaven cheek. He lets go of her hand, cupping her cheek with his large, square hand, for the longest time. Their lips meet in the softest kiss, and it feels as though they are momentarily suspended between worlds.

She pulls away first and gets out of the car, closing it behind her with a gentle click. The boys with the football are standing in front of the car, and when they see her, they break into applause and cheers. She feels mortified and she walks back up the road without a backward glance. It's not until she hears the engine start to purr and then roar away that she'll permit herself to look back at the spot Peter's car has just vacated.

Nicoletta goes back into the house and sits down heavily at the kitchen table; she can't hear her mother with the twins upstairs. Perhaps they're already asleep.

She writes up her notes from memory, then grabs her notebook, and with shaking hands she picks up the telephone receiver in the hall, dialling the number of the *Irish Sentinel*. 'Copy, please,' she says to the disembodied voice at the other end of the phone.

Chapter Twenty

The next morning, a Saturday, Nicoletta tiptoes downstairs and opens the shop so she can use the phone before her mother wakes.

She dials the *Sentinel*'s number by heart and asks for Dermot. His voice is muffled; she imagines him holding his hand over the receiver, to hide from prying ears.

'You're the talk of the place,' he says, half admiringly. He clears his throat.

'Can you pick me up when you've finished your shift?' There's a hopeful upwards inflection at the end of her question. 'I need you to drive me somewhere. Plus, it'd be nice to see you.'

'You know I can never say no to you,' he says, ringing off with a hoarse laugh.

The doorbell chimes later while Nicoletta is feeding the twins. Her mother appears in the kitchen with a frown.

'It's for you,' she says. 'Another man.'

By the time Nicoletta has dressed and arranged to leave the babies for an hour or so, Dermot is irritable. She can tell before she gets into the car where he's waiting for her.

She doesn't bother asking if he wants to come in and meet the twins, or her mother and aunt. He doesn't speak until they're circling St Stephen's Green. He's been circumspect, thus far, choosing his moment, she suspects. It comes when they're at the Earlsfort Terrace side of the Green, hovering beside the pavement. A car slows, then skids around them, beeping its horn. Dermot swears under his breath and puts his hazard lights on. They blink with an air of impatience.

'Still love to make an entrance, I see,' he says, a little gruffly.

'Thanks for coming.'

'Where'd you want to go, then?' His tone is gentle. 'I thought we could go for lunch. You could do with some feeding up.' A young couple walk by hand in hand, the girl's hair almost covering her bell bottoms, her face turned towards her companion as he leans in to hear whatever it is she's saying. They might be students at the nearby university, though the term is over; maybe they're repeating exams. He laughs and tucks a palm around her waist. Nicoletta feels a twinge of envy. She remembers how her father had encouraged her to study there but it never happened in the end. She snaps back to the present and drags the overflowing file out of her bag.

'Fairfax House in Blessington?'

Dermot turns right across as though he wants to shake her. 'Where the owner of our newspaper lives? Nic, are you mad? They'll never talk to us, and we'll be in a steaming pile of shite.'

Nicoletta grips the file from her bag in both hands. 'The

owner of the other part of the *Among the Ruins* painting, don't forget.'

Dermot opens a window and lights a cigarette. 'Tell me to mind my own business, but what you're doing is avoiding reality.'

She exhales shakily. 'Thanks for the tip.'

Her acidic response is not lost on him. He reaches back and pats her shoulder. 'Look, I really don't think you should doorstep the Dennehys. Besides, they're probably abroad. They only live in Ireland one or two months of the year.'

She shoves the file back in her bag. 'What about Holloway House in North County Dublin?'

His face clouds as he indicates right and pulls off into traffic, narrowly avoiding a motorcyclist. 'That story you wrote last night? You want to talk to the dead girl's parents? Nic, no way. I'm not taking you.'

'Yes,' she says with a hiss. She rolls down her own window and breathes in a mouthful of exhaust. 'Don't tell me Helen Leonard's painting going missing doesn't scream The Rook's handiwork,' she says.

They've stopped at a set of traffic lights. Nicoletta inclines her head; Dermot is looking back at her with strange intensity. She thinks she can detect something indiscernible in his eyes. Maybe pity. Or alarm.

'It screams you need a good night's sleep,' he murmurs, as the stream of cars winnows forward. 'Look, Miss Sarto.' His tone is artificially jovial. 'Let's go to Groome's on Cavendish Row. We'll have the mixed grill and a drink or two. I'll drop you home after. How does that sound?'

She sighs inwardly. It does sound nice. Sort of like old times. But there's something not quite right, she can't put her finger on it. All she knows is that she has to try and speak to Meredith Field's parents while the story is still fresh. This could be her only chance. She decides to play the ace in her pocket.

'Dermot, you never came to see me when the twins were born. You never contacted me when I was on maternity leave. I thought we were better friends than that.'

His face remains impassive as they approach another set of traffic lights. He stops. 'I told you, Nic. I'm not really a baby person. And besides, Barney mightn't have liked it.'

She bites her lip. 'So, it was about Barney? That's where your loyalty lies?'

He gives her a sideways glance before the road draws his gaze straight back ahead. 'Not everything is about you, Nic,' he says quietly.

'Of course not. But having two babies and returning to work sort of is about me? Me and Barney, of course. Though more about me.' She tries to make light of it, but she can't hide the hurt which has crept into the back of her throat. They sit in silence as he circles back around by Amiens Street Station, getting ready to do another loop.

'I came to see you because you asked me. I didn't come to get a hard time,' he says finally, waving to another driver who has let him pass a parked bus.

'I just thought ...' she falters, looking out the window at the grey streets and wispy grey sky.

'You just thought what?' He looks genuinely confused.

'I just thought we were better friends than that. I

thought we knew each other better. After everything that happened.' She lets the weight of the last part hang between them. He scrubs his eyes. She can see his left eye is bloodshot.

'What's going on with you?' She twists her hands in her lap. He doesn't answer. 'You're the one who needs feeding up, Derm,' she says, as gently as she can.

He flicks her an irritated glance and pulls into a space behind a parked bus, putting his hazard lights on.

'Jesus, what do you want from me, Nicoletta? Yes, we are bloody friends. I'm here, aren't I?' He tries to rake his fingers through his hair, as if by force of habit, though it's gelled down flat. He gives it a pat instead.

'Why don't you just drop me home?' She gives him a grim smile. He doesn't return it.

'Hey, come on, don't be like that,' he says finally, opening a window and lighting a cigarette. 'There's no need to be so intense about everything.'

'There's no need to drop me home,' she says at last, her voice in her boots. 'I can easily walk from here.'

'Ah, Nic.' He grabs her hand in both of his and squeezes it painfully close. 'Don't be like that. Of course we're friends. I've ... Things have been quite tough for me lately. But I'm okay. I'm okay,' he repeats, checking in his rear-view mirror. The bus has pulled off and an angry driver is gesticulating behind them. Grumbling, he turns off the hazard lights and heads out onto the road.

'Where're we going?' Nicoletta asks. She looks at him expectantly.

'You tell me!' Dermot says, tapping ash out the window

and driving at unnecessary speed towards the North Strand.

Nicoletta looks at him. 'I don't want to go home just yet,' she says. She can feel her eyes filling up again and she curbs the tears with the heel of her hand.

He turns to look at her, his face contoured with panic. 'Jesus, what's wrong? You're upset. I've made you cry. Brilliant. Just brilliant.'

She shakes her head. 'It's not you, Dermot. It's everything lately.'

He swallows, as though the sensation is excruciating. 'Tell me where you want to go. I'll bring you wherever you want in the world. Your choice.'

She looks straight ahead. 'Holloway House. Home of Meredith Field's family.'

They don't speak for the rest of the journey.

Chapter Twenty-One

The familiar fizz of nervous excitement spikes at the city limits, where the asphalt and concrete of brand-new housing estates give way to dark swathes of green. Nicoletta isn't sure what to expect, or even if they'll get past the front gate of Holloway House. Her hands tremble as she checks her face in her compact. The dark circles under her eyes look more pronounced in the unforgiving June light. Dermot doesn't say a word, which makes her nerves even worse, like a fist clenched in her stomach.

She looks up. They've reached a large black gate. Dermot glances sideways at her, his face closed and impenetrable.

'I'm staying here,' he says. 'You're on your own, Nic. This is a bad idea. If you've any sense you won't set foot outside this car, and we can go home now.'

He pauses, during which time Nicoletta takes a deep breath. 'Can you stay here for a minute? I'll try the gate.'

'Jesus, Nic,' Dermot says sharply, before reluctantly cutting the engine. There's deathly silence; nothing but the birds singing. Nicoletta stands on the grassy verge, cow parsley and buttercups making it feel very rural. She's sure she can smell manure. It should be a soothingly picturesque scene, though her heart is hammering in her chest. She tries the big black gates. They don't budge an inch due to several large padlocks securing them in place.

A high stone wall adjoins the black gates of Holloway House and runs as far as the eye can see on either side. Nicoletta picks the side running away from the direction they'd come from and starts following it. There has to be a way in somewhere. The road is narrow, and she sticks closely to the verge in case a car appears unexpectedly at her side. Eventually she comes to a gnarled stump. It must be the carcass of an ancient tree, as old as the original house, culled to make way for others. It appears high enough to use as a launching platform, its precious few branches still curling out at precarious angles in wispy entrails. Nicoletta heaves herself up on to its base. A sapling has rooted itself in the dead tree and budded little pea-green leaves. The wall is rough against her palms. She crouches on the wall, in her flared jeans and sweater, hardly daring to peek over at where she'd land. The ground below is carpeted with rotting foliage and brambles. It's a wooded area, with tall straight trees spaced evenly apart. Nicoletta hears an engine growl in the distance. She steps back onto the flattened old tree and lets herself drop as gently as she can onto the rotting undergrowth on the other side. She turns over awkwardly on her right ankle, the one she hurt before, on the way to The Rook's house, before righting herself and standing up, brushing down her jeans.

She looks around, hoping to see the house in the distance, or some sort of outbuilding: a landmark to walk towards. But this place must be so big that the wood goes as far as the eye can see. She starts walking uphill, dragging the bad foot with a slight limp over the uneven soil. Eventually the trees start to thin out into slightly boggy ground. She stops, her shoes squelching in protest, as she thinks about where to go next. A flat, silvery line has materialised into the horizon ahead, as though just cast there by some playful woodland sprite. It's the Irish Sea.

Nicoletta wades forward, the ground slightly marshy here, the sun low and soft in the sky. She is momentarily filled with a feeling of déjà vu, as though she is standing at the edge of the world, the only person on earth. She looks down over the expanse of land unfolding below, mist rising off the water in lazy dribs and drabs, like a patchwork tablecloth. It ends with a house. It sits, exuding entitlement, as though it has always been there. Three stories high, hunched by a huge, pillared portico over the front door, it goes on lengthways as far as the eye can see. Mullioned windows wink at her in the morning sun. She stops counting them after ten. There's a clock tower at the left-hand corner, scorched and jagged from a recent fire. That must be the arson attack that was reported in the papers, for which The Birds were believed to be responsible, but it was never proved. No one has so far registered her presence. She cups her eyes with her hand, slowly scanning the building, taking in the once-magnificent stonework, now covered in patches of moss, the crumbling chimney stacks, the crows and jackdaws lined up on the roof looking out over their terrain. It doesn't immediately strike her as the kind of place from where expensive *objets d'art* might be looted. From here, she doesn't know what to make of it. It reminds her of the carcass of some once powerful animal, now alive with insects, ripe with decay. Beautiful by its own imperfect metric.

At the summit of an artificial peak, a lawn starts to roll down towards the house. Nicoletta is still mired in soggy ground, drenched as far as her knees. She lifts a leg, and the ground tries to suck it back. She's knocked off kilter, putting out her right hand to steady herself. When she stands up, she cups her eyes again. She looks down; her legs are streaked with mud. She knows she must look a fright, but she is anxious to speak to whoever she can before she gets kicked out of here. Not a soul disturbs her as she walks across the dew-covered lawn. She passes the fire-damaged clock tower, and what looks like an added-on wing, lower, more modern. She comes to a set of three granite steps, which lead to a light-coloured wooden door. There's no bell or knocker. She takes a deep breath before rapping briskly, the wood making her knuckles smart. She holds her breath. After a minute or two, she hears footsteps.

A man opens the door, wearing a button-down brown cardigan over tight-fitting beige trousers and what look like riding boots. He looks slightly alarmed when he sees Nicoletta's bedraggled state, the muddy rivulets streaming out of her shoes.

'Hello. Could I speak to Ted or Eliza Field, please?' she asks with a shiver. The breeze is starting to get to her.

'Not now,' the man says. 'Haven't you heard the news about Meredith? They're devastated.'

'Yes,' Nicoletta says. 'I'm very sorry,' she continues.

'I'm a reporter for the *Sentinel*. I've come to ask about Meredith.'

The man's expression is mild, his eyes pale like boiled sweets, but he's still standing there, barring her way.

'I hope they catch whoever is responsible. Such a beautiful young girl. It's tragic,' she adds quickly.

'They won't,' he says shortly, stepping out beside her and closing the door behind him, before locking it with a key from his pocket.

'I believe Meredith was found with a valuable painting. The other half is still missing, believed stolen. Have you heard of *Among the Ruins*?'

He returns the key to his pocket and starts walking, then stops, indicating for Nicoletta to catch up.

'I really can't talk. I've to go and bring some horses in. I'll walk you out, Miss ... ?'

'Sarto,' Nicoletta replies quickly.

'Miss Sarto. I can't tell you anything. And you should go.'

He bids her a curt goodbye at the entrance to a wide U-shaped yard, with horses whinnying and whickering to each other. The sound is comforting, though Nicoletta isn't sure why. She stops and listens. She can hear someone singing. The voice is soft, female, perhaps it's not meant for public consumption. Instead of taking the path back around the perimeter of the property which leads to the curving driveway, back to Dermot and the girls, she follows the man who'd let her in, taking a sharp left, through a yellow bricked archway and into the yard. All the stable half-doors are closed and horses' huge curious eyes blink at her, intrigued by this new sight. The singing is coming from the furthest door at the end. It sounds like a lullaby; the kind you'd sing to a colicky baby. There is no horse's head sticking over the door, and Nicoletta thinks she catches the refrain of 'Rock-a-Bye Baby'. She is drawn towards it. She boldly walks up to the stable door and raps on the freshly lacquered wood. The singing stops. Nicoletta peers over the top and sees a shining flank. She can't see anything else. The horse stomps over and sticks its head out, nuzzling the top of her head. Nicoletta jumps in alarm. Horses are nervy, unpredictable creatures in her limited experience. She doesn't know what to do.

'Hello? Is anybody there?' she asks, her voice echoing in the enclosed space like a bell.

'You're scaring her,' an indignant, girlish voice says from the straw-filled cavern beyond. 'Step back. How'd you like it if I came to your house and barged my way in?'

Nicoletta is momentarily stuck for words.

'I'm sorry,' she says at last. 'I'm not used to horses.'

'I can see that,' the voice replies. A blonde head appears beside the horse, regarding Nicoletta cooly through powdery blue eyes. The face matches the voice. 'They can sense that. They smell fear.' She laughs, a gay little tinkle. Nicoletta takes a step back. The woman's pupils are huge; she's not acting normally.

'Go on,' she says, suddenly serious. She puts an arm around the animal's muscular neck. The gesture strikes Nicoletta as strangely possessive. 'She won't bite.'

Nicoletta hesitates. She isn't sure if the woman is

addressing her, or the horse. She feels uncharacteristically frozen to the spot.

'Put your hand out,' the woman says, flicking a glance at Nicoletta. 'Stroke her, just above her nose. Talk to her. Act like you've done it before, for heaven's sake.'

Nicoletta unroots herself and squares her shoulders, with what she imagines is an air of rigid nonchalance. She steps forward and her fingertips connect with the velvety part just above the horse's nose. The animal's nostrils quiver and she snorts, but she seems to tolerate Nicoletta's bolder attempt at patting her.

'She must like you,' the blonde woman says with a shrug, disappearing into the gloom.

'What's her name?' Nicoletta calls, a semitone more boldly than she feels.

'Lucy,' the woman says, reappearing again and unlatching the door. She joins Nicoletta in the yard, a hard hat under her arm, relatching the stable door one-handed. She shakes out her hair and squints against the sun, facing Nicoletta. 'Who are you?' She emits a sound, low and muffled, like a sob. 'I told Joe not to let anyone in. God knows how you got through the gates.'

'Nicoletta Sarto. I'm a reporter from the *Irish Sentinel*.' Nicoletta proffers her hand, as gingerly as she had initially approached the horse.

'Eliza Field,' the woman says, not taking her hand. 'Aren't you going to tell me what you're doing in my yard, uninvited?'

'I heard singing,' Nicoletta says, feeling foolish immediately after. 'You have a lovely voice.'

Eliza leans her lower back against the wall, as though it's the only thing standing between her and total collapse. She's slim to the point of emaciated, wearing skintight stained jodhpurs and a cobalt woollen sweater that makes her eyes look disconcertingly blue. She gives Nicoletta a penetrating look, bordering on contempt.

'I meant, why did you come to my house?'

Nicoletta squares her shoulders again, echoing her approach of a few minutes before to Lucy, who is watching this exchange with nostrils flared.

'I'm terribly sorry about Meredith. The Gardaí believe she was murdered.' She stumbles over the ugly word, and Eliza visibly flinches, as though Nicoletta has delivered a blow too far. Eliza looks to the horse, who widens its eyes. She sinks to her haunches and sits on the straw-flecked flagstones.

'Meredith was in trouble long before she was found. I don't know. She was my only child, but we hardly knew each other.' She speaks falteringly.

'How do you think she came to be in the possession of *Among the Ruins*?'

'What's that?' Eliza sounds lost, like a little girl. Her head lolls on her chest. Nicoletta wonders if the kindest thing would be to just leave.

'It's a valuable painting,' she explains. 'The other half was stolen from Fairfax House earlier this year.'

'I really have no idea. I hadn't seen Meredith for at least a year before she died.'

'Why did you wait so long before reporting her missing? The Gardaí were only alerted to her disappearance three months ago,' Nicoletta asks, afraid she is pushing it too far.

'She stole from us,' Eliza says, slowly, raising her head to eye level. 'We found out some things.' Her hands clench and unclench in her lap, and Nicoletta wonders if she'd ever understand the pain this woman is feeling. She hopes she never does.

Nicoletta tries to keep her face neutral. She's imposed for too long.

'Thank you, Mrs Field. I won't intrude any longer. I'm sorry for your loss.'

Nicoletta squelches a few steps away, suddenly mortified at her muddy, dishevelled appearance, and anxious to get back to Dermot. The astonished-looking horse watches her leave with a gentle snort. When she's back at the pathway from the house, she hears the singing start up again.

It's a long walk back around the perimeter of the property and down the road, back to the wall where she'd climbed in. It takes her several attempts to haul herself back over and onto the road. Her shoes have dried but her legs are still saturated. She feels a rising anxiety about getting out of here. She needn't have worried; Dermot's car is parked in exactly the same place outside the padlocked black gates as it was when she left. She slides into the back seat gratefully and catches sight of herself in the wing mirror.

'The state of you,' Dermot says sharply, turning to look at her. 'You look like you've been dragged through a hedge backwards.'

'I have,' Nicoletta says, opening the door again and taking off her shoes. She lets the muddy water drain away on to the pockmarked ground, before putting them back on her feet with a squelch. She crosses to the driver's seat. 'Thanks for waiting,' she says, still out of breath.

'Want to go home?' He starts the engine, and her teeth begin to chatter. She feels a bit foolish. How is she going to explain the length of her absence and her advanced state of dishevelment to her mother and aunt?

'Mind if we stop at a pub? I'd like to use the Ladies'.'

The narrow winding road that meanders beside the stone wall demarcating Holloway House straightens and widens when they reach a T junction, leading back to the main road and on to Dublin. The Santry Arms is a dim-looking pub with windows that appear impenetrable to daylight, opaque like the bottom of a bottle of stout. Dermot seems at a loss as to where to park.

'Leave it on the footpath,' Nicoletta says. 'There's no one around.'

'I'm staying here.' Dermot rests his palms on the steering wheel as Nicoletta grapples with her handbag and squelches out of the car.

The bar is practically deserted apart from a pair of elderly men perched on high stools reading their respective newspapers and drinking their respective pints. Nicoletta sees one of them has the *Sentinel* with her story as the front page. She leaves a trail of water through the lounge as she goes out towards the toilets. An unpleasant smell is emanating from the Gents'. A dusty payphone adjoins its entrance. She freshens up in the Ladies' as best she can, before going back into the lounge and lingering over the warmth of the fire.

She's just about to drag herself away when a man appears through the bar, flinging the connecting door open so hard that it bangs against the slightly stained wallpaper behind it.

'Do you own that black saloon on the footpath?' He's panting slightly, red in the face. He's about forty, with thick curly dark hair and a long bumpy nose that looks as though it might have been broken once or twice upon a time.

'My friend owns it. We're just leaving,' Nicoletta says.

The man breathes so hard it sounds like a snort. 'You're completely blocking the way for my deliveries.'

Nicoletta clears her throat. 'Very sorry,' she says, gathering her handbag over her wrist. 'We'd heard such good things about this place. Are you the owner?'

The man nods. He manages to rock his whole body in the process.

Nicoletta holds out her hand. 'Nicoletta Sarto. I'm a reporter for the *Irish Sentinel*.'

The man shakes it. 'Davin Smith. I'm the proprietor here.'

Nicoletta hesitates, thinking of Dermot back in the car. 'Can I buy you a drink?'

Smith sticks out two fingers and a tiny woman materialises, taking their order. When the drinks arrive, Nicoletta dives in.

'We've just come from Holloway House. I suppose you heard the sad news about Meredith Field?'

Smith chews his lower lip as though considering. 'Bad business,' he says finally, taking a sip of Guinness.

Nicoletta hears Dermot's engine roar pointedly outside, and she knows she doesn't have much time.

'Did you know Meredith?' She takes a polite sip.

Smith pops open a bag of crips. 'I suppose.' He makes a face before he starts munching. 'She was a History of Art student at UCD. Didn't get on with the parents, if I remember rightly.'

'Did you know her well?'

Smith's eyes are large and trusting. Not unlike those of a horse.

'No. She was in here a few times last summer with a boyfriend of hers. John something. I remember because she drank pints.' He takes a disapproving sip of his drink.

'What was he like?' Nicoletta asks. 'I'm sure he's very upset.'

Smith shrugs. 'I haven't seen either of them since. He may not be still on the scene. Looks like they were mixed up with a bad crowd.' He raises his face from his drink with a pleased look. There's a faint creamy residue on his upper lip.

'John Lanigan. That was the boyfriend's name. I remember because he wrote me a bad cheque and asked me to cash it for him.'

Nicoletta makes a mental note of the name and exchanges further pleasantries with Smith before saying her goodbyes. She stops at the bar on the way out for a packet of crisps for Dermot. When she arrives back at the car, Dermot's hands are clenched over the steering wheel.

'Made a bit of headway,' she says, passing him the packet of crisps. 'Got the name of Meredith Field's boyfriend. I'm going to look for him.'

She can see a familiar burly figure smoking in the doorway, perhaps waiting for them to move the car.

'You're pretty taken with this story,' Dermot says, squishing the empty crisp packet with his fist. 'But life isn't how you'd like it to be, Nic. Not everything gets tied up with neat bows. For the last time, I'm asking you to be careful. Leave it.'

Nicoletta reaches for the file still in her handbag, ignoring his warning.

'Why?' Nicoletta shoves all the pages back in the file. Dermot doesn't answer. Instead, he starts the engine and reverses slowly out onto the road, narrowly missing a yellow-painted wheelbarrow planted with an array of red and purple flowers.

'Have fun,' he says, staring straight ahead. 'Enjoy spending time with your parents and aunt, and the twins. Sort yourself out. Enjoy your one and only precious life.'

She pretends she doesn't hear him.

'Where to now?' His reflection when he turns to her is grave.

'Home, sweet home,' she says with a laugh.

She glances at him sideways, but his profile is rigid and expressionless. He switches on the radio, turning the volume up high. It stays on a stream of advertisements for what seems like ages. Nicoletta folds her arms, happy to let the inane jingles about furniture sales and package holidays fill the awkward silence between them all the way back to Fairview.

Chapter Twenty-Two

After a frosty reception from Daniela following her excursion with Dermot, Nicoletta spends the rest of the weekend walking up and down the road with the girls in their double pram. By Monday, she's dying to return to work, more specifically to keep going with her story. The morning goes quickly enough, as she gets dragged into an editorial meeting with Price. Eventually she makes her escape at lunchtime, fleeing down the stairs and crossing O'Connell Bridge at breakneck speed. It's not a day for shopping, and the department stores look empty, the mannequins in the window of Clery's unusually naked, their shiny bare limbs obscene in the dull afternoon light. The newspaper sellers hawk their wares from their habitual spots, screaming about nurses' strikes, emigration, another possible heatwave. It's all just become background noise. Not the real story, the one that she can feel rattling around in her bones. Nicoletta hurries while the urge to do so is still fresh. She circles back around a newsagent's at the corner of Burgh Quay and goes to a payphone. She dials Pearse Street Garda Station. Garda O'Connor himself answers the phone. His voice sounds neutral, like it always does.

'Let me buy you lunch,' she says, by way of greeting.

'All right, grand,' he says. 'Ricci's? What time?'

'Now? See you in a few minutes.'

'I'll be there as soon as I can.'

She's there before him, and she takes what she's come to regard as their usual table. When he arrives, his face breaks into a cautious smile when he sees her.

'Well,' he says. 'This was a nice surprise.'

They order tea and sandwiches and neither says much until after they've eaten and the waitress, the same one as before, has taken their plates.

'So,' she says. 'Thank you for letting me know about Meredith Field and the painting.'

'No problem,' he replies, observing her from across the table, his hands folded in front of him. 'I saw your story. Hope it didn't get you into trouble?'

'I don't think so,' Nicoletta says, shaking her head. 'Thank you for trusting me.'

He acknowledges what she's said with a close-lipped smile.

'I wanted to ask you: how do you think Meredith Field's body found its way into the Dublin mountains?' she asks, opening a sachet of sugar and emptying it into her half-filled cup.

O'Connor unfolds his hands, twisting his lip, as though disappointed. She stirs the hot tea and takes a sip; it's disgustingly sweet. 'Did she go there voluntarily, where she met her death, or was she brought there? And any sign of the gun that killed her?'

O'Connor puffs out his cheeks. 'We haven't found the gun. But judging by a shell we found, it looks like it was fired from a Webley. And we found a burnt-out red Ford Fiesta about a mile away from where Miss Field was left. There was a sticker on the window. The vehicle had been rented from D. Mooney's Garage at Mountjoy Square.'

Nicoletta scribbles the information down on a scrap from her handbag. When she looks up, O'Connor is putting on his jacket with tight precision.

'What's wrong?' It's a direct question, and it catches him in the eye with blunt force.

He sighs. 'Look, Nicoletta. I've told you all that. Now, perhaps it's best if I don't tell you anymore. You're not even meant to be working on this story. You could get yourself in a lot of trouble.'

She bites her lip and reaches for her bag. They both stand up at the same time. 'Is that the only reason?' Another direct question, which lands like a bullet.

He sits back down, splaying his palms in front of him, as though showing his hand at cards. 'I like you, Nicoletta. You know that. So, perhaps it's best we don't see each other anymore.' He stands up again and walks out, as though he hadn't been expecting an answer at all.

She heads back the way she'd come from initially, turning right at Parnell Street. Mountjoy Square is a dilapidated Georgian enclave north of O'Connell Street, bookended by tenements on either side. D. Mooney's garage is tucked away in the far corner of the west end. Nicoletta trots along the railing bordering the park in the centre, mentally rehearsing how she'll play this. The most likely scenario is that nobody will tell her anything. But you never know. We live in hope, she thinks, grimly sidestepping an ageing dog turd blanching at the edges. Children play skipping on the green, chanting an unfamiliar rhyme.

D. Mooney's shopfront has a large sign above a double garage door. Nicoletta can hear a radio blaring from the workshop within. She knocks, but no one answers. Eventually, she pushes open the small wooden door at the side. It takes a moment for her eyes to adjust to the gloom. Rows of cars, vans and bikes sit in varying degrees of repair with parts trailing out of them. A row of shiny metal links splays over on the floor, putting her in mind of spilled intestines. A man slides out from under a red Cortina. He doesn't acknowledge Nicoletta but continues whistling along to the radio. After a moment or two, Nicoletta realises that he's waiting for her to speak.

'Are you D. Mooney?' she asks in a bright voice – too bright.

'Nope,' the man says, eyeing her for a bit. She can't decide if he's young or old. He appears to be neither, though his demeanour suggests that of a teenager.

'Well, do you know where I could find him?'

'Nope.' The man slides out and spits something on the ground beside him. Nicoletta resists the urge to shudder.

'I really need to speak to him.' A note of annoyance has crept into her voice. 'Could you tell me when he'll be back?'

'Couldn't really say,' the man chuckles. 'Unless he's the second coming.'

'Well, I really need to speak to him,' Nicoletta repeats. 'Could you pass on a message for me?'

'Not really. I'm not a psychic.'

'Look, can you tell me where he is?' Nicoletta finally begins to lose her temper. The man notices and his expression becomes sombre.

'He's dead.' He tosses a rag onto a pile beside the momentarily static radio. 'Why'd you want to speak to him? Does he owe you money, is that it?'

'No, no, nothing like that.' Nicoletta sighs. She holds out her hand. 'My name's Nicoletta Sarto and I'm a reporter for the *Sentinel*.'

The man doesn't take her hand. He takes out a cigarette and lights it, before sitting down heavily at a small table inside the corner beside the door, crammed with papers. A jumble of invoices and receipts vie for space with crumpled confectionary wrappers. 'What's a reporter want with poor Des?'

Nicoletta takes a step behind, feeling the reassuring outline of the breeze-block wall at her back. The wave of tiredness that has just enveloped her is telling her this wasn't such a good idea. It's followed by the rising swirl of claustrophobia in her chest. She takes a deep breath, aware the man is watching her while she composes herself, hating the foul proximity of his cigarette.

'Are you all right?' he surprises her by saying, after a long pause.

He gets off his chair and proffers the vacant space. There doesn't seem to be another one. Nicoletta gratefully sinks down into it and allows her breathing to return to normal.

'I'm sorry,' she says, fanning her face. 'I have twins at home. They're only five months old. Not getting much sleep.'

A rueful smile lifts the man's face as he perches on the table, his face angled earnestly towards Nicoletta, shiny with perspiration. He's younger, or perhaps older, than she'd thought, in and around late thirties.

'I know how that goes.' He matches her laugh with a chuckle that turns into a cough. He reaches across her to extinguish the cigarette in an ashtray he takes from the shelf on which the radio sits. He flicks it off. The room is quiet and still. A child's shout from the nearby green floats into earshot.

'What can I do for you? You said you wanted to see Des?' He steeples his palms together, as though imploring her.

Nicoletta balances her bag in her lap, gripping the handles. 'I'm writing a story about the murder of a young woman called Meredith Field. Believed to be linked to a series of robberies. Of valuable artworks. Ray Hall, known as The Rook, is behind them. Perhaps you've heard of him?'

The man stands up. Nicoletta knows she is about to be shown the door.

'Yeah, I've heard of him. And I've already had the cops here asking about the burnt-out car they found in some field. How'd I know about that?'

Nicoletta nods. 'I understand, Mr . . .'

'It's Mooney. Phil Mooney.' He opens the door behind her and indicates for her to step out. She gratefully gulps in the fresh air as she emerges into the street.

'Was Des Mooney your father?' Nicoletta calls through

the door, as Phil flicks the radio back on and prepares to get back under a car.

He looks up, something sharp about his expression. He comes back to the door and observes her through the gap. 'My uncle,' he says with a shake of his head. 'Died three months ago. Heart attack. I've been sorting through this mess ever since.'

'I'm sorry about your uncle,' Nicoletta says simply.

Phil gives a gruff nod, acknowledging her condolence. He starts shutting the door, the gap narrowing to a slit.

Nicoletta puts her hand around it, testing it. She puts her face into the gap.

'Can you remember anything at all about that car? A young woman was killed. If you could remember anything it would be a big help ... in getting justice.'

There's silence and she's not sure if he's heard her. She sees his elbow turn, his back sidestep to the messy table, where he sits down. He flicks through a leather-backed ledger, slowly and methodically, before picking it up and carrying it back to where Nicoletta's nose is wedged through the gap in the door.

'Des died at the end of March,' he says, turning pages. 'His paperwork is a joke. Couldn't lay my hands on this when the cops called. Not that they seemed too bothered. He had a load of files stored in the jacks and there's water damage on some of them.'

He runs his finger over something and calls it out.

'Says here Des leased that car to John Lanigan, with an address given as 24 Leeson Street. No other information. He paid in cash.'

He closes the door, and Nicoletta hears a key turn in the lock. The rain starts as she passes the green area; the children have already cleared off. It steadies into a welcome drizzle, trickling into the dried-up flowerbeds and yellowed grass. Nicoletta raises her face skywards, in affinity with the dusty city. She doesn't want to go back to the newspaper.

Chapter Twenty-Three

The weather has started to break by the time Nicoletta reaches the intersection of Stephen's Green with Leeson Street. The rain has segued back into hot, sullen clouds. She trails along the street, looking at the numbers. Eighteen, twenty, twenty-two, twenty-four. Except number twenty-four is a pub called McBurney's, generally frequented by a young, student crowd.

It's the tail-end of the usual lunchtime rush, but the pub is busy, the bar lined up with what look like regulars, stoically sipping pints and reading papers in contemplative silence. One or two of them look up when she enters and she smiles at them, which drives them back into their papers and pints. Framed sepia photographs adorn the walls of past patrons of note, the only colour being a print of the entirety of a bearded all-male Irish folk group, raising their drinks solemnly at the camera.

Nicoletta hasn't eaten since breakfast, and she can hear her stomach match the rumble of the thunder from outside. She goes into the lounge, ordering a ham sandwich and a lemonade on her way. The barman promises to deliver them directly over to her table. She sits for a few moments, observing a large group of young people who sit around on low stools, empty glasses in front of them. They look like students: casually dressed, long-haired, in jeans and sweaters, some in T-shirts, bags of books by their sides. One of them, the only woman Nicoletta can see, gives her a curious look. A blue headscarf holds a mass of dark curls off the woman's face.

Nicoletta's lemonade and sandwich arrives, and she gratefully demolishes them. She can feel eyes on her and when she sees the female student go into the adjoining bar, she drains her lemonade and stands up, following her at a safe remove. The woman stands at the bar, resting one elbow on the polished ledge, drinking a glass of tap water the barman begrudgingly hands over.

'I'm not serving you a pint. We don't serve pints to ladies at this establishment.' He picks up a cloth. 'Anything else?' the barman asks pointedly.

The woman hands over a crisp note from her pocket. 'Change for the cigarette machine.' She holds it between two fingers, not seeming the least bit fazed by the barman's attitude.

The barman dings open the cash register in a pantomime of inconvenience. 'Don't have change,' he says, going to serve one of the old men. 'Change is for paying customers only,' he calls over his shoulder as a parting shot.

Nicoletta opens her purse. 'I have plenty of change,' she murmurs, before the woman can go back to her friends. 'I'll get these for you. To make up for your man being such a prick.'

Without waiting for an answer, she heads out to the cigarette machine, which she instinctively knows is located through a creaking door beside the Gents' toilet. A stale odour of urine mixed with chemical toilet cleaner permeates the air. She stops, realising she doesn't know which ones to buy. For a moment, she thinks she's lost the woman student, but then she hears the door creak.

'Are you a Guard?' The woman indicates the cigarette machine window for Players.

Nicoletta slots the coins in one by one. 'Nope. Why do you ask?'

'Because we've had one or two of those in here, asking us questions.'

'Ah, I see.' The cigarettes shoot out of the funnel like a prize at a funfair. Nicoletta brandishes them with a flourish.

'What are you, then?' The woman hesitates before accepting them, regarding Nicoletta with yellowish hazel eyes, the hue brought out by the blue headscarf.

'I'm a journalist,' Nicoletta replies. 'Nicoletta Sarto is my name. I'm the women's pages editor for the *Sentinel*.' The feel of the words in her mouth never gets stale.

'Cool,' the woman says, accepting the small rectangular packet. 'So, I wasn't wrong then.'

'Wrong about what?'

'About you being here to ask questions.'

Nicoletta waits a beat or two while the girl opens the packet and selects a cigarette with care, before lighting it and blowing out smoke with a whoosh of contentment. 'Do you know John Lanigan or Meredith Field?'

The girl pauses, the cigarette halfway back to her mouth. 'What about them?'

Nicoletta remains impassive. 'Meredith is dead.'

The girl nods solemnly. 'I know. I saw it in the papers.'

'Then you'll have read my story,' Nicoletta says smoothly. 'I'd like to talk to John. Do you know how I could get in touch with him?'

The girl shrugs.

'What is John studying?' Nicoletta asks, narrowing her eyes against the smoke and trying not to be obvious about it.

'History of Art, and Modern History, same as me,' the girl says. She's about to wander off, when Nicoletta places a fingertip against her elbow.

'Do you have some time to talk to me?'

The girl's eyes narrow. 'I'm supposed to be studying for a repeat. What do you want to talk about?'

Nicoletta prays she has some cash left in her purse. 'John Lanigan, preferably. But we can talk about whatever you want. I'll treat you to lunch.'

The girl brightens and strides over to where her bag is flung in a corner. She doesn't say anything to the other students and Nicoletta tries to melt into the background.

When they're out the door the girl looks at Nicoletta expectantly.

'Is it true what they're saying?'

Nicoletta blinks. 'What are people saying?'

The girl waves a beringed hand. 'Oh, you know. That John killed Meredith.'

'Who's saying that?'

The girl shrugs.

'Go to the Taj Mahal on Baggot Street.' Nicoletta rummages in her bag for some money and presses it into the girl's hand. 'Wait for me there. I have to make a quick phone call.'

The girl nods, and Nicoletta wonders if she's making a silly mistake in trusting her. But she's desperate for information about John Lanigan, and this girl was surely far more likely to trust her than a Guard. 'What did you say your name was?'

The girl smiles, as though she can sense Nicoletta's hesitation.

'I didn't,' she says boldly, tucking the money into the back pocket of her jeans. 'It's Debbie.' She gives Nicoletta a casual wave and Nicoletta jogs to the nearest telephone box.

She slides a coin into the metal slot and waits for a faraway dial tone, before asking the operator for Pearse Street Garda Station. Garda O'Connor takes a while to come to the phone. He answers with a muffled cough, and she can hear voices in the background. When he hears her voice, his tone sounds neutral. Nicoletta skips awkward pleasantries.

'Garda, off the record, does the name John Lanigan mean anything to you?'

He exhales noisily. 'Yeah.'

Nicoletta twists the cord around her finger. There's a pause, and she can imagine Garda O'Connor glancing around to see who is listening. She feels a pang in her chest. He has taken a risk in helping her.

'He was Meredith Field's boyfriend,' he says in a rush. 'And accomplice. They burgled Holloway House in North County Dublin, the home of Meredith's parents. Her parents kept it out of the papers. A file relating to their part in the burglary of Fairfax House and the murder of Garda Larry Grehan went missing from the office of the Director of Public Prosecutions during a recent break-in. Meredith was estranged from her parents before that. We think she was working for The Rook.'

'Did John kill Meredith?' Nicoletta asks in a rush.

'I doubt it.' He rings off before Nicoletta can thank him. She thinks about calling her mother, and rummages in her bag for more coins, but they're all gone. She'll just meet this girl, and then she'll go home to her own girls. The pang of loneliness that she'd felt during the conversation with O'Connor is pushed down by an impenetrable ball of guilt.

Chapter Twenty-Four

Debbie is waiting for her at a corner table of the Taj Mahal, a small but bustling restaurant at Baggot Street Bridge. Despite the name, the place is run by a middle-aged woman with steel-coloured hair and steely eyes to match, named Mrs Rafter. To Nicoletta's knowledge, Mrs Rafter hasn't ever been in possession of a Christian name. A tiny marble replica of the Madonna of Bruges sits on the counter, blankly observing the surrounding proceedings. Mrs Rafter rests on a high wooden stool behind it, back against the wall, her eyes darting back and forth, never appearing at rest in her head. She stands up to take a payment from a workman in paint-spattered blue overalls. They exchange a brief word, before Mrs Rafter resumes her perch, eyes scanning the room. Nicoletta walks down a narrow aisle between tables, right down to the end. As she approaches Debbie, a plate of the Taj's signature pineapple and bacon on toast makes its way in front of her, via a young waitress whose arms are piled high. Nicoletta sits down opposite her. It occurs to her that Debbie might just be using her for a free meal and mightn't have any information of note to impart. She'll just have to see.

'I was sure you'd stood me up,' Debbie says by way of greeting, in between mouthfuls. 'You were ages.'

Nicoletta makes a non-committal noise.

Debbie wipes her mouth with a corner of a paper serviette. 'Do you want something?' she asks, summoning the waitress with a magnanimous wave.

Nicoletta orders a scotch egg and toast, another signature Taj dish, and two pots of tea. The place is emptying now, the lunchtime buzz petering out as office workers make their way back outside. Debbie exchanges an awkward nod with a long-haired student with a bushy beard at the next table, before averting her eyes and focusing on her food. When her plate has been picked clean and she's almost finished her tea, she extracts a cigarette from the pack Nicoletta had bought her.

'I don't know if I have much to tell you.' Debbie is avoiding eye contact with, but is simultaneously hyperaware of, the male student near them. Nicoletta wonders how she knows him. She plunges in; it's sink-or-swim time.

'How well do you know John Lanigan?' she asks, taking a slug of tea.

Debbie shrugs. 'Not that well,' she admits in a bright voice. She nods at the next table. 'My ex-boyfriend is listening,' she mouths.

Nicoletta flicks a glance sideways. The young man is nursing what appears to be a cold cup of coffee and is studiously ignoring Debbie. It strikes Nicoletta that he's listening in and has been for the duration. This has been a waste of her time.

Debbie drains her tea and bends close to Nicoletta's ear.

'All I know is he came in here all the time. That's why I suggested it.'

Nicoletta nods, cupping her hot mug, unsure of what to do with her hands at times like these. She can't take notes; that might spook this girl.

'He ate here for free. Mrs Rafter, the owner of this place, was his landlady.' Debbie whispers urgently as she stands up. 'I've to go. Thanks for lunch!'

'Wait,' Nicoletta says, trying to keep the desperation out of her voice. 'Where is John now?'

'Haven't a clue.' Debbie shoulders a fringed tan bag and darts out the door without looking back.

The bearded student at the next table slams his cup down on the table and follows her to the door, before realising that he hasn't paid. He makes an abrupt turn back towards Mrs Rafter, who has him in her sights. When he's left, the restaurant has emptied out even more and Nicoletta thinks about her next move. She gazes out the fogged window. She should go home, she knows that. Get some sleep. But to go home now would be to concede defeat, to slam the lid back on Pandora's Box and walk away from this story. She extracts her purse from her bag and approaches the cash register. Mrs Rafter stands, unsmiling, her eyes taking Nicoletta in, all in one practised sweep, from her toes to the crown of her head.

'I'm paying for everything together,' Nicoletta says quickly, pre-empting any cutting remark from Mrs Rafter about Debbie. 'What did she have?'

'Quite a lot,' Mrs Rafter says with a dry chuckle.

When the substantial amount has been totted up and

Nicoletta has settled the bill, she pauses, before Mrs Rafter returns to her perch.

'This is beautiful,' she says, indicating the miniature statue of the Madonna and child.

Mrs Rafter peers over the counter. 'Oh, that,' she replies, tucking a lock of salt-and-pepper hair behind her ear. 'It's a replica, obviously,' she laughs. 'Don't think I could afford the real thing somehow.'

'Who's the artist?' Nicoletta asks, in a bid to keep her talking.

'Michelangelo,' Mrs Rafter says, ringing up the order. 'I went to Rome on a trip with my sister last year. Brought it back from a souvenir shop in the Vatican. The real statue is in a church in Belgium.'

She clears her throat, looking at Nicoletta as though this long speech may have overworked her throat.

'I've never been to Rome,' Nicoletta ventures. 'Though my mother was born there.'

Mrs Rafter looks interested. 'Oh?'

Nicoletta extends a hand. 'Nicoletta Sarto is my name. I'm a reporter for the *Irish Sentinel*.' She rests her hip against the counter, thinking she's going to be dismissed at any moment.

Mrs Rafter's takes her hand briefly, her expression inscrutable. 'Do you know,' she says, changing the subject, 'at the end of the war, the Germans smuggled the statue out of Belgium wrapped in mattresses in a Red Cross truck.'

'When was it returned?' Nicoletta enthusiastically takes up the baton of this change of course.

'A year later. It was found in an Austrian salt mine, and then the Belgians got it back.' Mrs Rafter locks eyes with Nicoletta for a moment or two that feels like a moment or two too long.

Nicoletta looks down. She can feel the countertop digging into her hip.

'I'm writing a story about two missing paintings, actually. *Among the Ruins.*'

'Oh? Turned up here after the war, did they?'

'No. Not that I know of.' Nicoletta shakes her head slowly. She's not sure how much to divulge. But it's hardly top secret. It's been in all the papers, thanks to her story about Meredith Field, and Helen Leonard's part in *Among the Ruins* turning up along with Meredith's body. And Nicoletta is desperate for information about John Lanigan. She decides to share some of what she knows with Mrs Rafter in the hope of receiving a *quid pro quo*.

'They're believed to have been stolen.' She pauses. 'By a criminal known as The Rook. Ray Hall.'

'Didn't he kill a Guard?' Mrs Rafter gives a brisk nod as some students pile over to pay for their meal. Nicoletta knows she'd better act fast.

'He was acquitted. Mrs Rafter, I believe you were John Lanigan's landlady. Do you know where he is now?'

Nicoletta keeps her voice low, so the students don't hear, but Mrs Rafter's hand flies to her throat. 'Why? You don't think he was involved with this Rook character, do you?'

'I don't know anything for sure,' Nicoletta says noncommittally. Her hip is really bothering her now. She takes an involuntary step back from the counter.

Mrs Rafter keeps her eyes focused on Nicoletta. She holds her gaze, though it's making her uncomfortable. 'I haven't seen John in months. I don't think he sat the exams. I had to ask him to leave.'

'Why's that?'

Mrs Rafter snorts. 'He was keeping all sorts of undesirable company.'

Nicoletta hangs on, her fingertips pressing into the cold plastic counter. 'Like who? Did you know Meredith Field, his girlfriend? Her body was found a few days ago.'

Mrs Rafter's gaze drifts to the impatient students queuing to pay behind her. She sucks in a short breath, like a child drinking lemonade through a straw, then wrinkles her nose.

'Yes. Quite a pair, they were. I'm sure the university could give you his parents' address. You can tell them he owes me a month's rent while you're at it.'

And with that, she switches her focus to the queue behind her and Nicoletta is dismissed. She walks out into the afternoon sunlight and starts back towards Stephen's Green.

Chapter Twenty-Five

Nicoletta pauses at University College Dublin at the corner of St Stephen's Green, situated at Newman House, an eighteenth-century palazzo-style mansion originally designed as a private house for a wealthy rake, taken over by Cardinal John Henry Newman in 1854 as the new Catholic university. In another life, she might have once been a student here. The steps up to the door are jammed with odd pieces of furniture – end tables, stacking chairs and old-fashioned desks with inkwells grooved into the wood – and several overalled men are busy loading these onto a nearby van. The overriding effect is one of constant activity.

'What's going on?' she asks a man with close-cropped black hair in pristine blue overalls who appears to be directing operations. He is doing more shouting and pointing than shouldering heavy loads, it appears to Nicoletta.

He turns to her in surprise. 'Fuck's sake,' he barks, with a mock sob, as a chair leg gets scraped along the pavement by a young lanky fellow with a cigarette hanging out of his mouth. 'Moving to the new campus in Belfield.' He nods meaningfully at Nicoletta, before rushing forward to admonish the youngster and grab the chair off him.

There aren't any students around, but the place is busy enough. Nicoletta drifts up the granite steps and waits for a space to squeeze through the wide door. She imagines what it might have been like, coming here every day, meeting people her own age, learning new things. Instead, there had been a fork in the road, and she hadn't taken the turning that might've led her here. She peers a little wistfully around, at the slightly musty smell pervading the air. This is what learning smells like. She's startled back to reality by the sight of two trousered legs sticking out of a little alcove under a stairway. A dark head pops up, narrowly missing bashing itself on the lip of the solid mahogany desk, and Nicoletta sees it's a young woman kneeling on the floor on the far side of the desk, laboriously labelling cards and filing them in small wooden boxes at her feet. Nicoletta clears her throat, and the girl blows her fringe out of her eyes.

'Can I help you?' Her voice is clipped, though courteous. The kind of voice that oozes education and doesn't have to fake confidence.

Nicoletta hesitates.

'I'm looking for John Lanigan. He's a student here, studying History of Art and Modern History.'

The girl puckers her chin and sits back on her haunches.

'All the students are long gone now for the summer,' she says. 'The exams finished ages ago. As you can see, it's bedlam here now as we're moving.'

Nicoletta shakes her head in frustration, but she doesn't move to go. The girl picks up a box of cigarettes from the floor beside her and lights one, offering Nicoletta the open pack. She takes one, for the sake of lingering and keeping the girl talking for another few minutes.

'Could he be repeating an exam?' Nicoletta asks, awkwardly blowing out smoke into the learned air.

'I don't really know.' The girl shrugs. 'Not sure I'd be able to tell you even if I did. Student records are meant to be confidential.' She looks at Nicoletta with naked curiosity. 'Is it an urgent matter?'

Nicoletta hesitates again, before scrubbing at her eyes with her knuckles and emitting a loud sigh. 'It's, well, it's a personal matter.' She gives the girl a meaningful look. 'I asked John's landlady, and she said he's moved on. I've got no other way of contacting him. And I need to let him know something.' She takes a drag on the cigarette for effect and sinks down beside the girl, who offers her a half-empty china teacup to use as an ashtray.

'Isn't that always the way? They're all the same,' the girl says with a wink, extinguishing her half-smoked cigarette into a hiss of cold tea.

'Yeah,' Nicoletta agrees. 'They're all the same.'

The girl crawls back to her position with all the tiny wooden boxes and flicks around opening and closing them between thuds and shouts of heavy furniture being lifted by the workmen all around them. 'Bedlam,' she mouths back at Nicoletta.

'John Lanigan, History of Art. What year?' She asks.

Nicoletta shrugs.

The girl shakes her head. 'Maybe he's not worth it,' she offers, arching a shapely eyebrow.

'Maybe.' Nicoletta stands up, brushing down her dress. 'Are there any teaching faculty around at the moment?'

The girl wrinkles her nose. 'Just one. Dr Celine Rault, a member of staff in History of Art. She had to get out to a café because the noise here was driving her potty.'

'I see,' Nicoletta says, still hovering, her ears pricked to the nth degree. 'I'd like to speak to Dr Rault,' she says, more businesslike now.

'She's grading exams,' the girl says, with a suspicious widening of her eyes.

Nicoletta scrubs at her eyes again. They have started to stream from all the dust in this tiny alcove.

'Ah, don't go upsetting yourself,' the girl says. 'I get it, you're desperate. He's done a runner, leaving you in trouble. Give me one minute.'

She flicks through a sheaf of cards until she finds what she's looking for, then she copies the information onto a sheet of paper she rips out of a pad.

'Dr Rault is probably at the Silver Teapot on Dame Street,' the girl murmurs, pressing the sheet onto her palm. It has been folded into a neat square, which Nicoletta deposits into her bag.

'Thank you,' Nicoletta says, feeling guilty at how she's duped this girl. 'You've been very kind. Maybe someday I'll learn my lesson.'

'I doubt Dr Rault knows where your fellow is,' the girl says with an impatient toss of her head, returning to her task. 'But there's no harm in asking, is there?'

'No, never any harm in asking,' Nicoletta replies, turning on her heel and escaping into the burnished sunlight of the mid-afternoon, which seems too bright after the cheerful gloom of the university.

The Silver Teapot belies its moniker, which evokes genteel grandeur and high tea, with crustless cucumber sandwiches. Instead, it's a mostly empty greasy spoon just beside Dublin Castle with oily condensation on the windows and a red-and-white tiled floor which has seen better days. A red setter with huge soulful eyes rests its head on the floor with a martyred air beside a tinny transistor radio tuned to local news. Nicoletta stops to fuss over the dog, while she can get the lie of the land. There is no waiter or proprietor in view. Celine Rault isn't hard to spot among the clientele as she's the sole customer in the place. She sits alone with a stack of papers and a large aluminium pot of tea in front of her, twirling a pen between her fingers and staring into space. Nicoletta croons at the dog and cradles its ears, and sure enough, the dog turns on its back to have its belly rubbed. Animals always seem to like Nicoletta.

Celine peers over at the red setter. 'Oh, it's you. The reporter who got kicked out of the Creightons' estate sale.'

Nicoletta colours as she approaches the table and can feel herself being appraised. Celine is wearing the same long shapeless red tunic, to match her long, red-brown hair. She looks contemptuous. 'Shy all of a sudden, are we?' She goes back to her papers.

'I'm looking for John Lanigan,' Nicoletta says, a little too loudly. Luckily, there's now only one other person in the café, who looks like they might be the proprietor. 'I believe John was one of your students?'

'He was.' Celine gives a brisk nod, not inviting Nicoletta to join her. 'Though why I should talk to you about him is anyone's guess.' She strokes the dog's ears.

'Did he sit the exams?' Nicoletta finally asks, indicating the pile of papers in front of Celine.

Celine hesitates, her surprisingly full mouth jutting out the bottom lip, giving the impression of a child sulking.

'I can't tell you that,' she says with finality. 'It would be a gross breach of privacy. Do you understand what that means? I don't suppose you do.'

She doesn't wait for Nicoletta's answer, turning back to her papers. Nicoletta hangs on, dancing from foot to foot. The café's proprietor, a young woman, has come out into view wiping down tables. She seems to know Celine, as a look passes between them as she fiddles with the transistor radio and switches it to pop music. T.Rex's 'Children of the Revolution' comes on and the dog closes its eyes.

'Did you buy anything at Creighton's?' Nicoletta asks.

Celine flicks her a scornful glance. 'It was all complete tat. Why?' she laughs. 'Were you hoping for an heirloom of some sort?'

'You haven't even asked me why I'm asking about John Lanigan,' Nicoletta points out, giving it one last shot.

'Why's that, then?'

'A young woman, Meredith Field, was found murdered in the Dublin Mountains alongside a missing painting, believed to have been originally purchased at Rault's Gallery. The woman was John Lanigan's girlfriend.'

'I read your little story about that.'

'Did you know Meredith Field?'

Celine gathers up her papers and dumps them in a large tan satchel under the table. 'She was a student of mine. She came to a party at the gallery once. Stole some money while she was there too, but of course I could never prove it.'

'Who do you think killed her?' Nicoletta is aware she sounds slightly breathless, but she doesn't care.

'I can see we're not going to get any peace here either,' Celine says to the dog, clipping on its lead.

Nicoletta hurries out after her. A stiff breeze has rolled in from the sea, slicing through the illusion of summer. Celine starts walking at a clipped trot down Dame Street and Nicoletta struggles to keep up.

'Hey,' she calls, feeling out of breath.

Celine doesn't stop.

'Your father's death must've been a terrible shock,' Nicoletta shoots, wondering if this will land. 'Do you think his death could have been murder, instead of suicide? And do you think John Lanigan had anything to do with Meredith Field's death?'

Celine wheels around with three-hundred-and-sixty-degree force. The dog whines at the sudden yank on its collar.

'I'll be making an official complaint to your editor about you,' she says. 'How dare you ambush me like this?'

'Did your father mention the *Among the Ruins* paintings at all?' Nicoletta calls.

Celine takes a step towards her, her face flushed with

fury. Nicoletta is by her side in a flash. 'Do you think John Lanigan was involved with The Rook as well?'

'Fuck off.' Celine snarls, before she starts walking away. Her brisk pace quickly turns into a sprint.

The dog takes one last longing look at Nicoletta before being dragged along beside its owner.

Chapter Twenty-Six

Nicoletta is at her desk early next morning, her knuckles blanched against a mug of coffee, when a call comes through from the switch. She hadn't slept much the night before. The twins had kept her awake, and once they were settled, she hadn't been able to drop off. She kept hearing a faint tapping on the window. Experience had taught her it was an ancient overgrown cherry blossom tree from the pavement, but in the depths of the night it became an invisible assailant, set on targeting her at her most vulnerable.

She picks up the phone, hopeful it might be O'Connor.

'Mr Leopold Slift,' the efficient older woman at reception says clearly, taking her time over each syllable.

'Miss Sarto,' a deep, pleasant voice intones once the call has been transferred. 'I hope this is a good time.'

'Hello, Mr Slift,' Nicoletta replies, putting down the mug too quickly and slopping cooling coffee all over her desk. 'It's a great time, actually.' She mops up the coffee with an ineffectual paper tissue she plucks from her bag. 'What can I do for you?'

'I've found something out that may be of interest,' he

says, his voice seeming further away than it had previously, as though he has turned away from the receiver. 'Perhaps you could pop down to my office at some point today. I'd rather not divulge anything over the telephone.'

'I'll be there in ten minutes,' Nicoletta says, but the receiver has already gone dead.

She scrambles for her bag, grabbing her coat and throwing it over her arm. She's about to leave when she hears a throat being cleared in her vicinity.

'Where're you going?' It's Price, his arms folded stiffly against his barrel-shaped chest.

'Just heading out,' Nicoletta says, in an attempt at sounding breezy. 'On a story.'

'Oh?' Price raises an eyebrow. 'Which story might that be?'

Nicoletta puts one arm into the sleeve of her coat, focusing away from the fury that's headed her way.

'Look at me when I'm speaking to you,' Price mutters in a low, dangerous voice. No one in the newsroom – not the two reporters at the typewriters, nor the three copy takers nearby – bat an eyelid at his tone.

Nicoletta forces her eyes onto his. She smiles, but he doesn't return it.

'Is it a story for the women's pages?' He inclines his head. Nicoletta notices a vein throbbing in his shiny forehead. She realises that she's playing a zero-sum game.

'Sort of,' she says, getting her other arm into the coat sleeve and making a big deal of doing up the buttons. 'It's about a woman who was murdered. Meredith Field. I'm sure you know the name.'

She looks at Price. He doesn't blink for the longest time. 'That is a story for the news desk,' he says finally, speaking quietly but with unmistakable menace. 'Not for you. Stick to the women's pages from now on.'

Nicoletta unbuttons her coat but doesn't take it off. She sits back down at her desk, vibrating with rage. But she won't give him the satisfaction of emotion. She fiddles with a pen, making a big deal of opening a notepad. She turns her head. He's still there, observing her. She straightens her shoulders and reaches for her in-tray.

She can see him in her peripheral vision, turning to walk away, then he appears to change his mind and stops.

'By the way,' he says, louder this time, for the benefit of the assembled audience. 'Duffy wants to see you at two o'clock. There's been some sort of complaint. Do you know what that's about?'

'No,' Nicoletta says, in a quiet but defiant voice.

Price makes a tutting noise. 'I'm sure there's a very wide remit for what it could be, in that case. See you at two.' He walks away, his footsteps heavy and deliberate. Nicoletta waits until she hears Duffy's office door close before she stands up and gets a cloth for her spilled coffee.

At one o'clock exactly, she flees from her desk and half runs to Leopold Slift's office at Grafton Buildings. There's no one at reception and he's at his desk when she bursts in. He looks mildly surprised to see her.

'I had to wait to come at lunchtime,' she says. 'Long story.'

'Not a problem, Miss Sarto,' he says, indicating for

her to sit down opposite him. 'I was loath to say what I had to say over the telephone. You know how it is.'

She sits, smoothing her skirt under her, setting her bag on her lap, taking out her notebook, and opening it with her pen poised. When she looks up, she notices his eyes on her.

'Don't have much time,' she explains briskly.

'Ah right,' he says, flexing his fingers and leaning forward. 'Let's get right to it, shall we? Unless you've time for a cup of tea?'

She nods. He busies himself with the kettle in the corner.

'Won't take a minute,' he calls over his shoulder. 'You look like you could do with it.'

She gratefully accepts the heated china cup, holding it carefully in her hands as though reluctant to relinquish it to the desk in front of her, lest it be taken away.

When he sits back down, she feels slightly calmer. He takes a drink from his own cup and smiles at her pleasantly over its rim.

'Thank you for inviting me here,' she says, quickly. 'Can I ask, how much is your fee for helping me with these enquiries?'

Slift puts down the cup, a smile lifting the corners of his mouth. 'Oughtn't you decide first whether or not my information has been of use?'

Nicoletta takes a gulp of hot, fragrant tea. She considers this.

'What did you find out?'

'I asked around among a few contacts about your Mr Antoine Rault, the provenance of the *Among the Ruins* paintings, and, of course, our friend Ray Hall, aka The Rook.'

'Who did you ask?' Nicoletta puts down the cup, pen ready to transcribe for her dear life.

Slift wipes moisture off his clean-shaven upper lip with a handkerchief from his pocket. He splays his hands on the desk in front of her.

'I can't betray their confidence, Miss Sarto. I'm sorry. It's delicate. Completely off the record. You'll have to trust me. Do you?'

Nicoletta looks up from her notebook, momentarily lost for words. She thinks of the kind faces of Slift and his wife, who had told her the truth, and helped her, when neither act must have been particularly convenient for them. She nods vigorously.

'I trust you,' she says.

'Well then,' he says, draining his tea and wiping his lips with the handkerchief from his pocket. 'Antoine Rault was not who he said he was.'

Nicoletta frowns. 'How can you be so sure?'

He gives her an apologetic smile. 'I really can't say.'

'Then who was he, really?' She checks her watch. Time is ticking on until her meeting with Duffy, Barney and Price. He must sense the urgency in her voice, or maybe he wants to get this meeting over with rapidly, because he stands up and takes the cups over to the kettle and stacks them beside some other used crockery.

He stays standing, opening a window and lighting a cigarette, blowing the smoke outside.

'Of that I'm not quite sure. I have it on good authority,

he was a young member of the French Resistance when he found some paintings in a barn outside Paris. He fled to Dublin during the war and set up an art dealership here. The *Among the Ruins* pair of paintings are purported to be from the hand of a now well-regarded Viennese painter, as you know.'

'Purported?' Nicoletta leaps on the word, seeing where this is going.

'Indeed.' Slift extinguishes his cigarette under the tap and disposes of the stub in a wastepaper basket. Leaving the window open, he makes his way back over to the desk and sits down. He gives her another apologetic smile. 'The paintings belonging to Pat Dennehy, and Helen Leonard, the ones given them by their father Tom Leonard, which The Rook was so keen to get his hands on, are reproductions. Though convincing. They had your Miss Leonard's father completely fooled when he bought them.'

Nicoletta sits for a moment, taking this in, before checking her watch and shoving everything back into her bag. 'I'm so sorry, I have to dash.'

She shakes Slift's hand across the table. 'So, they're fakes? Then where are the genuine articles? If there are any?' She is reluctant to leave mid-conversation, but her job is on the line if she's late to the meeting.

Slift raises his hands in a 'search me' gesture.

'Miss Sarto, you are dealing with dangerous individuals, with no respect for human life. I'd bow out if I were you. Before it's too late,' he says with a kindly smile, as he stands up and walks her to the door.

She's halfway down the stairs when she looks back and

sees his anxious brow peering down at her, his hands dug into his pockets. She turns on her heel and doesn't stop running until she's back at the office.

Chapter Twenty-Seven

She's sweating and out of breath when she makes it back to the newsroom with two minutes to spare. Ann looks up from scribbling furiously on a loose sheet at her desk, blowing stray bits of fringe out of her eyes with heavily glossed lips.

'They're waiting for you. In Duffy's office.'

'Thanks,' Nicoletta replies, frantically swabbing at her shiny face with a tissue and dragging a comb through her hair.

'Come here,' Ann says, motioning for Nicoletta to step forward. She takes a plump bottle of perfume from her desk drawer and liberally spritzes its contents in the air around Nicoletta. She closes her eyes as she's enveloped in a cloud of descending sickly-sweet-smelling mist.

'You're grand, off you go.' Ann gives her a wink, and Nicoletta strides off towards Duffy's office, her shoulders back, her confidence restored by Ann's unexpected kindness.

The door is closed when she approaches, and she can hear a low murmur within. She raps sharply on the glass, and a gruff voice tells her to come in. Duffy is behind his desk when she steps inside, his chin in his palm. Price and Barney are perched on chairs on the other side of the desk, with a third vacant seat angled slightly away beside the window. Price and Barney don't stand up or acknowledge her.

'Nicoletta!' Duffy growls, getting to his feet and gesturing towards the empty chair. 'Take a pew, that's a good girl.'

She smiles at Duffy and obeys his command, sitting down and tucking her feet under the chair. She places her handbag beside the window. When she looks up, she glances sideways at Barney, but he won't meet her eye. Nor will Price. Instead, they both keep their gazes straight ahead, focused on Duffy.

He taps the table rhythmically with both palms, as though he's banging an imaginary set of drums. 'Well now, how are you?'

Before she can reply, he clicks his tongue and leaves it lolling out the side of his mouth, eyeing her as if she's a particularly tasty morsel. 'We're concerned about your well-being, Nicoletta.'

'Oh?' Nicoletta clears her throat, which has gone very dry all of a sudden. It must have been the sprint back from Grafton Street. She smiles. 'I don't think there's anything to be concerned about.'

Duffy doesn't return her smile. Instead, he closes his eyes and puts up a hand. 'It's my turn to talk, my dear. You'll have a chance to have your say, but first you have to listen. Got it?'

She acquiesces with a polite nod. Inwardly, she's seething. She knits her fingers together on her lap to stop them trembling. Price gives her a furtive smirk, but Barney keeps focused straight ahead.

'Your behaviour is erratic, you're never at your desk, you are continuing to pursue a story that you were expressly told to stay away from. We've had a complaint from Celine Rault that you've been harassing her and her mother in the aftermath of Antoine Rault's suicide.' He bangs a fist lightly on the desk to emphasise each point. 'You're just not doing the job you were hired to do.'

He looks at her from underneath wriggly brows. 'Everyone's entitled to a life outside this newspaper.' He gives Barney a meaningful glance. Price smirks, then looks down at the floor. 'But when that private life bleeds into your professional life here in this office and interferes with your ability to do the job you're being paid to do, I have a serious problem with that.' He puffs out his cheeks glumly. 'I'm afraid, Nicoletta, I'm letting you go. You have until the end of the week to work out your notice.'

Nicoletta doesn't react. She's aware of three pairs of eyes on her, studying her. She sighs.

'Can I speak now?' She doesn't wait for permission. 'I think it's grossly unfair that I'm clearly being punished in a professional capacity for the breakdown of my relationship with Barney.'

Barney splutters. 'Come on, Nic. You aren't coping with the demands of the job and your domestic duties. As the boss said, your behaviour is erratic, to say the least. Go and spend time with your kids.' He pauses, then whispers, as an aside, as though he can't quite help himself: 'Liam is devastated, by the way. Are you ever going to contact him? And apologise for the way you've abandoned him?'

Nicoletta shakes her head in disbelief. She picks up her bag, stands up and backs out in the direction of the door. Before she goes, she addresses Duffy. 'I'm going back to my desk to work out my notice. Thank you for all the opportunities. And I'm sorry it didn't work out.' She ignores Barney and Price, closing the door quietly behind her.

As soon as she's back in the newsroom she makes a sharp right turn for the stairs that leads to the library. Dolores is sitting on her perch, reading that day's *Irish Independent*. She looks up in surprise when she sees Nicoletta.

'Dolores, can you find me everything you have on file about Tom Leonard, Louise Leonard and Ray Hall? I'll wait.' She knows there must be some evidence of a link between the Leonards and The Rook, if only she can find it. Meredith Field was most likely working on The Rook's behalf, sent to Helen Leonard to retrieve the painting, otherwise how would she have known what to look for?

Forty-five minutes later she leaves with a sheaf of cuttings secreted in a manila folder wedged into her bag. She arrives back in the newsroom, her head held high. Dermot is at one of the typewriters. He looks ashen, grey pouches pronounced under his eyes. She grabs his arm.

'Free for a drink?'

He shakes his head. 'Can't, sorry.' He meets her eye. 'Another time, Nic.' He squeezes her hand. She sits down heavily at her desk and, on impulse, dials Louise Leonard at the Law Library. By some miracle, she gets her on the phone. Louise must get the urgency in Nicoletta's tone because she agrees to meet her for a drink at the Bailey.

She grabs her coat and leaves before anyone can stop her. It starts to drizzle on the lonely walk up Westmoreland Street, and she doesn't bother opening the umbrella in her bag or covering her head with a scarf. The numbness starts to dissolve with the feel of the rain on her face, droplets frizzing her hair. The worst has happened. And yet she feels emboldened with every step as she marches towards College Green.

When she gets to the Bailey on Duke Street, she pauses at the doorway, bracing herself for seeing people she knows, having to make small talk with the ones she can't get rid of. But the place is mostly empty: post-lunchtime rush; the student crowd has cleared out for the summer. She doesn't want to be disturbed until Louise arrives. She orders a coffee, craving something warm and sweet, and opens her bag, surreptitiously taking out the manila file and spreading its contents across the table once her coffee has arrived and she's certain she isn't being observed. There are easily hundreds of clippings, in chronological order, from the 1940s to present day. They relate to Tom Leonard's career as a barrister, Louise Leonard's career as a barrister, and Ray Hall's career as a criminal. Nicoletta steels herself with a gulp of bitter coffee and applies herself to the task with laser focus. She doesn't know what she's looking for. This is the only chance she'll have to look at this file before Dolores starts looking for it back, as word will have reached her by now that Nicoletta has been sacked and had no business asking for *Sentinel* clippings in the first instance. There is a dizzying amount of data to take in. Nicoletta crosses her legs at the ankle and swings them back and forth against the scruffy banquette, enjoying the solitude, the blindingly strong coffee, the fact that no radio is playing in the background to intrude on her concentration, apart from the odd clang or bang from the bar area.

She shuffles on to a photo of newly qualified barrister Louise Leonard BL, one of only two women in her class at King's Inns, who'd scored the highest exam results that year, her father's arm around her shoulder. It's a dazzling puff piece, the unnamed '*Sentinel* reporter' praising the young Louise's family background as the daughter of 'well known senior counsel Tom Leonard Junior' and the granddaughter of 'politician and businessman Tom Leonard Senior'. It didn't mention Senior's efforts in the 1916 Rising, nor his subsequent fortune amassing in South Africa in the '20s. Funnily enough, it also omitted any mention of Louise's female antecedents in any meaningful sense, other than the reporter praising the young Louise's brains and style.

She yawns and checks her watch. It's been forty minutes since she left the office. She's about to stand up and visit the Ladies' when Louise herself rushes towards her, all apologies. Before she can tell her not to, she's back with two gin and oranges.

'Might as well,' Louise says with a wink, as she takes a gulp of the watery-looking concoction and takes off her jacket, its lapels severely cut against her soft white throat. She looks softer, younger, without it. She hangs it from the back of her chair. 'So, tell me everything. You sounded so mysterious on the phone.'

Nicoletta feels a wave of emotion rise and rise, until it stops somewhere in her chest, an unruly, tentacled thing. Following this story had been a huge mistake. It's time to cut her losses and ask Louise to help her.

'I've been sacked,' she says, taking a swig of the gin and instantly feeling better.

'By the *Sentinel*?'

Nicoletta nods.

'Why?' Louise watches her steadily from across the table. Does she really see her? It doesn't matter, Nicoletta decides. She'll take what she needs from this conversation. And that will be that.

'I went after the story about your aunt's carer. Meredith Field, it turns out her name was. Who was murdered. And The Rook.'

Louise frowns. 'You wrote that exposé about the nursing agency hiring unqualified nurses to care for the vulnerable elderly. Which I'm hugely grateful for, by the way. But what does The Rook have to do with my aunt Helen?'

Nicoletta takes a fortifying swig of gin. She's beyond caring. 'Oh, come on, Louise. You're not that naïve. The Rook already has one half of the painting belonging to Helen's sister Pat Dennehy. Meredith Field was found with Helen's painting. By the way, I have it on good authority that this was a forgery.'

She sits back and folds her arms. Louise doesn't bite.

'How do you know that?' She narrows her eyes.

'I have it on good authority, as I've said. Antoine Rault was not who he said he was.'

Louise drains her gin. She emits a tiny belch, and

eyeballs Nicoletta, as though daring her to draw attention to the fact. 'Of course Rault wasn't who he says he was. No harm in being queer, though, is there? That didn't feed into the rest of his life, surely.'

It's Nicoletta's turn to frown. 'Wasn't he cautioned in the District Court for moving a stolen painting through his business? One that was stolen from Holloway House and linked to The Rook?'

Louise waves a ringless hand. 'I don't know. I do know that you seem to have got yourself into a spot of bother, and that's unfortunate.'

There's silence for a minute or two. Nicoletta takes another gulp of gin. 'Could you put in a good word for me with Maureen French at the *Chronicle*, or any of the others? I need a new job.'

Louise drains her drink and eyes Nicoletta steadily. 'Sure,' she says. 'Leave it with me. You'll hear from me.' She puts back on her jacket and shakes Nicoletta's hand with a solemn movement.

'Thank you for meeting with me, Nicoletta. And just as a precaution, I'm going to get the painting that was found with Meredith Field's, ah, body, assessed. If it is indeed a forgery, then what has all this death and destruction been for, eh?'

The question must be rhetorical, because she snatches up her bag and walks off before Nicoletta can attempt an answer.

Chapter Twenty-Eight

She enters Pearse Street Garda Station like a greyhound out of a starting trap and asks for Garda O'Connor at the front desk. Not allowing herself to feel anything so self-indulgent as hope. She doesn't know what she's going to do yet, but she hasn't written anything off either. A middle-aged man, his hands bound in front of him in handcuffs, snores from one of the seats beside the desk, his stained lapels flapping violently as each exhale increases incrementally in volume. The young Garda at the desk, a steaming mug at his elbow, a glowing two-bar heater by his side, doesn't register familiarity at the sound of her name. She exhales in relief.

She considers the last few hours. Maybe she subconsciously wanted to be fired. Maybe she purposefully made sure she couldn't hack it. The Guard indicates for her to sit beside the drunk man. She slides onto the cold gridded metal, crossing her legs at the ankle while the young Garda presses buttons in front of him and speaks intermittently in a low, respectful voice. Nicoletta shivers. The afternoon hasn't yet heated up; it's as cold as winter.

The man beside her is crescendoing up a symphony of snores. Nicoletta uncrosses her legs. It's only a matter of time before he wakes himself. She looks at her watch and waits. And waits. A couple of times she thinks about leaving, but she can't bring herself to stand up and walk back on to the street. But she doesn't want to be alone with her own thoughts. She pictures Garda O'Connor's face, the kind eyes, the stoic set around the jaw. She owes him her life. *But that's not why you're here*, she reminds herself. She shifts uncomfortably in her seat. The man beside her wakes up with a start, his eyes popping comically wide, his neck sticking out to survey his surroundings like a startled turkey. He wipes drool from his mouth with the back of a bony hand and eyeballs Nicoletta. She pretends to be deeply involved with rearranging the pleats on her skirt.

'Are you on the game?'

She starts, not sure if she's heard correctly. She stands up and approaches the young Garda at the desk, looking at him from under her lashes. He's talking to someone on the phone and seems to have forgotten she exists. He doesn't even register her standing in front of him. She clears her throat.

'What's the going rate these days, love?' the drunk man slurs.

She spins around in a flash of irritation. '*Far* out of your budget.' His head lolls back and he re-enters noisy slumber. Whether or not he heard her retort isn't clear.

'Miss Sarto.' She wheels back around to see O'Connor leaning against the door frame, an amused twist to his lips. 'To what do I owe this honour?'

Her chest surges with joy at the sight of him, his eyes shrewd, flinty as arrowheads. But she stays rooted to the spot. 'I'd like to talk to you about ... something,' she says, carefully, glancing behind her at the front desk. The young Garda is studiously pretending not to be listening intently to what they're saying. 'Not here, or now, obviously,' she says, more quietly. 'I'm sure you're busy. But I didn't want to say it on the phone.'

'I see.' He coughs into his hand. 'I'm actually finishing up a shift here.' He indicates the coat over his arm.

He gestures for her to step outside, onto the cold grey pavement.

'Well,' he says, and smiles. It lifts his whole face. 'How've you been?'

'I got fired from the *Sentinel*,' she says softly, half afraid the words might get carried off on the breeze. 'And just so you know, I'm never going back to Barney. Never ever,' she laughs, a dry, hollow sound filling her throat. 'Never, ever, ever. I just wanted to tell you. Okay, bye.'

She starts to walk away, then she feels the weight of his hand on her shoulder, rooting her to the spot.

'Nicoletta,' he says, the word like music from his mouth. He's hardly ever called her by her first name before. She turns; the movement is excruciatingly slow.

'I've the car over there,' he says, indicating a side street. 'I was about to go home. Come with me. We can talk.'

They don't talk much in his car, a bottle-green Ford Escort. Nicoletta fidgets with the seat belt, unsure if she's done the right thing; being here, after all that. Whereas Barney's driving had been all skating corners at dangerously wide angles, O'Connor is a meticulous, instinctive driver. Nicoletta looks out the window, at the city going by, greys, browns and greens running down the glass like heavy rain. Eventually he pulls in at the middle house of a neat red-bricked terrace between Ranelagh and Rathmines. He lets the engine run for a ruminative few moments, as though he too is having second thoughts. Then he looks at her; in this light his eyes are slate blue. She unclicks her seatbelt and gets out of the car, not sure what to do with her hands. She shoves them in her pockets, her handbag dangling off one wrist and hitting her thigh in an awkward rhythm as she follows him to the crimson door. He unlocks it and indicates for her to go ahead of him. She stands for a moment, looking around, while he enters a room at the top of a short corridor. There are framed photographs lining the hall, sepia wedding portraits of, she presumes, his relatives. Surely not of him, but a sudden uncertainty shrouds her as she approaches the door he'd just gone through. It leads to a wide, open-plan kitchen, clean, bright. He's standing at a counter, filling an electric kettle at the sink.

'Do you live here alone?' She feels at once like they are two strangers who have just met, and also like she's known him all her life.

'Yep,' he says, turning his head as the kettle comes to the boil. He pours water into a cup and stirs, indicating the sugar bowl. She shakes her head, exhaling slowly.

'Are you married?' The question seems gauche to her own ears, yet she needs to know now, in plain English, before they go any further.

'No.' He picks up the steaming cups and carries them over to a scrubbed-looking wooden table beside a glass door through which molten morning sunlight is streaming.

'I can close the blinds if that light's too strong?'

She shakes her head, impatient to get this conversation out of the way. 'Have you ever been married?'

His eyes meet hers for a moment. There's an understanding in them, though nothing has yet been said. 'Never,' he replies, sipping his tea.

'Why?' The word scorches her tongue as she takes a gulp of tea, almost wishing she could spit it out.

He smiles, lifting his face to the stream of sunlight. 'Never met the right woman.' He looks up at her. 'You?'

She bites her lip, looking down over the gilt-edged rim of her cup. 'I was engaged to Barney, and we have two children,' she says, her voice dropping to a whisper. 'It's a bit of a mess.'

He nurses his tea between both palms. 'You sure you don't want to work things out, no? For the sake of the children. Rosa and Cara, isn't it?'

Nicoletta bobs her head in a miserable nod. 'No.' She looks up at him. He is studying her intently. 'I won't go back there. But I can't live at my mother's forever.' She takes another scalding gulp of tea.

'You could stay here for a bit,' he says thoughtfully, putting down his cup. 'You and the two girls. There's plenty of room, sure.' His eyes widen. 'Just until you get yourselves sorted out, like. Strictly as friends, if you like.' He sits back, waiting for her reaction, his face raised in expectation.

She sets her cup down on the table. 'I couldn't do that,'

she breathes. 'The three of us here, taking up space, intruding on your tidy life.'

He seems to consider that for a moment. Finally, his mouth curves in a faint smile. 'Has it ever occurred to you that maybe I'd enjoy the company?'

She shakes her head. 'It'd be too much,' she says, putting down her cup.

'All right,' he says with a wave of his hand. 'The offer's there. What did you want to talk to me about?'

She hesitates a moment. 'I have it on good authority those paintings are fakes.'

'Who told you that?' He puffs out his cheeks.

'I can't tell you that. I've already been fired, so my last action on this story is that I'm going to doorstep The Rook and get his reaction.'

He gives his head a slight shake. 'That's a really bad idea, Nicoletta. He's dangerous. Besides, haven't you lost your job at the *Sentinel*? Who would publish the story?'

She scrapes back her chair and stands up. 'I'll worry about that when it looks like I have something to publish.' They look at each other, neither wanting to break the invisible thread binding them in the moment. 'Thank you for the tea.'

'You're more than welcome,' O'Connor says, pushing back his chair and standing up.

He walks her through the sparse, spotless hall. At the door, she pauses. 'You're a good man.' She stands on tiptoes and presses her lips to his cheek. It feels smooth and familiar. She doesn't wait for his reply before she's out the door, and down the path. She looks back when she's halfway down the road and he's still standing in the doorway, his face half obscured, so she can't tell whether he's still looking at her.

The journey home seems to take an eternity. By the time she reaches Fairview, the day has warmed up. Swathes of cobalt blue streak the sky, as if drawn by some bold cosmic paintbrush. Rossella opens the door to her parents' house before Nicoletta has even rung the bell.

'Your mother is worried sick,' she hisses, a warm speck of saliva landing on Nicoletta's forehead. 'And Barney's been ringing the shop all day looking for you.'

'I'm sorry,' Nicoletta mumbles, feeling lightheaded whether from hunger or exhaustion, she's not sure which anymore. 'There was nowhere for me to call.'

'I bet there wasn't.' Rossella takes Nicoletta's coat roughly from her shoulders and throws it onto a hook. It immediately falls to the floor in a crumpled heap. Neither of them makes any move to pick it up.

Nicoletta follows Rossella meekly into the kitchen. When they reach the door, instead of opening it, Rosella wheels around, her sheer force inching right up against Nicoletta's face, though Nicoletta is easily a head taller. 'Those babies are exhausting your poor mother. You can't just dump them on her like that.'

Nicoletta gulps. 'I've been busy with work. I was working on a story. I can't just drop it. It seems to be finished now anyhow ...' She trails off. Rossella's eyes are narrowed.

'Funny, that. Barney said you got fired today. So, what exactly was the work thing that was so important?'

Nicoletta reaches a brazen hand behind her aunt and twists the door handle. Before she pulls it fully open, she pauses. As though reading her mind, Rossella scowls.

'I haven't said anything to your parents if that's what you're worried about. Let you tell them yourself.'

Nicoletta exhales silently as they file into the kitchen. Her father is at the kitchen table with a newspaper spread in front of him, shining his shoes.

'Well,' he says with a smile. 'Our intrepid reporter.'

Nicoletta manages a thin smile, the guilt enveloping her in a noxious cloud.

'Hi, Dad,' she says, hugging him from behind, cheerier than she feels. 'You're back. What's been happening?'

He looks down at a shoe, mid-rub. 'Your mother's upstairs with the girls. It's quiet, so she must've finally got them to sleep.' He winks.

Nicoletta nods. 'I'll go up now. Swap places with her.'

He indicates the chair in front of him. 'Take a seat. There's tea in the pot. Your mother will be down soon.'

She does as he suggests, sitting back with her fingers curled around the mug, as Rossella bangs around at the sink clearing up. She should really be upfront, tell her parents that as well as having nowhere to live, she's now been sacked.

'Dad, I have to go into work in the morning, but I should be home early. Do you think that would be okay with Mam? Just for one more day.'

'Of course,' her father smiles, buffing his shoes with balled-up newspaper. 'If it helps you, then of course.'

Nicoletta ignores Rossella's snort of disapproval from the sink as she clangs a dripping pot onto the draining board.

'I'm going home,' she says, addressing Ettore, wiping her hands on her skirt. 'It's been a long day.'

Nicoletta stands up. 'I'll walk you out.'

In the hall, Rossella snatches up her coat and handbag, then draws Nicoletta into a rough hug.

'I'll tell them tomorrow,' Nicoletta says shortly, as Rossella bangs the door behind her.

'Tell us what?' Her mother is standing midway down the stairs.

Nicoletta takes a sharp breath. 'Tell you that I've found somewhere to live. We'll be moving out. Thank you for all the help.'

Relief softens her mother's face. 'Not at all,' she says, taking a couple of steps down and sitting on the bottom step. 'The girls are asleep,' she says.

Nicoletta sits down beside her.

'Where will you be living?'

'I have a couple of possibilities,' Nicoletta lies. 'I'm paying a visit tomorrow morning.'

'That's great,' her mother sighs, patting her shoulder. 'Now, go up and get some sleep. You must be exhausted.'

Nicoletta heads upstairs and gets into her single bed without turning on the light, even though the twins are surely asleep in her mother's bed and no sound emanates through the wall. She closes her eyes, her mind rolling over each possibility with relentless clarity. She waits a long time for sleep to come. She wakes at sunrise, washing and dressing before the babies stir. She can't bear to look in on them as she tiptoes past her mother's room, down the stairs and out the door without saying goodbye.

Chapter Twenty-Nine

She walks into town, her feet remembering their way to the *Sentinel* offices at Burgh Quay by rote. Once she reaches O'Connell Bridge, she pauses. A malodourous mist hangs resolutely over the river in the still of the early morning, as though betraying the events of the night. She turns right, following the glittering murk of the river up as far as Kingsbridge station, without any idea of where she should go. Once there, she leans against the low boundary wall and wraps her arms around her middle. A dray horse carrying large barrels of something – milk? Guinness? – clip-clops past, before it skitters sideways in her direction at the blare of a car horn, startling her out of her funk.

There are goosebumps on her arms, she realises, as she reaches into her bag for her notebook relating to this story. It has so far been strange and unexpected, and it has cost her job, but she takes out the pages anyway, leafing through them, until she finds what she's looking for. John Lanigan's parents' address is at the intersection between Ranelagh and Rathmines. She'll pay them a visit, she decides, crossing the road to the taxi rank at the station.

Why? she pleads with herself. *Go home. Ring Barney. Beg for your job back.* And for their relationship? She shakes her head, though there's no one else around. She can't go back there. But perhaps she should lie low, plan her next move. That would be the sensible thing to do. *Besides, John Lanigan's parents aren't going to tell you where he is, even if they know,* she reasons with herself. Although she'd like to ask them about John's girlfriend Meredith Field, and the shocking way she'd been found dead. Would they react to that? Would they tell her anything? Maybe they didn't even know their son's girlfriend. Both adults, students, free to see whomever they pleased, not living under their parents' roofs.

She exhales slowly, sticking her hand out for a small black Fiesta, inching its way forward first in the queue at the rank. The realisation sets in that she has nowhere to send a story even if she gets one. She's lost her job. It meant so much more than just somewhere she went every day. It had been her life for a long time. Louise Leonard's inscrutable face pops into her head. Meeting her had set this whole thing in train. She remembers how the other members of Women for Choice had been so admiring of her work on the Julia Bridges story. Maureen French from the *Chronicle* in particular. She yanks open the door and gets into the back seat. Perhaps she'd be giving Maureen a ring sooner rather than later to file some copy. Her guts tighten. She can feel this story taking shape, somehow, despite everything, its inky tentacles inching out further than she'd previously imagined they could. She asks the driver to let her out on Ranelagh's main street, just over the canal. Once she pays him, she realises she has no money left.

John Lanigan's home address is a smart Edwardian villa in the middle of the swathe of red-bricked dwellings that comprise Ranelagh and Rathmines. The garden is gravelled and neatly kept, with minimum fuss or foliage in evidence. Before she can give in to the sinking feeling of wrongness in the pit of her stomach, Nicoletta crunches her way up the front path and rings the bell. She doesn't trust herself not to change her mind and turn tail. There's a faint rustle, whether it emanates from the slight breeze which has risen over the course of the early morning, or from deep within the house, Nicoletta is unsure. She takes a deep breath and stands her ground. She has all the time in the world. She rings the bell again after a gap of a respectable couple of minutes, clasping her bag to her side, as though for comfort. She can hear faint footsteps, then silence, as though someone is behind the door, but won't reveal themselves. Nicoletta rings the bell again. The door opens a couple of inches, and she catches a gleam of fair hair, drawn back off a pale, high forehead.

Then the person opens the door fully. A girl of about sixteen stands in the doorway in stockinged feet, holding a slice of toast in her hand. She swallows before she speaks.

'We're not buying anything,' she says, brushing crumbs from her lips.

'I'm not selling anything,' Nicoletta says with a smile. 'Don't think I'd be very good at it anyhow.'

'Why's that?' the girl asks. She shifts her weight to the

other foot. She's wearing plaid shorts and a cream camisole, from which a hanging thread is loose. Nicoletta longs to snip it.

'I don't know,' Nicoletta says, still smiling. 'I'm not very good at lying. And you have to be a liar to be a good salesman. Trying to convince someone to buy something they don't need.' She exhales, wondering if she should regret this little digression. But the girl is smiling, showing a row of small white teeth.

'I lie all the time,' she says, with a happy little shrug. 'Especially to Mummy. But I try to be good.'

Nicoletta feels a prickle of shame in her chest. She hasn't yet told this rather trusting girl who she is or why she's here. And she's about to deliver bad news about her brother's girlfriend having been murdered, unless the girl already knows about it. Nicoletta smiles at her again. There is something fey about her, an innocence that was not discarded back in childhood.

Nicoletta holds out her hand. 'Nicoletta Sarto is my name. I'm a reporter. Could I please speak to your mother, if she's available?'

The girl blinks. 'You're a reporter? So, telling the truth is your job. You literally can't lie.'

Nicoletta feels her fingers curl around the leather strap of her bag across her shoulder. It's her turn to shrug. 'That's exactly right,' she says. 'I literally can't lie.'

'Mummy's having a rest,' the girl says suddenly, taking a final bite of toast, and taking an age chewing and swallowing. Her large blue eyes glisten. 'What do you want to speak to her about?'

Nicoletta hesitates. But this girl is all she's got at this precise moment.

'It's about John Lanigan.'

The girl's face goes white, and she goes to close the door. 'We haven't seen John in months. Go away now.'

Nicoletta manages to jam her bag into the closing gap. 'Wait. Did you know John's girlfriend, Meredith Field?'

The girl's eyes open wide. 'I know Meredith,' she says quietly. 'Wait, why did you say, "did you know Meredith", like you were speaking in the past tense?'

Nicoletta makes a split-second decision. 'Meredith was found murdered in the Dublin mountains,' she says in a rush. 'It's been all over the newspapers.'

The girl's small hands curl into fists. 'I don't read the newspapers,' she says, pressing them forlornly to her chest.

'I'm very sorry,' Nicoletta says, feeling awful.

The girl shakes her head, as though deflecting the ineffectual condolence. 'You'd better come in. Mother's taken two Valium so she'll be out for the count for hours.'

She opens the door wide, and beckons Nicoletta to follow her down the hall.

The house is shabbier inside than its gravelled paths, freshly painted borders and shined windows on the exterior would suggest. The girl leads Nicoletta into a small breakfast room wallpapered with peeling navy vertical stripes. The effect is to make Nicoletta feel slightly queasy. Her stomach rumbles loudly, and she looks at a point above the mantlepiece until it stops. There's a muddy brown and green painting of hunting dogs and horses. They look pretty miserable. It's the kind of thing she can't abide. She wonders if it was expensive. It probably was. She also wonders if it came from Rault's Gallery. It probably did. That doesn't make it any more pleasant. She waits to be told where to sit. But the girl slumps down on the rug next to the ashen fireplace, side on to Nicoletta, hugging her knees to her chest, her lips moving, as though she's crooning to herself in some manner of self-soothing. Nicoletta perches on an uncomfortable high-backed wooden chair beside the door. She supposes it might be an antique, expensive like the painting, though to her it just looks old and worn.

'Are you all right?' she says at last to the girl's profile.

There's no answer.

'What's your name?' she tries again.

The girl swivels around, as though just remembering Nicoletta's presence.

'Nancy,' she says, standing up and coming over to the chair beside Nicoletta.

'Nancy Lanigan, or ... ?' Nicoletta asks, uncertain of how to play this.

'Yes,' Nancy agrees, cautiously swiping a hand down her face like a cat.

'What's your relationship to John Lanigan?' Nicoletta asks again.

Nancy looks at Nicoletta as though this might be the most absurd stroke of the day yet. 'He is my brother.' She sighs. 'My half-brother, but I'm not supposed to say that. Mummy was widowed when she met my father.'

'And where, er, is he? Your father?' Nicoletta heaves her notebook out of her bag and opens it on her lap.

The girl blinks at Nicoletta, then looks down at her

stockinged feet with a blush, like it was a staring contest. 'At sea,' she says, waving a hand to indicate an expanse of ocean.

'I see,' Nicoletta replies, not sure she really does at all. 'What does he do there?'

'He's a sailor,' Nancy says with a laugh, as though Nicoletta has just pulled the funniest punchline yet.

Nicoletta writes a line or two, then stops. 'Is it all right if I write down what you say to me? I won't use it in a story if you don't want me to.'

Nancy frowns. 'It depends.' She looks at Nicoletta from under her lashes. She will be a handsome girl, someday, Nicoletta decides. But for the moment there is something rather unformed about her face, like unmoulded clay.

'Depends on what?' Nicoletta says, briskly closing the notebook.

'On what you can do for me.' Nancy rummages in her shorts pocket and comes back with a slim pack of cigarettes. She lights one and goes to sit cross-legged at the fireplace to smoke it.

Nicoletta exhales through her teeth and tosses the notebook back into her bag. 'I haven't got any money,' she says, standing up. 'If that's what you're after. But I understand this is an upsetting time. You've just found out your brother's girlfriend was murdered. You were fond of her?'

Nancy laughs. 'Oh God, no. No way.'

It's Nicoletta's turn to blink. She sinks back down into the uncomfortable, high-backed chair.

'Why did you ask me in, Nancy?' She speaks slowly. Nancy remains puffing away on her cigarette, blowing plumes of smoke up the chimney, considering the question.

'I wanted to find out what you knew,' she says, tossing the butt into the ashy mess in the grate. 'Of course, I read the newspapers and of course, I saw the news about Meredith. You could hardly miss it in the *Sentinel*.' She rises and sits back down beside Nicoletta, looking pensive. She suddenly looks much younger, her chin trembling with the effort of keeping up the act. Nicoletta wonders if she might actually be a couple of years younger than sixteen. Someone who has played the part of a grown-up for so long she has almost taken on its mantle as a second skin. Almost, but not quite. She surprises Nicoletta by grabbing her hand. It's a small, clammy palm that meets Nicoletta's, and she can't bring herself to pull away.

'They don't think John did it, do they?'

Nicoletta is so taken aback by the heartbreaking directness of the question that she lets the silence go on for a beat longer than she means to. 'I don't know much about the Garda investigation,' she finally replies honestly. 'I'm not involved in anything to do with that. What I am involved in is speaking to people who knew Meredith. Just to give some sense of who she was before she was taken away so senselessly.' She smiles, hoping she sounds convincing. 'I'm sure the Gardaí are examining all angles. You mustn't worry. Do you happen to know where John is?'

Nancy shakes her head so vigorously that her slight body judders with the motion. She doesn't let go of Nicoletta's hand. 'He's seven years older than me. A student at university. He comes and goes, does what he likes. I never know where he is.'

Nicoletta lets another beat elapse. 'Why did you dislike your brother's girlfriend?'

Nancy gives her head another shake. 'She was a user. I knew she'd do John wrong, and she has. I don't know how, I just know John wouldn't be in this mess if it weren't for her. He'd have sat his exams. He'd have a future.'

Nicoletta gently detaches her hand from Nancy's and extracts her pen from her bag in one neat movement. 'Do you think John had something to do with Meredith's death?' she asks, raising an eyebrow. Nancy visibly falls to pieces at the suggestion. She raises trembling fists to her eyes, her shoulders heaving.

'John wouldn't hurt a fly,' she breathes hoarsely, scouring away the falling tears with her knuckles. She sits back on the chair opposite Nicoletta, composing herself by lighting another cigarette. This time she doesn't bother going over to the fireplace to displace the smoke up the chimney. She looks so childlike, holding the cigarette in her hand. Nicoletta tries to remember the name of that horrible book she'd once read, the William Golding one about the children killing each other on an island. *Lord of the Flies*. But she didn't think there were any girls in it. This girl wouldn't be out of place in that setting. All pretences at civility gone. She'd probably had to fend for herself her whole life, a child playing by adult rules. Her eyes level with Nicoletta's, and she sits for a minute or two, smoking. 'John wouldn't do something like that,' she says, her voice carrying a pleading note in it.

'Where is John?' Nicoletta asks evenly, pen poised.

Nancy bites her lip and looks down at her nails. 'He

said he was going away for a while. To England, I think. He told Mummy, not me. I get everything second hand, including news.' She gulps, which turns into a cough.

Nicoletta doesn't write anything. Instead, she puts her writing materials back in her bag and stands up, holding out her hand. 'You should tell your mother how you're feeling. That you're worried about John. I'm sure she'll do her utmost to reassure you.'

Nancy snorts wetly. She doesn't take Nicoletta's hand, instead crossing over to the fireplace and tossing the butt. 'I'm sure she won't,' she says, in an ironic singsong voice.

Nicoletta pauses. She feels dreadful imposing on this vulnerable girl and just leaving her like this, distraught.

'Tell you what,' she says. She takes out her notebook and writes down the address and telephone number of Sarto's shop. She can hardly give her the *Sentinel* address now. 'If there's anything you want to speak about, in relation to John, or Meredith Field, that you remember, or anything else at all, you can come and see me.' She folds the page and presses it into the warm little palm, before seeing herself out into the red-bricked street.

Chapter Thirty

She turns a corner, then another. The streets are composed of warren after warren of similar-looking houses, all lined up in neat rows, their chimney stacks aligned in one endless loop. Her footsteps echo smartly on the wide paving. There aren't many people around yet. She has lost her bearings, but she keeps on walking, thinking she might be somehow closer to Rathmines than Ranelagh. As though drawn towards it by some magnetic pull, she finds herself on Grosvenor Avenue, with its rosy-hued Victorian villas, the path uneven thanks to the roots from the evenly spaced plane trees shading the handsome houses from prying eyes. She keeps walking until she reaches the end house, with its slightly shabby exterior compared to the others around it. Before she can stop herself, she walks up the short, gravelled driveway and rings the bell, just as Barney had only a few weeks beforehand, though now it seems like a lifetime ago. As far as she is aware, Barney has never got past the front door. A wave of reckless abandon washes over her as she rings the bell again. She's sure she can do better than he ever did.

The door is finally opened by a dark-haired, slim girl of nineteen or twenty. Her eyes are heavily kohled and her feet are bare. She doesn't say a word, just looks Nicoletta up and down, waiting for her to speak. Nicoletta remembers the dark-haired girl she'd seen at the window when she'd visited here with Barney, and wonders what relation she could be to Ray Hall. His wife? Sister-in-law? Her mind snags on what Barney had mentioned about The Rook being in a ménage à trois with two sisters and inwardly scoffs. Barney isn't always right. But still, she wonders.

'Yes?' the girl says, as though exasperated by Nicoletta's silence. 'Are you just going to stand there and gawp all day or what?'

'I'm looking to speak to Ray Hall, if I could,' Nicoletta says, holding out her hand. The girl doesn't take it. 'Nicoletta Sarto is my name. I'm a reporter.'

The girl looks Nicoletta up and down again, taking everything in, from the slightly rumpled smock and jeans to the bare, tired face. 'You don't look like the usual type who come around this way.'

'Oh, how's that?' Nicoletta asks, hoping to keep her talking as long as possible.

The girl scratches her cheek thoughtfully. 'Well, you're a lady reporter for starters.'

'There are quite a few of us,' Nicoletta says with a wry smile.

The girl shakes her head. 'None that want to speak to my . . . to Ray anyway, that's for sure.' She cocks her head to the side. 'Who do you write for anyhow?'

'I'm freelance at the moment,' Nicoletta says quickly.

She resolves to call Maureen French with this story for the *Chronicle* if she manages to get an interview with The Rook. Barney was right about something at least: it is like trying to get an audience with the Pope.

'Ray isn't in at the minute,' the girl says, scratching her cheek again, the door closing.

'Right, okay,' Nicoletta says, a desperate tremor creeping into her voice, 'why don't I give you a note that you might be able to pass on to him, when he comes home? I'll wait around for a bit.' She fishes in her bag for a pen and paper before the girl can answer. The door closes in her face. She scribbles a line on the page.

Dear Mr Hall,

I am writing to request an interview with yourself this morning at your earliest convenience. I am a very fair and conscientious reporter. I would like to hear your perspective on things. Thank you.

Yours sincerely,
Nicoletta Sarto

She folds the page in half and writes 'Mr Ray Hall' on the back, before sliding it under the door. Then she goes back to the gate and waits.

She taps her foot against the pavement, her nerves wired to infinity. She doesn't know if she's being incredibly brave, or incredibly foolish. She won't know until after the fact. She shifts her weight to the other foot. A row of haughty-looking crows on the telephone wire in front of her flap and squawk when, after twenty minutes have elapsed, she turns sharply and walks halfway up the street. She turns back when she realises that her window of opportunity might come at any moment and then clang shut just as suddenly. She only has one chance. When she comes back, she leans against the gate, her back to the house. After a minute or two, she turns around, squinting at the house side-on. She hates uncertainty. And unfortunately, with this job comes plenty of it. It sits on her chest, uncomfortable, a weight she can't quite shift. She exhales wearily. She decides she'll give it half an hour more, then go home.

The thought of her mother and Rossella minding the twins pierces the dense weight in her chest with a stab of guilt. Her father is home now, Rossella will soon return to her own home, and it will be business as usual for Sarto's Newsagents, with her mother working in the shop, and her parents resuming the steady rhythm of life as it always has been since she moved out. She's thinking of leaving the futility of this endeavour to people with no such worries, when she hears the click of the door and light footsteps on the gravel. She turns around to see the girl from earlier approaching her. Her dark fringe has separated – whether from the heat or exertion, it's hard to tell – and she waits until she's right up in front of Nicoletta before she speaks softly and quickly.

'Ray will see you in five minutes,' she says, biting her lip.

Nicoletta gulps. 'Really? Thank you.' She can't resist asking. 'Why?'

'He says you have the most beautiful handwriting he's ever seen,' the girl almost whispers over her shoulder, so that Nicoletta has to lean forward to catch it.

She follows the girl up the path to the front door, but the girl stops and indicates Nicoletta to follow her around the side of the main house. 'He's in the pigeon house,' she explains, stopping in front of a thick laurel hedge, its glossy green leaves shooting outwards in all directions.

'Oh?' The hedge is so thick that Nicoletta steps back and feels the rough hue of a granite windowsill jammed into the small of her back. She almost loses her footing but follows the girl to a flat, grassy clearing at the back where a high, wooden beamed structure stands on stilts, with a narrow ladder leading up to it. The girl points. 'He's up there.' She shrugs.

'I didn't catch your name,' Nicoletta says to the girl.

'I didn't give it,' the girl calls, as though she can smell the whiff of desperation in Nicoletta's voice, as she stands all alone in the back garden, apart from the faint cooing coming from the little wooden shed. The girl doesn't give her a backward glance as she makes her way around the side of the house, then disappears into the jungle-like foliage of the hedge. Nicoletta takes a deep breath, while she can. Then she hears a low, male-sounding cough echoing from within and she steels herself to start ascending the ladder.

When she reaches the top, she has to bend forwards in an awkward semi-crawl, to fit through the small, square opening in the wooden structure. It takes her eyes a moment to adjust – not only to the lack of light, but to the smoke, the ripe smell of bird droppings, and the inescapable feeling of a dozen pairs of eyes blinking out at her in the gloom.

It takes a while to ascertain that he's sitting on a small

stool at the back. He doesn't stand up or move at all. She can sense him basking in her discomfort, observing her from his perch like another of his pigeons. He must be small in stature, though Nicoletta doesn't remember him being quite so compact the time she'd seen him outside his house with Barney. The extremities of his limbs are in shadow, as are most of the planes of his face. Only his eyes are noticeable: gleaming like wet pebbles, they remind her of those of a neighbour's cat from when she was a child. She tries to remember what happened to the cat. The thought occurs to her that even the chubbiest, clumsiest of cats are wilier, more flexible and far more intuitive than their fittest human counterpart.

'Hello,' she calls cheerily, aware she is red in the face and feeling like she might explode out of her skin, keen to regain some sort of upper hand. 'Mr Hall. Thank you for agreeing to speak to me.' As she dips her head in an uncomfortable turn, she doesn't see any other stools available for her use. Without being asked, she half sits, half crouches on an upturned cardboard box halfway down the row of cages, aware it could give under her weight at any moment, leaving her in an undignified heap. The birds coo and flutter overhead, giving her the creeps.

'Miss Sarto, welcome to my office,' he says, in a low, husky voice, his eyes never leaving her face, so close she can almost feel the warm secondary smoke from his pipe curling its way into her lungs. This is too intimate, she decides, seeing the folly of her ways. She should have told Garda O'Connor she was coming here. Or someone, at least. But would The Rook have agreed to see her any other way? With a creeping sense of unease, she remembers that the childhood neighbour's cat, Pebbles, maybe so called after its distinctive gleaming eyes, had been squished on the road by an evening newspaper van.

The Rook blinks, as though reading her very thoughts. Nicoletta squares her shoulders, urging herself to get a grip. All he can sense is whatever it is she's putting out. And she needs to take control of the situation.

'Do you spend a lot of time up here?' Her tone is brusque, but pleasant. She hopes she doesn't sound as terrified as she feels.

'Yes,' he says, with a pale flash of teeth. 'It's where I do my best thinking.' He leans forward, extinguishing the pipe. She tries not to cough. 'You know, a lot of reporters have asked me for sit-down interviews over the years.'

'Why do you think that is?'

He shrugs. 'I've led an interesting life.' He rests his elbows on his thighs. 'Haven't I?' He doesn't blink.

She coughs politely, pretending to think, inching towards the open window at her back, until her breathing returns to normal. 'Yes,' she says, with an emphatic nod. 'You surely have. Do you mind if I take notes?'

He waves a hand, several rings glinting like gunmetal. She uncaps a pen, then realises she can't really see what she's writing anyway. She recaps the pen and keeps it in her lap.

'I'd like to start by asking you what you think about the *Among the Ruins* painting that was stolen from Helen Leonard turning out to be a fake?'

'How is that relevant to me?' he snarls. He gets to his

feet and, to her fascination, he only has to stoop slightly to avoid bumping his head.

Nicoletta digs her fingernails into her palm. 'Oh, that must be my mistake, so. Do you not have the other one?' She aims for sounding breezy, in actuality coming across as anything but. She gives an involuntary nervous giggle. It's out of her mouth, a twittery avian tick completely foreign to her ears. Heat rises on the back of her neck, but she ploughs on heavily. 'In which case, your one must be a fake too.'

He sighs loudly, as though it pains him to be dealing with such petty, venal concerns. 'Let's go back to the beginning.' He sits back down on his stool and relights the pipe. 'And put that pen back in your bag. If I say anything memorable, I'm sure you'll remember it.'

They sit facing each other, the smoke filling the space between them, not speaking, for a long moment. Nicoletta begins to feel slightly lightheaded from the lack of air. She knows her lungs are going to pay for this later. For now, she grits her teeth and stays where she is.

'Where would you like to begin?' Nicoletta asks finally, when the silence becomes too much for her to bear. She's never been good with long-drawn-out quiet. Nature abhors a vacuum. Isn't that what one of the nuns at school used to say when she said she didn't believe in God? She doesn't have any questions prepared, but she's heard Barney talking about this man and his brothers often enough to feel she knows about them. Everybody does.

'I don't know. Just ask me questions and I'll see if I want to answer them.' He waves the non-pipe-holding hand in a gesture of nonchalance. One of the birds at Nicoletta's right twitches and flutters at the sudden movement, and several more follow suit. Their cooing is intruding into her thoughts. This surely isn't going well. She is unusually tongue-tied, and she feels the urge to hurl herself back down the ladder onto the grass below. She presses her lips together. What is it even for? She has nowhere to file the story if she even does get one worth writing about. Her shoulders relax, the stress leaving her body. She can leave anytime she wants to. Can't she? Maybe now would be the time.

She twists her hands together and sighs. He quenches the pipe and sets it down by his feet. Nicoletta tries not to let her eyes follow the motion.

'You're very jumpy,' he says. 'And you're not wearing a wedding ring.'

'That's because I'm not married,' she says. 'Never have been. And I'm not sure if I ever want to be,' she adds boldly, feeling the adrenaline spike in her veins.

'Is that so?' He chuckles softly. 'Yet you're a mother. To twin baby girls.'

'How'd you know that?' she shoots back.

His shoulders twitch in a gentle shrug. 'I make it my business to know a lot of stuff. Some of it isn't my business but I know it anyway. Tell me, Barney won't marry you, no?'

Nicoletta feels a prickle of heat spiral down her collar. 'I left him,' she says flatly. 'Whatever he says. It's the truth he doesn't want to get around.'

'Did he get you fired?'

Nicoletta looks at him in surprise. 'How on earth do you know about that?'

He holds his hands up. 'You're very defensive.' He coughs.

'I've had to be,' she says. 'Besides, isn't attack the best form of defence?'

'It depends,' he seems to consider the question.

'On what?' she presses.

His eyes seem to take her in and she looks down quickly. 'On what the end goal might be. What's your end goal here, for example? With this interview.'

'To find out the truth.' The answer is automatic, as though she has been rehearsing it. Though of course she hasn't.

He takes the pipe out again and puts it to his lips. 'The truth comes at a price,' he says, taking it away from his mouth and waving in the dense air around him. 'The question is, are you prepared to pay it?'

She pushes her palms together, realising too late that her fingers are trembling. She exhales a shuddery breath. 'Am I interviewing you, or are you interviewing me?'

He laughs, slow, mirthless. She can't see most of his face, but she can see his eyes, never straying from her face. Playful, or ready to pounce?

'Where were you born?' she asks, the question falling out of her mouth bold and inevitable as projectile vomit.

'What does it matter?' He shrugs again.

Nicoletta sighs and stands up. 'If you're not prepared to answer any of my questions, I'm afraid I'll have to leave,' she says. 'It was lovely to meet you all the same.'

'I'm afraid I'll have to leave,' he echoes prissily, taking her off in an uncanny impression of what she'd just said. He laughs.

'All right. Chesterfield Buildings in Rathmines. That's where I was born. At home. Like everybody was then. None of these fancy hospitals.'

Nicoletta remembers the wild goose chase she'd undertaken to the local authority flats in Rathmines in search of Helen Leonard's nurse's reference, only to find the complex being demolished. Something pings in her head.

'Do you know Meredith Field? Or did you know her, I should say?' she demands, sounding way more confident than she feels.

'Who?' he says, his large eyes not blinking.

'The heiress who posed as Helen Leonard's nurse and stole the second *Among the Ruins* painting,' Nicoletta says impatiently. 'I think you know exactly who she is. Or was. She was murdered.'

'A terrible shame,' he says, blinking. 'I read about it in the papers. Same as everybody else.'

'I see,' Nicoletta says, after falling silent for a moment or two, allowing the cooing of the birds to fill the gap between them. 'A curious sort of person. An heiress who stole from her own parents.'

The Rook laughs. 'She wouldn't be the first or the last to reject what she grew up with. Isn't that what you did?'

Nicoletta bites her lip. 'Not exactly. I'm very close to my parents now.'

'Now?' He laughs again. 'I wouldn't say they were too happy with what you wrote about the Julia Bridges story.'

She shakes her head. 'Tell me about Chesterfield Buildings.'

'What exactly would you like to know?' he yawns. 'Isn't it your job to ask me specific questions? I can't be doing all the hard work here, you know.'

'All right.' She nods. 'Who was in your family at the time you were born?'

He shakes his head. 'People think they know my family. People think they know me.'

'And they don't?' Nicoletta holds her breath imperceptibly. Then she coughs violently, overtaken by the lack of fresh air. The Rook waits politely for her to finish before he continues.

'They know a version,' he says, in between sucking on the pipe. 'The version I give them. That's all.'

She can feel the prickle of heat in her neck again. 'What version are you giving me now?'

He smiles. A full-toothed, Cheshire cat grin, almost taking over his whole face. 'I haven't decided yet,' he says.

'I see,' she says, a tingle of danger starting at the base of her spine. It stays there, vibrating against her skin, not working its way up, but not going away either. A warning, or a stimulus. It emboldens her to look him dead in the eyes, which seem huge now, watchful as all hell. He rarely seems to have the need to blink. She wonders if that is deliberate, a frightening tic he has honed, rather than something that comes naturally. She takes such a deep breath, she almost swallows her own tongue. She knows what she is about to ask could go one of two ways. 'Did you kill Meredith Field, Mr Hall?'

He looks at her for a moment, his expression impassive.

Her breath rises in her chest as she decides she may as well ask all the burning questions on her mind. 'I think Meredith Field was working for you. Is that correct? Did she disguise herself as a nurse and steal Helen Leonard's painting, *Among the Ruins*? Did you then kill Meredith Field? I'd imagine how disappointing it must have been for you to find out that both paintings are fakes.'

He finally blinks, for the longest time. When he opens his eyes again, he takes the pipe out of his mouth. 'This interview is over,' he says, before slamming the bowl of the pipe into the mesh wire of the nearest enclosure. The sound is shrill, bleak. Like a badly tuned string instrument, or a siren. Nicoletta starts, and so do the birds, rising and falling back to their perches as one frustrated mass, their shrieks filling the enclosed space with a wall of noise. It occurs to Nicoletta that proverb or saying about birds of a feather flocking together. Does it mean they won't go anywhere without each other? Or that they recognise one another as being of their own species? Like finds like, maybe. Does that mean she is similar to Barney, their characters one and the same? Or perhaps she is more like O'Connor: determined, honest. She hopes it is more of the latter. The thought of O'Connor grounds her, as now the pigeons have gone from appearing to be benign, slightly noisy, smelly beings to something more sinister entirely. Their colourless eyes put her in mind of the trays of slimy fish, which she's only ever seen laid out on ice at the supermarket, cold and staring. They always gave her the creeps, she doesn't know why. She just knows she has to get away from here, from him. She almost dives headlong down the ladder and lands on the grass. It meets her with a crash, harder than she'd imagined it would, and she cradles the arm that had broken the fall, looking around for a way out.

She passes around the side of the house, falling into the overgrown laurel hedge before careening around to the gravelled driveway in front. The girl who'd shown her in is nowhere to be seen. A faraway dog whines, a man's voice booms, a door slams. The gate is slightly ajar from when she'd come in, however long ago that was, she isn't sure. She wrenches it open and makes her exit onto the footpath, the plane trees whispering in the breeze. A figure in a Garda car opposite eyes her curiously, before going back to staring straight ahead. She looks up at the circular window at the top turreted slant of the house. The girl from before is standing with her face pressed against the glass, dark hair pooling around her shoulders. Nicoletta walks down the road cradling her arm. She stops under the first plane tree and looks back. The face at the window has vanished.

Chapter Thirty-One

She walks home, not having enough taxi or bus fare in her bag. Nor any money at all. By the time she reaches Fairview, her arm feels as though it's on fire. She has lost all track of time, and she has forgotten to wear her watch, as she always does. She's surprised to see the clock at Clery's say only one o'clock as she passes. Not that much time has passed after all.

When she reaches her parents' front door, Rossella opens it before she has the chance to knock.

'Right, we need to have a chat,' she says, guiding Nicoletta into the empty kitchen, her small hand heavy on Nicoletta's painful shoulder, sitting her down at the table, busying herself filling the kettle and clattering out tea things. Nicoletta doesn't have the energy to object. When she hands Nicoletta a steaming mug, and seats herself opposite, her lips are pursed. She has the beginnings of her sister's frown lines tracking her forehead, Nicoletta notices. Though she seems to have resisted them for years.

'Your mother's worried sick,' Rossella says quickly, glancing at the door. She hasn't made any tea for herself.

'She physically can't mind two babies on her own.' She gives Nicoletta a meaningful look. 'They're fine, by the way. Not that you've asked. But they're upstairs asleep.'

Nicoletta turns to pick up the tea, but the pain in her arm hits her like a train.

'What is it?' Rossella frowns. 'Did you hurt yourself?'

'My arm.' Nicoletta doesn't want to say that she hurt herself jumping out of The Rook's pigeon shed. 'I tripped earlier. I'm sure it's just a sprain.'

Rossella shakes her head. 'You're sure of lots of things, Nicoletta, that's the trouble.' She catches Nicoletta's eye. 'Have you found somewhere to live yet?' Nicoletta thinks of Garda O'Connor's offer, but the reality is here, upstairs asleep in their cribs. She can't drag two innocent babies into a new mess.

'No,' she answers, relieved to finally be honest. 'I need a bit more time.'

'All right,' Rossella breathes. 'We're finally getting somewhere. You need more time. Of course you do, that's natural. Your whole life has changed.' She exhales again. 'The thing is, if you need more time, then you have to be here to help your mother out too. Especially now you've lost your job.'

Nicoletta avoids eye contact, instead keeping an eye on the clock above the door. It's somehow now three o'clock. Time has lost all meaning, she thinks, before remembering that her mother's clock hasn't worked in years.

'Don't worry, I haven't told them,' Rossella says, opening a pack of digestives and offering it to Nicoletta, who gratefully accepts two biscuits, barely pausing to crunch them in her mouth before swallowing them almost whole. 'That's up to you. In your own time.' She cups Nicoletta's cheek. 'This whole thing will be the making of you,' she says, standing up. 'Mark my words. You'll look back and remember how hard it is, yes. But you'll mark it out as a major turning point as well.'

Nicoletta nods, barely able to speak. Rossella doesn't seem to notice. 'I'll keep an eye on the two little ladies upstairs.' She bangs Nicoletta on the bad arm. 'Why don't you pop into the shop and give your poor mother a break?'

Nicoletta nods mutely, slurping the last of her tea and peeling herself off the chair to go through to the shop. Her mother is wearing her shop coat, leaning against the counter reading that afternoon's *Evening Press*, her dark hair spilling over the newsprint. The shop is empty.

She looks up when she hears the door open and shut. When she sees Nicoletta, she doesn't say anything, instead licking a finger before carefully turning a page and continuing to read.

'Hi, Mam. Why don't I take over now and you have a rest?' Nicoletta drags out a stool in front of the cash register and sits on it. Her mother closes the newspaper and replaces it on the rack. She takes off the blue shop coat with 'Sarto's' embroidered on the breast pocket and hangs it over her arm. She leaves without a word, heading back into the living quarters, and closing the door quietly behind her.

Nicoletta ducks and grabs the newspaper her mother had just replaced. But she can't take in the words that buzz in front of her eyes like flying ants. The fire in her arm has subsided to a dull ache. She stands up to search the shelves behind the counter for soluble aspirin, when the bell chimes above the door. She stands to attention, trying to look busy, on second thoughts wiping smudges from under her eyes. But the person who approaches the cash register is not a usual customer, most of whom she recognises by sight. It's Nancy Lanigan, John Lanigan's sister from earlier. Nicoletta blinks. It takes her a moment or two to place her here in this unfamiliar context.

'Nancy,' she says. 'What can I do for you?'

Nancy looks very slight and young away from her natural surroundings. The adult posturing of earlier with the cigarettes and the devil-may-care attitude has dissolved and left a bewildered child in its place. 'You told me to come if I remembered anything. Well, I did.'

'Oh?' Nicoletta feels a fizz of excitement wash over her weary bones. 'Why don't you come back here and sit beside me. In case any other customers come in, you see.'

'All right,' Nancy agrees, not seeming to think it strange that the reporter who interviewed her earlier is working in a shop.

'I'm just helping my mam out,' Nicoletta explains, as Nancy ducks under the counter onto the stool indicated by Nicoletta, the grown-up in charge. She assumes the role at once.

'Tell me, Nancy, what you've remembered.'

Nancy scrunches her fists together as though working herself up to thinking.

'It's about John,' she says, focusing all her attention on the open newspaper spread out on the counter.

'Yes,' Nicoletta agrees pleasantly. 'I assumed it would be.'

'And it's about Meredith too. She was a bad influence on John, and I'm not sorry she's dead.' Her eyes widen, as though waiting to be struck down for such a terrible utterance. 'She was working for a criminal.'

'Oh?' Nicoletta pats her arm, waiting for her to continue. None of this is news to her. But there might be some useful nugget of information within.

Nancy takes a long, shuddery breath. 'John and Mer were blackmailing someone.'

'Any idea who?'

Nancy rocks forward and almost falls off the stool, before Nicoletta reaches out an arm to steady her. Just then, the bell chimes and Mr O'Brien ambles in, picking up each of the newspapers in turn for a free read, before he plumps for his usual *Evening Herald*, waving at Nicoletta as he plops it on the counter.

'Who's this?' He gestures towards Nancy.

'A friend,' Nicoletta says shortly.

He clicks his tongue as she rings up his purchase. 'Isn't it great to have so many friends.' He lingers for a moment or two, but Nicoletta stands up and pretends to rummage on a nearby shelf until he leaves. She comes back to where Nancy is hunched on the stool, almost immobile. 'Listen, Nancy,' she says in a whisper, 'I'm going to ask you a few questions. Try and answer them as well as you can, as honestly as you can. I won't use your name in anything I write. You have my word.' She pauses. 'How old are you?'

'Fifteen,' Nancy says in a hoarse whisper.

'Okay.' Nicoletta grabs a Cadbury's Dairy Milk from the counter and makes a mental note to put some money in the till for it later. She unwraps it, and breaks off two squares, handing them to Nancy. 'Have this,' she says.

Nancy wolfs down the chocolate. 'Right,' Nicoletta says, tearing off a long ream of paper from the receipt roll and picking up a pen, leaning against the counter. 'We don't have much time. Who were they blackmailing, Nancy?'

Nancy swallows the chocolate. She looks up at Nicoletta. 'I don't know,' she says. Her teeth are covered in chocolate.

'How do you know they were blackmailing someone, then?' Nicoletta whispers furiously.

'John told me, the day before he left for England.'

'What did he say?' Nicoletta writes England in capitals on her receipt roll.

'He said they'd got sick of working for someone else. They decided to make a bit of money their own way.'

'Why was he telling you this?' Nicoletta thinks to herself that John Lanigan sounds like a very foolish young man, if it were true that he was working for The Rook, putting his sister in danger like that by involving her.

'He wanted me to know where he was going. He said he was finished with it all, with Mer, whatever scam they were pulling. He was going to go to England to work for the summer and repeat the exams when he got home.' Nancy breaks off another bit of chocolate. Her cheek bulges. Nicoletta keeps an eye on the door, but there are no customers. On impulse, she walks to the door and hangs the 'we're closed' sign facing out. She races back to Nancy and pats her shoulder. 'You're doing great, Nancy,' she says.

'So, what did John say, exactly, when he said they were blackmailing someone?'

Nancy hesitates and swallows. 'I don't know if you know, but Mer came from a very wealthy family. But they'd stopped giving her money.'

Nicoletta nods impatiently. They're going around in circles. And if word gets out to her mother that she'd closed the shop unauthorised, she'll be in big trouble.

'John didn't actually tell me they were blackmailing someone,' Nancy says finally. 'He just said he was sick of being pushed around. He didn't want anything more to do with whatever scam he and Mer were involved in, he said.'

'So, what happened then?' Nicoletta tries to keep her voice calm.

A tear rolls down Nancy's cheek. 'I missed John terribly. He didn't leave any forwarding address or contact details. I didn't know when he'd be back. Mummy can be very difficult. So then, one day, I was in Bewley's on Grafton Street, and I saw Mer leaving. I followed her.'

'I see,' Nicoletta says slowly. 'Where did she go?'

Nancy puffs out her cheeks. 'She went to Pearse Street. She was walking quickly. When she got to the station, she got on a train, going to the seaside. I was right behind her, but she didn't look up once. She got out at Monkstown station and so did I.'

'Was she meeting someone?' Nicoletta asks.

Nancy hesitates. 'I'm just telling you with Mer being dead and all. I thought maybe the person she met might have done something to her. It's terrible.'

'Yes,' Nicoletta agrees. 'It is. Absolutely awful. But it doesn't answer the question of who she was meeting.'

'It was a woman,' Nancy says loudly. 'She went into the car park of The Stag pub, overlooking the sea. She saw this lady – long hair, a pale red colour. It looked dyed. They seemed to know each other.'

Nicoletta looks at Nancy in surprise. 'Oh,' she says casually. 'You say they knew each other?'

'The woman handed Mer a bag, a holdall of some kind. The type you might use for carrying a sports kit. Then they argued. The woman shouted at Mer. I kicked an empty beer tin then by accident and they looked my way, so I had to hide behind a car, and I don't know what happened then. When I looked up, they'd gone. But maybe I should go to the police, in case this woman is the one who killed Mer. What do you think?'

Nicoletta nods. 'You should absolutely tell the Garda what you've just told me. Would your mother accompany you to talk to them?'

'I doubt it,' Nancy replies, taking cigarettes out of her pocket and lighting one without asking. The chocolate appears to be all gone. 'She's in bed most of the day.'

Nicoletta chews the inside of her cheek. She can hear a rapping on the glass. She knows she has to reopen the shop. 'You're sure the woman you saw seemed to know Meredith, and she had long, pale red hair?'

Nancy blows a smoke ring and nods in assent. Nicoletta smiles. 'I have to get back to these customers, Nancy. But thank you for coming to see me. I'll be in touch soon.'

Nancy reluctantly uncurls herself from the stool and

follows Nicoletta to the door. Nicoletta opens it and sees her into the street, before flipping the sign to 'open'. Two irate regulars are peering in through the shutters. As Nicoletta rushes back to the cash register, she calculates how long she'll have to stay before she can leave again. Nancy had said that the woman Meredith Field had met, presumably the last person, or one of the last people, she'd seen alive, was known to her and had pale red hair. Nicoletta stabs her finger into the till and rings up a bunch of grapes for an old lady who seems to know her name, but Nicoletta doesn't have a clue who she is. Hadn't Meredith Field been a History of Art student at UCD? And Celine Rault is the head of the department there. Nicoletta thinks about Celine: her laconic air, long tunic and rows of tinkling bangles. And the dyed-looking red hair, ironed dead straight, which falls to her waist. Could she have killed Meredith Field for Helen Leonard's *Among the Ruins* painting?

Chapter Thirty-Two

It's late afternoon by the time Nicoletta can get away again. The shop has been almost empty for most of the afternoon, but she soldiers on sitting at the counter sweating in front of the evening newspapers until five o'clock, at which point she pops back to the kitchen to tell Rossella she has to go to a job interview. She squashes down the lump of guilt somewhere deep inside, somewhere she can't reach. She reasons that she is homeless, jobless, and single, and she has to get out there and sort her situation out for her daughters. She'll deal with them later. She hears the thwack of a football smacking a wall on her parents' street when she walks out into the bright afternoon and she feels horrible. She hasn't seen Liam since she left Barney. He must be wondering where she's gone, but she hasn't so much as sent him a word after her departure. Maybe it's better this way? She resolves to call him the next day. *But what good will that do?* She doesn't know how to answer. She won't have any solutions for him, only more grown-up-sized problems he could do without.

The bright afternoon has an underlying sharp breeze

which skitters into every corner. High summer is over, and the evenings are getting incrementally shorter again. She could tell Rossella hadn't believed her about the job interview. So, she'd doubled back and applied some garish lipstick of Daniela's which she found in the bathroom, and didn't suit her colouring, to make it more plausible. She'd taken this, along with some soluble aspirin, before any questions were asked, for her aching shoulder. Then she'd backed out the door and made a break into town. She avoids Burgh Quay, O'Connell Bridge and Westmoreland Street. She doesn't want to bump into any former colleagues, or worse, Barney. By taking a circuitous route she's not properly familiar with, she finds herself on Westland Row, opposite St Andrew's Church, where her parents had been married, umpteen years before. She thinks about the intervening years. Had they ever been truly happy? Now that she's a bit older and wiser, since the breakdown of her engagement to Barney, the arrival of the twins and the benefit of hindsight, she can see some of the good in their relationship. How Ettore hadn't been Daniela's first choice, but he had loved her anyway because he always had. They worked hard and minded each other. Perhaps that was enough. She would never know what that was like now. She and Barney hadn't worked out, and she is too proud to go back. Not that she would dream of it in a million years. But she's running out of options.

She crosses onto Nassau Street and keeps walking until she reaches Rault's Gallery. The same dull paintings of rural hunting scenes are still in the window. She remembers the painting she'd seen when speaking to Nancy Lanigan and wonders again if it came from here. Nicoletta shudders. This type of stuff gives her the creeps. Adrenaline shoots into her veins. Not knowing what to expect, the most intoxicating feeling of all. Uncomfortable for some. Until you lean into it.

She rings the bell. It echoes forlornly in the surrounding silence. She doesn't know what the opening hours would be for a place like this, but it looks shut. There's nothing. No footsteps or lowered voices. She bangs the door, heaving the brass knocker down on the maroon painted door.

A few seconds later, a window above her head is raised a couple of inches and she can see a face peering down at her.

'What is it?' It's a man's voice, thick with sleep.

'I'd like to speak to Celine Rault. Or Agatha Rault please.'

'About what? They're not available,' the man snaps.

Nicoletta improvises. 'It's about a painting. The one in the window. With the waggly tail.'

The man doesn't seem to appreciate her attempt at humour. He slams down the window and Nicoletta waits for what feels like an eternity until he unlatches the door, his shirt only half buttoned, his hair standing on end.

'I'm sorry to disturb you,' Nicoletta begins. 'I don't know what your opening hours are.'

'We're closed,' the man huffs. He has a funny little nailbrush moustache that he keeps touching, as though newly grown and something he is self-conscious about. He scowls at Nicoletta. 'And that painting isn't for sale.'

'Pity,' Nicoletta says, after a beat. 'What's it doing in the window, then?'

The man looks at her as though she's an imbecile. 'It's already been sold. Good day.'

'Wait,' Nicoletta shouts.

The man looks at her in alarm. He's not much older than she is.

'Can you show me around? And maybe I could see if there's anything else I'd like.'

He scowls again. 'I thought you said you wanted to speak to Mrs or Dr Rault.'

Nicoletta gives what she hopes is her most winning smile. 'You said they're not available. So, you'll have to do instead. Maybe you'll do even better.'

He doesn't pass any remark at this, just sighs wearily, as though this sort of thing happens all the time.

'All right, then. Come in.' He opens the door a fraction to accommodate her, and she steps through into a dark hallway. He walks ahead, indicating for her to follow him.

'Mind the step,' he calls abruptly, as she stumbles down into a small, dim room with a plush blue carpet, lined with paintings of all shapes and sizes.

Nicoletta stands for a moment in the middle of the room and walks around, pretending to scrutinise each one.

'This is nice,' she says, stopping in front of a row of blue splotches on a white background. The man grunts, but she can feel his eyes on her as she continues examining each painting, exclaiming over each one. She can't blame him for being sceptical at her enthusiasm. She did burst in unannounced and spoil his nap.

She turns to face him. 'How much?'

He laughs, seeming genuinely amused. 'For what?'

'That one,' she says, going back to the first one with the blue splashes of ink. 'I see something different every time I look at it.'

He shakes his head.

'It's very expensive,' he mutters from the doorway.

'That doesn't answer my question,' she says with a playful smile. 'I'm sure it's only expensive to those who can't afford it.'

'And you can?' He looks her up and down, taking in the cheap shoes and handbag, the barely made-up face, apart from the slash of her mother's lipstick.

She finishes her lap of appraising the paintings before she answers. 'You haven't said how much it is, so I won't know until you tell me.' She holds out her hand. 'Nicoletta Sarto is my name.'

'And what do you do, Miss Sarto, that would enable you to afford a painting like that?' He says the words without malice, more with sincere curiosity.

'I'm a journalist,' she says. 'Or I was.'

'You were a journalist? I see.' He picks up a pen and unclicks it. 'What do you do now? Apart from almost breaking down the doors of respectable art galleries?' He is smiling, but she feels the need to explain herself.

'I'm a mother,' she says simply. 'And it's complicated. But I'm going to go out and buy a Sweepstakes ticket right now so that hopefully I can come back tomorrow and buy that painting. If that's what it is. It looks more like an experiment.' She gestures behind her.

He laughs unexpectedly. The sound erupts from his whole body. He takes her hand and shakes it solemnly.

'Louis Rault,' he says gruffly. 'That's my name. Since you've shared yours. Now we're even.'

She looks at him from under her lashes. 'I don't know much about art, I'm afraid.' She laughs. 'But you've got some lovely stuff here.'

He sits down heavily in a minimalist chair behind a desk with only a telephone and a ledger on it, rubbing his eyes. He looks up as though remembering she's there. 'Some of it is. Some of it is absolute dross. My father bought a lot of it. He didn't have very good taste.'

'Did he buy the one in the window? Of the dogs and horses?' Nicoletta asks.

'Yes,' he says. 'I hate that one. It's so ugly.'

He looks up at her and bursts out laughing again. The noise echoes around the confined space and vibrates off the ceiling. His laugh is so infectious she can't help but join in.

'I'm sorry to have disturbed you,' Nicoletta says at last. 'I can come back another time.'

He yawns. 'You're grand. I was actually just grabbing a few hours' kip. I don't sleep during the night. It's a bother.'

'That is a bother,' Nicoletta replies. She gives a polite cough. 'I don't sleep much either.'

He looks up, meeting her eye, before raising his fingers to his little moustache. 'Why's that?'

'I have two small babies,' she says. 'Twins. They don't let me. Plus, I've moved back in with my parents so it's all a bit fraught.' She sits down on the steep step into the room. This time it's her turn to rub her eyes. 'Maybe I should go home,' she finds herself saying.

His moustache twitches. 'Tell you what,' he says, 'let

me get myself straightened up,' he indicates his dishevelled appearance. 'Then let's go for a drink.'

'You and me?' Nicoletta opens her eyes wide in alarm, unsure of what she's got herself into.

'You and me,' he says, fluffing the moustache with his thumb. 'I didn't see a wedding ring,' he explains. 'And you said you've moved back in with your parents. So, I thought I might take a chance. Why not? You only live once.'

'What would your father have to say about it?' She knows she's fishing, but he doesn't seem to notice.

A flash of anguish crosses his face. 'He died suddenly a few months ago.'

'Oh, I'm sorry,' Nicoletta says. She means it. And now she feels like a heel for tricking him like this. But maybe he knows about his sister's involvement with Meredith Field's death, and the *Among the Ruins* paintings, and maybe she can get him to share any and all relevant information with her over a few drinks.

He throws a glum sort of smile in the direction of the blue splotches before gesturing for her to follow him into the hall. When they're out on the street, he takes her arm.

'Where would you like to go?'

'How about the Duke?' Nicoletta asks. 'It's nearby.'

When they get there, he finds her a seat in the lounge while he goes to get the drinks. He doesn't ask her what she wants, and she doesn't appear to mind. Whatever happens today, happens. When he comes back, he plops a glass of white wine in front of her, while he slurps on a creamy pint of stout. She takes a sip. Then another, and another. An excruciating silence falls between them, and Nicoletta is acutely aware of how difficult it's going to be to extract herself from this situation, now that she's in it.

'How long have you worked in the art business?' she asks, for want of anything better.

'All my life.' Louis flips a beer mat between his fingers and gives her an intense look. He wipes foam off his moustache. 'But not for much longer.'

'Why, are you leaving?' Nicoletta asks with genuine curiosity.

He looks down into the depths of his pint. 'It's not the same without Pa. After everything that happened.'

'What's everything that happened?' Nicoletta can't help but ask, draining her wine.

He gives her a cautious look. 'My father died. And well, you know. He left some debts. That sort of thing.' He gestures to her empty glass. She acquiesces with a nod.

Another pint of Guinness and glass of wine are duly delivered to the table. Nicoletta is feeling reckless. She thinks about going to the payphone in the alcove beside the bar and calling O'Connor. But something – maybe pride – stops her. What would you tell him? That you're out drinking with another man, still chasing after this stupid story that has cost you everything? She inwardly chides herself for being so foolish as she takes a huge gulp of wine. It hits her empty stomach like battery acid. She's not really used to drinking.

'Why'd you get fired from your newspaper job?' Louis Rault asks, rousing her out of her maudlin reverie.

She rubs her lips together. They're dry, and chapped, now that the smear of bright lipstick has rubbed off. 'I was looking into a story about the *Among the Ruins* paintings,' she says, looking him directly in the eyes. 'The ones your father sold to Tom Leonard Senior all those years ago. Turns out they're forgeries. Very good forgeries, but fakes nonetheless.'

His eyes widen, and he plucks at his upper lip, as though ruminating on what he's going to say next. 'I knew that was a cock-and-bull story about fancying the painting in the window,' he says at last. 'As soon as you said you were a journalist, I knew why you were there.' He shakes his head with a bitter laugh.

'I'm not a journalist anymore,' she says, matching his laugh. 'I was fired. So even if you told me anything, I've nowhere to publish a story of any sort.' She raises her almost empty wine glass and clinks his. He wanders off to get them more drinks and Nicoletta sinks back, wondering how she got here. There are one or two other women in the lounge, nursing drinks quietly. She realises they've been quite loud and raucous. Ah well.

When he comes back, they drink in silence. His moustache is covered in foam, but he has given up wiping it off. Nicoletta sighs. She turns and catches sight of herself in a mirror behind her. She looks gaunt, hollowed out, her eyes huge in her head, her hair standing on end. Her mother would be getting dinner. Probably complaining about her to high heaven to her father, Rossella, and anyone who would listen. *Go home*, she wearily admonishes herself. *Before it's too late.*

'I must go,' she says, half to herself, half to Louis Rault, whose knees are jammed into her thigh. Had they always been like that, or was this a recent development? She stands up, her legs wobbly. She bangs her knee off the side of the banquette she'd been sitting on.

'Wait,' Louis Rault stands up, putting a hand on her arm. 'Where are you going?'

'I have to go home to my children,' she says honestly. 'You're a nice guy, but this was a waste of time. I should drop this story now. Nothing good can come of it. Goodbye.'

She goes to leave, but he's squeezing her arm, almost pinching it between forefinger and thumb. 'Don't be a tease,' he says, his tone half-hearted in its admonition.

She shakes her head. 'I came for a drink with you. I didn't promise I'd jump into bed with you. Thank you for a pleasant time.'

He sits back down heavily on the banquette she'd just vacated and briefly shuts his eyes. For a moment, she wonders if he's going to drop off for forty winks. She rubs her arm where he'd pinched it. She fears she'll have a bruise there come tomorrow.

'You're right,' he says suddenly. 'I'm a prick.'

Nicoletta looks on in alarm as a single tear falls down his cheek. He doesn't bother wiping it away.

He takes Nicoletta's hand. She doesn't pull away. She wonders if he'd already been drinking all day – surely he isn't this messy after three pints?

'Forgive me,' he says, puffing out his cheeks. Nicoletta sits down on the banquette beside him. She furtively looks around but they're the only ones in the lounge now. It's emptied out, a window of calm before the after-work rush.

She's about to stand up and leave him there, when he draws her towards him and tries to kiss her. Her lips get mashed against his teeth, and she stands up. 'Good day, Mr Rault,' she says, craving fresh air.

'Wait,' he says. 'I'm sorry. I didn't mean it.'

'Okay,' she says, hovering, keeping an eye on the door.

'It's just, I've had a lot on my mind of late.'

She tries to look sympathetic. 'Of course, with your father dying. That must be very difficult.'

'Not just that,' he waves a long, pale hand. 'That girl who was murdered. The heiress.'

'Meredith Field?' Nicoletta asks, smartly, moving out of arm's reach.

'That's the one. The *Among the Ruins* painting was found with her, wasn't it?'

'Yes.' Nicoletta takes a deep breath and tries to sober up. 'Why?'

'That girl was blackmailing Pa.'

Nicoletta remembers what Louise Leonard had said about Antoine Rault being queer. Could that be why he'd been blackmailed? And could Celine Rault have killed Meredith because of it? She stands with her handbag over her shoulder, already on the move. 'Where does Celine live, Louis? I'd like to speak to her.'

'I thought you were going home to your children?' he scoffs. 'You're a tease. That's all you are.' He folds his arms, closing his eyes as though in blessed relief.

'Why did you tell me this about Meredith blackmailing your father?' She might as well ask.

He opens his eyes again. 'I had to tell someone.' He grabs

her hand and takes another lunge at her, but she's too quick for him. She's out the inner door to the bar, where she asks for the Dublin telephone directory. She finds an address for Dr Celine Rault at a flat on Pembroke Road and scribbles it down on a beer mat. Then she's out onto the safety of the street before he can catch up. She practically runs as far as Baggot Street before her lungs get the better of her. She stops, almost sinking to her knees in front of Carlo's, the restaurant where she'd met Louise Leonard and Maureen French weeks before. She's aware the next meeting must be on the horizon and she's meant to be the organisation's new secretary. The restaurant still looks shuttered and closed. She wonders what Louise has done or said, if anything, to put in a good word for her with Maureen at the *Chronicle*. She resolves to call Louise as soon as she can. The weight in her chest eases, and she stands up, steeling herself for doorstepping Celine. She has nothing to lose. Celine has already cost her the precious women's editor job at the *Sentinel* with her complaint about harassment. If it's a confrontation, so be it. Celine is most likely a cold-blooded murderer, after all. She's dangerous. Who knows what she's capable of.

Nicoletta feels as though she's floating above the pavement, her feet barely touching the ground. A bespectacled girl wearing a beret almost walks into her and her whole body constricts in fright. The girl looks alarmed, mouthing a quick apology, before rushing off. Nicoletta can't quite shake the feeling that she's being followed. Each gleam of headlights reflected in the long Georgian windows of Baggot Street feels like an accusation. Every businessman or secretary scurrying back to Pearse Street station after the working day appears as though they are taken aback by the very sight of her. She sticks her hands in her pockets and keeps walking until the street widens at Pembroke Road. Celine Rault lives in the ground-floor flat of a wide Georgian house opposite a popular pub at the Baggot Street end. There's no bell, so Nicoletta knocks on the door. She can smell cooking aromas and hears a radio blaring. She bangs on the door this time with her fist. Celine pokes her head out a window, her long red hair piled on top of her head. She's wearing a striped apron.

'What is it? You'll frighten the neighbours.' When she sees Nicoletta, she shakes her head and mutters to herself.

The door opens a crack a second later and Celine steps out onto the step, locking it behind her, as though Nicoletta were going to try and bolt in after her. She wipes her hands on her front. 'You again,' she says with a half-smile. 'Have you been following me? Do I need to make another complaint – to the Guards this time – not just to your employer?' She wags a finger at Nicoletta with another sly smile.

Nicoletta takes a deep breath, trying, and failing, to keep the blood from rising to her cheeks. 'Can you comment on the fact that you were seen meeting murdered heiress Meredith Field at The Stag pub's car park in Monkstown?'

Celine laughs, a nasty cackle. She steps towards Nicoletta. 'An unnamed source, eh? "Murdered heiress"? Once a tabloid reporter, always a tabloid reporter. Isn't that right? Though God knows who'd employ you now.' She goes to unlock her front door, but Nicoletta is too quick for her.

'I had a very interesting chat with your brother today.'

Celine turns around slowly and crosses her arms, hugging herself tightly, though it's a mild evening.

'My brother is a drunken fool. And clearly, you've been on the sauce too. Go home and sleep it off. You're embarrassing yourself.' Nicoletta is momentarily discombobulated. Is it nighttime? But then she remembers the commuters she'd seen on Baggot Street. She may have lost all track of time, but it's still early evening. There's a tinkle of broken glass from the pub across the road, and a laugh, then a shout. She longs to be there, among friends. Not here, on this path of destruction.

Celine pokes her in the hollow of her shoulder. Nicoletta is brought back to the present by the physical sensation of almost losing her balance.

'I'm not intimidated by you or your family,' she says, enunciating every word, suddenly aware of the several glasses of wine she'd tipped back a short while before. 'And this is a public area. I'm entitled to stand here if I want.'

Celine snorts. 'Well, I don't have to look at you.' She slots the key back into the lock, but Nicoletta calls her name. Celine cocks her head in irritation.

Nicoletta goes in hard. 'What comment do you have for my story on the allegation that you murdered Meredith Field?'

Celine fully turns back and blinks. 'What the fuck? Can I comment for who, exactly? Didn't you lose your post at the *Sentinel*? Now, get out of my sight or I'm calling the police.'

Nicoletta stands her ground. She doesn't care who's listening. Celine might though.

'I'm planning on calling the police myself. To tell them that you killed Miss Field.'

She's about to say something else, when Celine is in front of her.

'Why on earth would I do that? She was a student of mine.' Her teeth are bared in Nicoletta's face. The veneer of civility, the laconic air, the sophistication, is gone.

Nicoletta gulps. 'She was blackmailing your father. Because he was queer. And after he died, you wanted revenge. Isn't that what happened?'

A warm clump of Celine's saliva hits her squarely on the nose. Nicoletta doesn't blink, doesn't twitch an eyelid.

'My brother may be a drunken fool, but you're a foolish little trollop,' Celine says, measuring each word in vicious little sips. Her breath is sharp with wine. 'You can't even see what's in front of your own face. I didn't kill that girl.'

'Then who did?' Nicoletta utters a reply, through gritted teeth.

'My father certainly wasn't the only one being blackmailed. Maybe you should look closer to home and leave me the hell alone. Go back to the gutter where you belong.'

She's retreated through her front door and locked it behind her before Nicoletta puts a shaking hand into her bag and drags out an old tissue, scrubbing her face over and over. She looks up. A curtain twitches in an upstairs flat. She walks back onto the street with as much dignity as she can muster.

Chapter Thirty-Three

Nicoletta heads back towards the centre of town, her brain fizzing with possibilities. Celine had told her to look closer to home. What exactly had she meant by that? Anger and purpose override the exhaustion which has seeped into her bones, and with each step, she builds momentum until it carries her back to O'Connell Bridge as though she's a woman possessed. She finds herself inexplicably drawn back to Burgh Quay, despite the heartache and humiliation of the past few days. She still has all the clippings in her bag, from when she'd borrowed them from the library. She has no need of them now. Will this story come to anything? It seems to have fizzled like a damp squib in her hand.

When she reaches the door, Noel the doorman, her pal of old, puts down his paper to give her a solemn nod. He doesn't ask why she's there and she doesn't give a reason, other than to brandish the pile of clippings in front of her face. The familiar, slightly metallic smell of the newsroom knocks her sideways. It feels like she's never been away. A couple of heads are bent over the typewriters, clacking away, but it's quiet. If they see her, they don't bother acknowledging her. She's picked a good time, it seems. Dolores is getting ready to lock up when Nicoletta arrives at the top of the rickety steps to hand back the pages, which she's bundled haphazardly back into the furred manila file.

Dolores gives her a sympathetic look. 'Didn't expect to see you back so soon.' When Dolores accepts the file, Nicoletta realises her own hands are trembling. Dolores places it on the counter in front of her and begins putting on her coat and gathering up her things.

'Are you all right?' she asks.

Nicoletta sits down suddenly on a small footstool by the counter. Plenty of people had been adamant that they didn't want her following this story, all for varying reasons. Barney, out of pride, because it was his, and he doesn't like sharing. Duffy, because he didn't want to upset his boss. Her parents, Rossella and Joan, because she was being reckless, and it took her away from the time she should have been minding her children. She thinks of Dermot's recent weight loss, his sunken cheeks, the dark pouches under his eyes. He had been adamant that it was a bad idea. But he'd never said why. And now she really wants to find out.

She realises she's shivering when Dolores's gentle voice breaks into her thoughts.

'Is it cold out? Maybe the good weather is finally breaking.'

Nicoletta tries to speak but she can't get the words out. She closes her eyes and tries not to scream.

'I need to find Dermot,' she manages at last.

Dolores crosses over from where she'd been switching off the lights at the back, and looks at her, slightly alarmed.

'Are you sure you're all right?' Dolores gives Nicoletta a brisk pat on the shoulder.

Nicoletta shakes her head. 'I've had a shock. I need to find Dermot.'

Dolores makes a clucking noise with her tongue. 'I saw him earlier,' she says doubtfully. 'Not sure if he's still here. If he's not, we can put you in a taxi.'

'I've no money,' Nicoletta says simply. To hell with dignity.

'I can lend you some,' Dolores says, fishing her purse out of her bag. 'I don't know what's happened, but the right place for you is at home. Not here.'

Dolores gets behind the counter again, and with an efficient flick of her wrist dials a few notches on the phone and gets through to the switch.

'Dermot Mahon, please,' she says with a curt nod at Nicoletta. 'Send him up to me.' She shoves her purse back in her bag. 'Will Dermot bring you home, is that it?' she asks a bit more gently, putting down the receiver.

Nicoletta nods miserably. She doesn't know what to say. It's as though she has lost the power of speech.

Dolores clicks off the radio and settles herself back on her perch, waiting for Dermot. He doesn't materialise for another fifteen minutes. When he pokes his head around the door, Dolores walks over to greet him, where they confer in low voices for a minute or two.

'He's here now,' Dolores says, in a high, artificial voice, as Dermot offers her an arm and she stands up.

'I'll give you a lift home, Nic. What's up?' Concern etches the lines around his nose and mouth. Had they always been as deeply scoured into his flesh?

She shakes her head, taking his arm as they are ushered out the door by Dolores, who is finally able to lock up. She follows him down the stairs in silence, his keys jingling in his pocket. They walk through the newsroom, Dermot waving at someone. Nicoletta keeps looking straight ahead until the blessed relief of the cool stairwell.

'What's going on?' he asks finally, guiding her down the stairs, past Noel, who watches them go with a shake of his newspaper.

'I've had a rough couple of days,' she says, when they are out on the street, walking towards the lockup where he left his car off an alleyway around the corner. Her teeth won't stop chattering.

'You've been acting strangely,' he says, giving her an odd look. 'I think being let go from the *Sentinel* has been a blessing in disguise for you, Nic. Take the time off to deal with whatever is going on. Stop using work as a distraction.'

She opens her mouth to protest, then closes it. She feels numb, her limbs are rubbery and slow, the adrenaline of earlier has faded.

They turn into the alleyway, its walls dank and slimy with what she presumes to be excrement. Dermot twists a key in the padlocked gate, before putting a hand under her elbow to guide her into the passenger seat, and she lets him. When they're in the car, back on the quays, facing into traffic, she takes a shuddery breath.

'Did you only meet Antoine Rault once, Dermot? Or was it a bit more than that?'

He's indicating right. He looks at her eventually, as though it is he who has been awaiting an answer to some unspoken question. 'Where to, Nic? Your parents' house?'

'I don't want to go home, Dermot. Not just yet.' She looks sideways at his profile. His jaw is set.

'Fancy a glass of wine?' Her voice is light, but her hands are clenched in her lap, like an animal's claws. 'But nowhere busy. I'm not in a social mood.'

He purses his lips in acquiescence. 'Let's go to my place. I don't feel like seeing anyone either.'

She doesn't ask why. It seems redundant at this point to do so. There's plenty of time yet for her to let things unfold.

They drive in silence to his mews in Rathgar, a square modern-build plonked in the overgrown front garden of a large Victorian pile, not far from Grosvenor Avenue, where The Rook lives.

'I interviewed The Rook this week,' she says casually, as he pulls into the unlit street, his side hubcaps kissing the kerb with a gentle scrape. She looks up. The sky is blank: not a star peeks out at them. She feels utterly alone.

He cuts the engine, flipping up the hand brake, before finally turning around to look at her. He frowns.

'Isn't that Barney's story?'

Nicoletta shrugs. 'Barney doesn't own The Rook. Anyway, we had an interesting chat.'

'Did he pump you full of hot air about his ménage à trois and his troubled childhood? Barney's a sucker for that sort of thing,' he scoffs. 'Besides, I thought you'd given up on all that by now.'

'That's what a lot of people would like, isn't it?' It's her turn to frown. 'But maybe that's why I should keep going.'

He's looking at her intently, his eyes narrowed. Eventually, he laughs and puts his hand on the door. 'A bit late now, Nic. Who'd publish it? You've no job.'

She bites her lip, tasting blood. He curls a hand around her arm. 'I'm saying that as your friend. I'd never bullshit you. You've wasted enough time and energy on this story now. Time to let it go.'

He gets out and comes over to her side, helping her onto the pavement, crossing back to solicitously close the door gently after her, as though to soften the blow of what he's just said.

They walk to his front door arm-in-arm. He lets go of her to open the door and switch on lights. There's a musty, shut-away air in the hall. Half-filled cups litter the telephone table by the door. Nicoletta picks one up. It's left a light-coloured ring indent on the conker-coloured wood. She looks up. He's observing her with a half-smile.

'I don't need a wife, Nic. Just so you know,' he says with a laugh, though she can sense a heaviness underneath the playful tone.

It's her turn to laugh. 'Don't mind me. I'm no one's wife.'

He doesn't acknowledge that, instead going to the galley kitchen and opening a large cupboard. She can hear him rooting around, opening and closing drawers, as she takes a seat on a beige leather sofa in the small sitting room, adorned with a red throw hanging crookedly from the back. Her thighs stick to the leather.

He comes back with a chilled bottle of wine, a corkscrew and two glasses. He fills the glasses all the way to the top and they clink. He sets down his own glass on the coffee table, replacing the bottle in the fridge in the kitchen. When he rejoins her, he sits opposite in a matching leather armchair. She puts down her glass and wanders over to his record collection, scanning each one, letting her fingers trail over each sleeve, before deciding against putting on music. She picks up her wine glass. Dermot has drained his, so she does the same.

He stands up and draws the curtains, selecting a record and placing it on the turnstile, before heading back into the kitchen for more wine. Once he's topped up their glasses, he sits back and closes his eyes, nodding his head to the heavy baseline. Nicoletta lets the melody and heady feeling from the wine wash over her.

'This is just like old times,' she finds herself saying. Dermot opens his eyes.

'Yes, I suppose it is,' he says, with a smile.

She takes off her shoes and gathers her feet under her, cradling her glass. She looks at him directly. His eyes are half closed, but he's watching her.

'You never told me how you knew Antoine Rault,' she says, lobbing the question into the air between them like a live grenade.

He opens his eyes wide. 'Not everything is your business, Nicoletta. Why does it even matter?'

She lets her feet sink down into the plush carpet, stung by the sudden rebuke.

'I thought we were friends,' she manages finally. 'I should go.' She snatches up her shoes and handbag and visits the small WC in the hall. She puts her shoes on, and splashes cold water on her face, before lifting up her dress and sitting on the toilet, unleashing an endless stream of urine into the avocado-coloured bowl. When she's finished, she wipes, noticing that her period has started. At least she's not pregnant again. She tries to flush. The cistern emits a pathetic little *pffft* sound, like a child blowing raspberries. She tries again, and it's more of the same. She panics, not wanting to leave blood-smeared tissue paper and urine in Dermot's toilet. She rattles the handle, and nothing doing. She remembers her father showing her how to fix a faulty cistern years ago. She lifts up the heavy ceramic casing and, with a heave, sets it down carefully on the avocado-coloured floor tiles. She peers inside. There's something glinting in the shallow water, like a crocodile lurking in a swamp. She reaches in and lifts it out, weighing it in her hands. She's never held a gun before. It's lighter than she expected. Her hands are shaking so much she's afraid she'll drop it. She fiddles with a button inside the cistern and the toilet flushes. She plops the gun back where she'd found it and heaves the casing back on. She washes her hands and picks up her bag, ready to run.

Dermot is standing right outside the door waiting for her when she opens it. She starts babbling. 'I have to go,' she says, eyeing the front door. 'I have to get back to the twins.'

'Ah yes,' he says, crossing his arms. 'You're always thinking about the twins, aren't you?'

His well-aimed barb pierces her pride and snaps her back to the reality of the situation. She crosses her arms, hugging herself, despite the warm, stuffy atmosphere of the house. 'Is that a Webley in the toilet cistern, Dermot?' She remembers Garda O'Connor telling her the name of the gun that had killed Meredith Field.

He scrubs his eyes with the back of his hand. 'Yes,' he says finally, taking a step towards her.

She takes a step back into the tiny bathroom. 'Did you kill Meredith Field, Dermot?' She clenches her fists so he can't see that her hands are still shaking.

He bites his lip. 'When someone you love is threatened or harmed, you lose all reason. Tell me, wouldn't you kill for those twins of yours?'

She opens her mouth to speak, but the words won't come out. She nods vigorously instead, releasing a breath. This time the words form.

'Did you love Antoine Rault? Is that what you're saying, Dermot?'

He bows his head. 'When he died, I felt like I'd died too, honest to God.'

Nicoletta claps a hand over her mouth. 'You were being blackmailed by Meredith Field as well, weren't you? Over your relationship with Rault.' Slowly the pieces fall into place. 'Meredith Field was Celine Rault's History of Art student at UCD. She'd been to a party at Rault's Gallery, according to Celine, who suspected her of theft on the same occasion. Meredith must have been working for The Rook as a go-between in order to steal the painting from Helen Leonard, but perhaps she saw or heard something about your relationship with Rault that gave her ammunition for blackmail. You and Celine Rault both agreed separately to meet Meredith at that pub car park in Monkstown to give her one final payoff. But you couldn't leave it at that. You shot her. Why, Dermot?'

He shakes his head. Tears are coursing down his face, but he makes no move to wipe them away this time. 'Antoine had been investigated by the Guards for his involvement with The Rook and moving stolen paintings through his gallery. Everyone thinks that's what his suicide was about. But it was more of a reaction to the blackmail. That greedy little bitch just wanted money, she didn't care how many lives she destroyed. And when he died, she kept on asking me for money. So, I got rid of her.'

He sits down heavily on the hall floor, burying his face in his hands. Nicoletta unravels a roll of toilet tissue and hands him a wad. He dabs at his face. She sits down beside him, beginning to feel the walls closing in.

He grabs her hand, squeezing it painfully in both of his. 'If our friendship has ever meant anything to you, you'll pretend I never told you this. Walk out of here and go home. And leave me in peace.'

As calmly as she can, she picks up her bag, walks to the front door and lets herself out into the velvety night.

It's after midnight when she lets herself into her parents' house in Fairview. The key is in its usual spot under a flowerpot on the parlour windowsill. She creeps through the dark hallway into the kitchen, shedding her shoes along the way. She goes to the sink, fills a glass, and takes a long drink of water. Leaving the glass beside the sink, she tiptoes to the door which divides the house from the shop. Her parents never lock it. She pushes it open and turns on a light behind the counter. The shop is instantly flooded in a brilliant yellow glare. She shields her eyes with the back of her hand and crosses to the squat black telephone resting on the counter, snatching up the receiver.

She dials the number she knows off by heart. It's answered after a couple of rings.

'*Irish Sentinel*, copy department, how can I help you?' She tries to speak, but she almost chokes. She can't go back there, whatever happens. Besides, they wouldn't publish this particular story anyway, she's sure of it.

She slams the receiver back into its cradle. She picks it up again and dials Louise Leonard's father's house. Several rings elapse before a sleepy voice answers gruffly. It's Louise.

'Louise, it's Nicoletta Sarto. I'm sorry for the late call.'

'It's the middle of the night!' She hears what sounds like a rustle and a creak as Louise heaves herself into an upright position.

'Louise, I have an update on the story I've been working on. I can't tell you everything now, but it's very important that you let Maureen French at the *Chronicle* know that I'll be contacting the *Chronicle* news desk tonight, if I may, to file copy. Could you put in a good word? Now?'

'Don't you think you could've told me this in the morning?' Louise shrieks, before slamming down the phone. Nicoletta sits contemplatively for a few moments before she digs in her handbag for her contact book. She finds the number for Garda O'Connor at home and dials. He answers after a second or two, sounding wide awake. Perhaps he hasn't been to bed yet.

'It's Nicoletta,' she says. 'Sarto,' she adds, when he doesn't say anything.

'Well, I only know one Nicoletta. Hello,' he says cautiously. 'What can I do for you?'

'I have to tell you something,' she says. 'Now. I know who killed Meredith Field. But I'd rather not say it over the phone.'

'All right,' he says.

'I'll be there as soon as I can.' She rings off in a clatter.

She tiptoes upstairs and gives herself a wash, changing her clothes, checking in on the girls. They're fast asleep in her mother's room. She gives them a last regretful look and gathers up her things, grabbing a fistful of coins from the jar beside the bread bin in the kitchen. She's back out the door as quietly as she can before anyone wakes up.

Chapter Thirty-Four

When Garda O'Connor opens the door to her, he looks as cautious as he'd sounded on the phone. He's wearing fawn slacks and a green sweater vest over a light blue shirt.

'What's all this about?' he asks, as he beckons her through the tidy hallway, and into the large, open-plan kitchen.

He flicks on the kettle, before turning to look at her properly. 'Jesus, you're white in the face. Are you all right?' He takes her coat and ushers her onto a chair.

She wraps her hands around the steaming mug he gives her and takes a tentative sip before sucking in a deep breath and answering. 'Dermot Mahon just confessed to the murder of Meredith Field. I don't know what to do about it. You're the only one I trust to tell.'

He sits down heavily opposite her. 'Dermot Mahon from the *Sentinel*?'

She nods, allowing the grief to finally seep through to her top layer of skin. She manages to compose herself in order to continue. 'It turns out you never really know someone.'

He whistles. 'Tell me from the beginning.'

When she's finished, she bows her head and allows the tears to fall. She is grieving everything she thought to be true, the life she once had, the people she once knew. Eventually, she wipes her eyes with a tissue passed to her by O'Connor and looks up. 'I don't know what to do,' she says.

'There's only one thing you can do,' he replies, heading out to the hall where the telephone has its own table by the door. She follows him, attentive, as he picks up the receiver. She knew this was inevitable, but it is heartbreaking just the same.

'Are you going to arrest him?' She feels useless, just standing there.

'I'm not, but one of my colleagues is,' he says briskly, before talking into the mouthpiece for what seems like the longest time. When he hangs up, she realises she is shaking.

'I think you should get some sleep, Nicoletta,' he says.

He places his hands on her shoulders and kisses her forehead. 'You don't look well. You can have my bed. I have to go back in now, but I'll come home later. Get some rest.' She opens her mouth to protest but he is gone before she can get the words out.

She wanders back into the spacious open-plan kitchen, where there's a cosy sitting area in one corner, with a small couch propped against the wall looking out into the moonlit garden. It is small and square, with neatly tended flowerbeds and shrubbery. She can imagine planting things in the autumn, waiting for them to grow in spring. What would that be like? A regular, stable life. She draws the curtains on both windows, sinking down into the sofa, which is more comfortable than it looks. She drags down a crocheted throw from its arm and drapes it over her legs. She closes her eyes, not bothering to turn off the main electric light. She doesn't expect sleep, but the next thing she knows is that daylight is seeping through the curtains and some large-sounding rooks or jackdaws in the garden are making a racket. She pops her head up, not knowing where she is. O'Connor is seated at the kitchen table, fully dressed, nursing a steaming mug. He looks up when he sees she's awake.

'What time is it?' she yawns.

'Just after five a.m. I'm glad you slept.'

She sits up. 'What happened? Tell me.'

He scrapes back his chair and joins her on the edge of the sofa. 'Dermot Mahon is in custody. He's being charged in the Bridewell this morning with the murder of Meredith Field. I'm sorry, Nic.' He puts a hand on her shoulder as her face crumples. She swallows down her feelings, as he bustles around making her coffee. He hands her a fresh cup, and she carries it over to the table.

'Can I use your telephone?' she asks briskly, trying to present herself as businesslike as possible. 'And your bathroom. But not in that order.'

He waves her in the direction of the hallway. She scrubs herself at the bathroom sink, trying to massage some colour back into her cheeks. She cares what she looks like again, now that she's here with Garda O'Connor. She'll have to get more used to calling him Peter. But for now, in the context of the story she's about to write, he's Garda O'Connor.

Once she's changed, washed and partly made up, she drags a notebook out of her bag and sits back down at the kitchen table. She asks Garda O'Connor for all the necessary information, and an unofficial quote, to accompany her story, with which he obliges her. She scribbles for several minutes, before bringing her cooling coffee and open notebook into the hall. She places both on the hall telephone table and sits down in the little wooden seat attached to it. She shifts her weight; it's bloody uncomfortable. She dials the operator and asks for a number for the *Daily Chronicle*. Once she's dialled it, she asks to be put through to Maureen French on the news desk.

'Hello, Nicoletta.' Maureen's voice is crisp and alert.

'I have a really big story for you,' Nicoletta says, dispensing with any preamble.

'Yes, Louise Leonard called me at home at some ungodly hour and said you might.'

Nicoletta takes a strangulated breath. Her blouse feels too tight around her neck. 'Just so you know, I no longer work for the *Sentinel*. I'm freelance now.' She pauses.

'I heard,' Maureen replies. 'Word travels fast. That's of no concern to me right now.'

She can hear a deep voice shouting in the background, and a tapping sound, as though Maureen is clicking her nails or a pen lid against the mouthpiece.

'Well, aren't you going to spit it out, or do I have to drag it out of you?' Maureen asks with a laugh.

'It's an exclusive,' Nicoletta says a little hesitantly. 'I'm offering it to the *Chronicle* only, because of your sterling reputation as a journalist, and because you know Louise.

But if I do so, I'd like you to consider me for a permanent job.' She exhales. Maureen doesn't say anything. Nicoletta ploughs ahead.

'In summary: Dermot Mahon, a reporter from the *Irish Sentinel*, is about to be charged at the Bridewell after confessing to the murder of Meredith Field, the heiress from North County Dublin's Holloway House. Miss Field was involved with the criminal gang headed by Ray Hall, known as The Rook, who stole the *Among the Ruins* paintings, which have since been verified as being fakes. I have an exclusive on this, and I can file copy right now for the *Chronicle* if you wish.'

There's a beat of tinny silence and a click, and Nicoletta fears that Maureen has hung up on her.

Then there's a different dial tone and a chirpy female voice is on the line announcing the *Daily Chronicle's* copy department. 'Hello, Copy?'

Nicoletta grasps her notebook between both hands and reads out what she'd just written at Garda O'Connor's kitchen table. She speaks slowly, but efficiently. She doesn't recognise the normal-sounding voice reading out those terrible words as being her own. When she's finished, she hangs up and swipes her notebook onto the carpet. She rests her hot cheek against the cool reddish-pink wood of the table, and weeps.

Chapter Thirty-Five

Four months later – October 1970

Nicoletta and Peter are having breakfast at the kitchen table when the doorbell rings. Peter looks at Nicoletta, and she shrugs. She hears a cry from upstairs, then two sets of cries, and she leaps up, closing the newspaper in front of her.

'The twins are awake,' she says.

'I'll come and help you,' Liam says from where he's lying on the sofa in the corner reading a comic. They have all been living there for the last few months: Peter, Nicoletta, Cara, Rosa and Liam. Nicoletta had felt too guilty for leaving Liam; and when she asked him if he wanted to stay for a while, Barney hadn't stopped him.

'Thanks, pet,' Nicoletta says. 'What would I do without you?'

When they come back downstairs rocking a baby each, Peter is standing at the kitchen table. He places a small, rectangular parcel in front of Nicoletta and frowns.

'For you,' he says. 'It looks like it originally went to the *Sentinel*, and they then forwarded it on.' She hands Cara over to him so she can rip off the brown paper. It's a black-and-white photo. She squints at it in recognition. It's the one she'd been looking at in Seaview House, all that time ago, at the start of the summer, during the Creighton's Open House auction. Where she'd first met Celine Rault. In the photograph, Charles Creighton stands beside his daughter, Delia, who looks about six, as she looks grumpily at the camera from the back of a plump pony.

A note falls out onto the tabletop.

Thought you might want this. Delia.

Nicoletta can't help but laugh. It's bizarre, but not unexpected. She had always half thought she might hear from Delia again. Besides, nothing can put a dent in her happiness now. She is starting at the *Chronicle* the following week as a reporter. Maureen French had come through and offered her a job.

'I was thinking of taking a trip to Dun Laoghaire today,' she says to Peter, putting the photograph in her bag. 'There's someone I want to see.' She looks down at the note on the table. 'Not Delia. Although now that I mention it, I might pay her a visit too.'

It's a breezy walk from the train station at Dun Laoghaire to the mews at Seaview House where Delia Dawkins still lives. Nicoletta doesn't know why she wants to see her, other than to ask her why she'd sent her the photo. She knows from experience that Delia loves a confrontation, and she loves talking about herself, so even a brief encounter will surely yield a tell or two. Nicoletta is also certain that whether or not she is consciously aware of it, Delia is fascinated by Nicoletta's connection to the Creighton family. A bond which will bind them to each other forever, whether she likes it or not. She can't face losing another person from her life. Maybe fate has stepped in and offered her this connection just when she needed it. Just as Helen Leonard and Pat Dennehy were bound together by their lineage and the fake paintings their father gave them, so she is connected to Delia forever, whether either of them likes it or not. The side gate of Seaview House is unlocked. Nicoletta wrenches it open, taking the winding path through the rose beds, past the peacocks' shelter, to the blindingly white, low-roofed modern house at the end of the garden. The peacocks are nowhere to be seen.

She rings the bell before she loses her nerve. There's nothing. No one. She waits. Then rings again. The handle is turned and a gap of an inch or two is pulled open. A watchful child peers around the edge, silent. Waiting for Nicoletta to speak.

'Hayley? Isn't it? Hello.'

The girl furrows her brow. She couldn't be more than seven or eight, but her stillness makes her seem older. 'How did you know my name?'

'We've met before. Ages ago. You probably wouldn't remember.' Nicoletta waves a hand cheerily in the direction of the hall to distract Hayley's attention from what she really wants to say, which is: *before your father went to prison.* 'I'm a friend of your parents. Is your mam home?'

Hayley gawps at her. Then she turns her head. 'Mum!' she yells into the hall, then twists herself back in a quick, birdlike movement, as though she's loath to leave Nicoletta at the door unsupervised.

Nicoletta hears grumbling, then the approaching slap of sandals on a tiled floor. When Delia pulls the door back and sees Nicoletta there, she doesn't look surprised.

'Look what the cat dragged in!' she mutters under her breath. Hayley looks at her mother askance.

'Hayley, go and do your homework.'

'I don't have homework, I'm on my mid-term break,' Hayley says with mild reproach.

Delia sniffs. 'Go and read a book. Amuse yourself. I was always very good at amusing myself.'

Hayley rolls her eyes at Nicoletta, who can't resist a smile. She's clearly heard this unconvincingly mythologised version of young Delia many times.

'Okay,' Hayley says. 'Only I've read them all.'

'Well, go to the library or something,' Delia snaps. 'Let me talk to this lady and see what she wants.'

Hayley flicks her gaze from Nicoletta to Delia in confusion, before looking back to Nicoletta. 'She said she was a friend of yours.'

'That's right,' Delia says with a hint of sarcasm, as Hayley gives Nicoletta one last searching look, before brushing past her mother and disappearing back into the house. 'We're just one big happy family round these parts.'

She gives Nicoletta a slow once-over. 'Let yourself go, haven't you?'

She folds her arms against the breeze and steps out to join Nicoletta on the step, closing the door behind her. She's wearing a wrap-around dress in a petrol-blue jersey material, her hair loose around her face. The shadows under her eyes match Nicoletta's, and her collarbones stand out under the clinging neckline. Nicoletta feels a half-hearted stab of sympathy for Delia. Her own flesh and blood.

'What are you doing here?' Delia asks, taking out a pack of cigarettes from her dress pocket and lighting one, lowering herself onto the step, her skinny legs stretched out in front of her. She indicates for Nicoletta to do the same. 'I thought I made my feelings towards you perfectly clear the last time.'

'Why did you send me a framed photo of you and your father? With you on horseback?'

Delia blows out a stream of smoke. Goosebumps stand up on her arms. Nicoletta wraps her coat tightly around herself.

'Why?' Nicoletta asks again, watching the smoke curl itself into the reckless breeze. 'You gave me my marching orders last time and said you were calling the police.'

Delia gives her a wry smile. 'I felt bad about kicking you out that time. Mother said you were looking at it. No one else wanted it anyhow. It was that or the bin.'

'Thanks, I guess?' Nicoletta says, trailing her fingers along the gravel, tracing each bump as though it might contain a coded message therein.

Delia stubs out the cigarette and sticks the butt back in her packet. 'Don't want the peacocks to swallow it,' she explains. She turns back to Nicoletta.

'Is that why you're here? To ask me about some photo taken a thousand years ago?'

Nicoletta sighs. 'I don't know,' she says. 'I keep being drawn back here. I always wanted a sister.' She laughs. 'And I got you.'

'I suppose.' Delia's frowns, but her expression isn't hostile. 'I mean, you must have guts. To keep coming back here.'

Nicoletta stands up. Her legs are starting to cramp, and she is not comfortable in the slightest. She leans against the outer wall of the house. They both look straight ahead while Delia takes out another cigarette and smokes.

'I'll see you around,' she says, with a casual wave.

'Wait. What happened with Helen Leonard's nurse?' Delia stubs out the cigarette on the heel of her shoe and replaces it in the packet. The peacocks are still nowhere to be seen. She brushes down her skirt. Nicoletta nudges the gravel with her toe.

'She was killed. Murdered.'

Delia crosses her arms. 'Do you know who did it?'

Nicoletta nods. 'A former colleague of mine. And the painting that was found with her was fake.'

Delia whistles. 'All that, for nothing. What a waste.'

Nicoletta nods. 'Things don't always make sense.'

Delia reaches back for the door handle. 'I'd better go. Why don't you come back here sometime? Or I could come into town to meet you if you'd like to get away from this place? That wouldn't be so terrible, would it?'

Nicoletta smiles despite herself. 'That wouldn't be terrible at all.'

She hears Delia's feet slapping on the tiles, then a faraway inner door slams, and children's laughter from the beach drifts over on the breeze. The peacocks make a return and dance around her feet as she tries to make a dignified exit. When she reaches the side gate connecting Seaview House with the main coast road, she looks back at the mews, low slung at the rear of its garden. Back to where she started, with the Creightons. Hayley, the little girl, is visible through a downstairs window. From the safety of the street, Nicoletta looks back. The window has been swallowed by a dazzling wall of sunlight, but she still feels as though she's being watched.

She had arranged earlier in the week to meet Sadie Duggan, Helen Leonard's former housekeeper, at the pub at the top of Seaview Terrace. She checks her watch. She has a few minutes to spare.

There's no one in the pub but Sadie, who is nursing a pot of tea, and the same barman Nicoletta remembers from before. He flicks a cloth in her direction as she orders tea for herself too and joins Sadie in the lounge.

'What did you want to talk to me about?' Sadie cuts right to the chase, lighting one of her foul-smelling cigarettes.

'I need a childminder five days a week from next week when I go back to work,' Nicoletta says, pouring tea. 'I'm starting a new job. Would you be interested?'

Sadie nods vigorously. They agree terms, then lapse into companionable silence. Sadie drains her tea and picks up her bag.

'Sorry to be rude, but I've to head off. To Miss Leonard's house, actually. The family are selling it and I'm helping to clear it out.'

'Poor Miss Leonard,' Nicoletta says, as they walk out together.

'Yes. I'm working on the shed today. There's some amount of old rubbish in there.' She looks thoughtful. 'Do you have a garden?'

'Yes,' Nicoletta says, thinking of Peter's neat flowerbeds. 'I do now, actually.'

Sadie smiles. 'Would you like to take a sack of daffodil bulbs? I've nowhere to plant them, and they need to be planted in the next week or two. Otherwise, they're for the rubbish dump.'

Nicoletta claps her hands. 'That would be great. It would be a nice way to remember Miss Leonard. I've never planted anything before.'

'Okay,' Sadie says. 'It's a deal. Come with me now and grab them. They're not heavy, you can take them with you. Miss Leonard liked you a lot, you know. She told me.'

Miss Leonard's house is empty, clean, and devoid of furniture. It looks almost unrecognisable from before as they pass through on the way to the shed in the back garden.

The shed is a rickety wooden structure. Sadie pulls a string from the ceiling, and a dim bulb casts an uneven glow over a mountain of what looks like decades worth of old bicycle pumps, cracked flowerpots, yellowing books and broken furniture. Nicoletta stands in the doorway as Sadie bravely navigates her way to the back of the cramped space, where dozens of bags of bulbs and packets of seeds are stacked in varying states of decay and disorganisation. Sadie seizes on a knee-high brown sack with 'DAFFODILS' marked in thick black capitals on the front. She lifts it up.

'Jesus, it's heavier than I expected,' she says, dragging it to where Nicoletta accepts some of its weight.

'Let me just check to see what's inside,' Sadie says, fetching scissors from the kitchen to open it. 'Miss Leonard might have packed some old household items in it. I don't want to be giving you a pile of cracked plates along with everything else.'

She cuts the top of the bag and reaches in, pulling out two small rectangular shapes, individually wrapped in layers of plastic sheeting and brown paper.

'What's this?' Sadie asks Nicoletta.

'Maybe we shouldn't open them,' Nicoletta says. But Sadie is already ripping apart the packaging. The paper comes off the bottom right-hand corner of the first one to reveal a gilt frame. And over that is a clearly discernible signature. 'E Dunst.' The rest of the paper reveals two children standing in front of a house. Nicoletta shudders. It's creepy. It reminds her of Hansel and Gretel standing in front of the witch's house in the fairy tale.

'E Dunst. Edvard Dunst.' Nicoletta breathes. 'The *Among the Ruins* paintings. Are these the real ones?' She checks and the other one has the same signature. To her credit, Sadie doesn't turn a hair. They carry a painting each into the kitchen and place them on the table, while Nicoletta goes to the phone in the hall and calls Peter. She waits while he calls one of his colleagues at the station.

As they wait for the Garda to arrive, Nicoletta and Sadie sit on the front step, barely talking, Sadie chain smoking. A heavy rain shower sends them back inside and Nicoletta paces up and down the hall, her heels clicking against the parquet, her mind racing.

When the Garda has been and gone, taking the stolen paintings away with him back to the station, Nicoletta files copy for the *Chronicle*, then phones Peter, telling him what's happened. Finally, she can go home. As she walks back to the station, the sack of bulbs light under her arm, minus the two paintings, a rainbow pops up on the skyline, the sea unbelievably calm and glassy, the view perfect. There it is, barely tangible to the naked eye, a glimmer on the horizon: the truth. Undeniably beautiful by its own metric. She keeps walking towards it.

Acknowledgements

Multitudes of thanks are due to the amazing people at Simon & Schuster UK who have worked tirelessly on this book: Katherine Armstrong, Georgie Leighton and John Sugar in Editorial for their patience and insight; Jess Barratt in Publicity and Hannah Paget in Marketing; Katie Forrest for the beautiful jacket design and Victoria Denne for the thorough copy-edit. Thank you to the wonderful Sales team: Olivia Allen and Heather Hogan in UK Sales; Rich Hawton and the reps team; Maddie Allan, Alice Twomey, Robyn Ware and Rachel Bazan in Digital Sales; and Nicholas Hayne, Hannah Pocock, Claire Richardson and Sorcha Mulligan in Export Sales. To everyone at Gill Hess, Ireland – Simon Hess, Declan Heeney and Helen McKean, thank you for everything you do so well.

It's a pleasure working with you all.

Dream agent Sheila Crowley: thank you for steering me in the right direction; thanks also to Helena Maybery, Sabhbh Curran, Anna Weguelin and Theo Roberts at Curtis Brown.

All the readers, booksellers, Bookstagrammers, fellow

authors and reviewers who gave my debut, *Where They Lie*, so much support: it meant more than you will ever know.

Writing friends and colleagues, you're the best: special mentions go to Susan Stairs and Jamie O'Connell, as well as Sam Blake and all the Irish 'Murderesses' (as we call our crime writers' WhatsApp group).

To my family, and my ever-supportive in-laws, thanks for being my cheerleaders.

And Chris and Hannah, for everything: I couldn't have done it without you.

WHERE THEY LIE

CLAIRE COUGHLAN

SHORTLISTED FOR THE AN POST IRISH CRIME NOVEL OF THE YEAR

Dublin, 1943

Actress Julia Bridges disappears. Her body is never found.

Dublin, 1968

The bones of Julia Bridges are discovered in a back garden. Nicoletta Sarto, an ambitious junior reporter for the *Irish Sentinel*, investigates the mystery of Julia's disappearance, drawing her into the tangled underworld of the illegal abortion industry.

But some stories remain a mystery for a reason, and it's not long before this one stirs up buried secrets from Nicoletta's own past. Secrets that perhaps should stay buried . . .

'A thrillingly dark and atmospheric tale, richly evocative of its time' **John Banville**

'This isn't just a mystery novel: it's a window into a vanished world' **Tana French**

AVAILABLE IN PAPERBACK, EBOOK AND AUDIO

SIMON & SCHUSTER